THE BREAKING EARTH

FIRST

A hair-raising novel about the end of the world in our time.

THEN

Noted space scientist G. Harry Stine ticks off a few of the all-too-likely ways that Mother Earth might put paid to that annoying little upstart, *homo sapiens.*

FINALLY

SF superstar Frederik Pohl, author of *Gateway, JEM,* and *Beyond the Blue Event Horizon,* gets down to the specifics of

The Breaking Earth

(Don't miss it!)

Other novels by Keith Laumer available or soon to be available from TOR Books:

The House in November (Sept. '81)
Worlds of the Imperium (Nov. '81)
Planet Run (mid-'82)
(with Gordon R. Dickson)

THE BREAKING EARTH

Keith Laumer

With Afterwords

by

Frederik Pohl

and

G. Harry Stine

A TOM DOHERTY ASSOCIATES BOOK

PINNACLE BOOKS
NEW YORK

This is a work of fiction. All the characters and events portrayed in this book are fictional, and any resemblance to real people or incidents is purely coincidental.

THE BREAKING EARTH

Portions of this book have been published separately:

Catastrophe Planet, © 1966 by Keith Laumer.

"Shaking Up Space" was originally published in the Summer 1980 edition of *Destinies,* © 1980 by Frederick Pohl.

"This Dynamic Planet" © 1981 by G. Harry Stine.

A Tor Book

First printing, June 1981

ISBN: 0-523-48503-4

Cover illustration by Rick Sternbach

Printed in the United States of America

PINNACLE BOOKS, INC.
1430 Broadway
New York, New York 10018

CATASTROPHE PLANET

CHAPTER ONE

I held the turbo-car at a steady hundred and forty, watching the strip of cracked pavement that had been Interstate 10 unreel behind me, keeping a sharp eye ahead through the dust and volcanic smog for any breaks in the pavement too wide for the big car to jump. A brand-new six-megahorse job, it rode high and smooth on a two-foot air cushion. It was too bad about the broken hatch lock, but back in Dallas I hadn't had time to look around for the owner. The self-appointed vigilantes who called themselves the National Guard had developed a bad habit of shooting first and checking for explanations later. True, I had been doing a little informal shopping in a sporting goods store—but the owner would not have cared. He and most of the rest of the city had left for points north quite a few hours before I arrived—and I needed a gun and ammunition. A rifle would probably have been the best choice, but I had put in a lot of sociable hours on the Rod and Gun Club thousand-inch range back at San Luis, and the weight of the old-style .38 Smith and Wesson felt good at my hip.

There were low volcanic cones off to my right,

trickling black smoke and getting ready for the next round. It was to be expected; I was keeping as close as the roads allowed to the line of tectonic activity running along the Gulf Coast from the former site of New Orleans to the shallow sea that had been northern Florida. Before I reached Atlanta, sixty miles ahead, I would have to make a decision; either north, into the relative geologic stability of the Appalachians, already mobbed with refugees and consequently drastically short on food and water, to say nothing of amusement—or south, across the Florida Sea to the big island they called South Florida, that took in Tampa, Miami, Key West, and a lot of malodorous sand that had been sea bottom until a few months before.

I had a hunch which way I would go. I have always had a fondness for old Scotch, sunshine, white beaches, and the company of sportsmen who did not mind risking a flutter at cards. I would be more likely to find them south than north. The only station still broadcasting dance music was KSEA at Palm Beach. That was the spirit for me. If the planet was going to break up—all right. But while I was alive I would go on living at the best speed I could manage.

The map screen had warned me there was a town ahead. Just a hamlet which had once had ten thousand or so inhabitants, it would be a better bet for my purposes than a big city. Most of the cities had been stripped pretty clean by now, in this part of the country.

The town came into view spread out over low hills under a pall of smoke. I slowed, picked my way around what was left of a farmhouse that had been dropped on the road by one of the freak winds that had become as common as summer squalls. A trickle of glowing lava was running down across a field from a new cone of ash a quarter of a mile off to the right. I skirted it, gunned the turbos to hop a three-foot fissure that meandered off in a wide curve into the town itself.

It was late afternoon. The sun was a bilious puffball that shed a melancholy light on cracked and tilted slabs of broken pavement. In places, the street was nearly blocked by heaps of rubble from fallen buildings; hoods and flanks of half-buried vehicles, mud-colored from a coating of dust, projected from the detritus. The downtown portion was bad. Not a building over two stories was left standing, and the streets were strewn with everything from bedsteads to bags of rotted potatoes. It looked as though the backlash from one of the tidal waves from the coast had reached this far, spent its last energy finishing up what the quakes and fires had started.

Clotted drifts of flotsam were caught in alley mouths and doorways, and along the still-standing storefronts a dark line three feet from the ground indicated the highest reach of the flood waters. A deposit of red silt had dried to an almost impalpable dust that the ragged wind whirled up into streamers to join the big clouds that rolled in endlessly from the west.

Three blocks east of the main drag I found what I was looking for. The small street had failed even before the disaster. It was lined with cheap bars, last-resort pawnshops, secondhand stores with windows full of rusted revolvers, broken furniture and stacks of dog-eared pornography, sinister entrances under age-blackened signs offering clean beds one flight up. I slowed, looked over what was left of a coffee and 'burger joint that had never made any pretense of sanitation, spotted a two-customer-wide grocery store of the kind that specialized in canned beans and cheap wine.

I eased off power, settled to the ground, gave a blast from the cleaner-orifices to clear the dust from the canopy and waited for the dust to settle. The canopy made crunching noises as I cycled it open. I settled my breathing mask over my face and climbed out, stretching stiff legs. A neon sign reading Smoky's Kwik-Pick was hanging from one support and creak, creaking as the wind moaned around it. I heard the distant soft *buroom* of masonry falling into the dust blanket.

As I reached the curb, the dust lifted, danced like water, settled back in a pattern of ridges and ripples. I spun, took two jumps and the street came up and hit me like a missed step in the dark. I went down. Through a rising boil of dust, a clean-cut edge of concrete thrust up a yard from my nose with a shriek like Satan falling into Hell. Loose gravel fill cascaded; then raw, red clay was pushing up, a foot, two feet. There was a roaring like an artillery bombardment; the pavement hammered and thrust like a wild bronco on a rope. The uplifted section of street jittered and danced, then slid smoothly away, squealing like chalk on a giant blackboard. I got to hands and knees, braced myself to jump. Then another shock wave hit, and I was down again, bouncing against pavement that rippled like a fat girl's thigh.

The rumble died slowly. The tremble of the ground under me faded and merged with a jump of my muscles. There was not much I could see through the dust. A little smoke was curling up from the new chasm that had opened across the street; through the mask I caught a whiff of sulphur. Behind me, things were still falling, in a leisurely, ponderous way, as though there were no hurry about returning what had once been the small city of Greenleaf, Georgia, to the soil it had sprung from.

The car was my first worry; it was on the far side of the fissure, a ragged two-yard-wide cut slicing down into the glisten of wet clay far below. I might have been able to jump it if my knees had not been twitching like a sleeping hound's elbow. I needed a plank to bridge it; from the sounds of falling objects, there should be plenty of loose ones lying around nearby.

Through the smashed front of a used-clothing emporium two doors down, I could see racks of worn suits of indeterminate color, powdered with fallen plaster. Behind them, collapsed wall shelves had spilled patched shirts, cracked shoes, and out-of-style hats across a litter of tables heaped with ties and socks among which tones of mustard and faded mauve seemed to predominate. A long timber that had supported the ends of a row of now-exposed rafters had come adrift, was slanted down across the debris. I picked my way through the wreckage, got a grip on the plank, twisted it free to the accompaniment of a new fall of brick chips.

Back outside, the dust was settling. The wind had died. There was a dead, muffled silence. My plank made an eerie grumbling sound as the end scored a path through the silt. I found myself almost tiptoeing, as though the noise of my passing might reawaken the slumbering earth giants. I passed the glassless door of Smoky's Kwik-Pick, and stopped dead, not even breathing. Ten seconds crept by like a parade of cripples dragging themselves to a miraculous shrine. Then I heard it again: a gasping moan from inside the ruined store.

I stood frozen, listening to silence, the board still in my hands, my teeth bared, not sure whether I had really heard a noise or just the creak of my own nerves. In this dead place, the suggestion of life had a shocking quality, like merriment in a graveyard.

Then, unmistakably, the sound came again. I dropped the plank, got the pistol clear of its holster. Beyond the broken door I could make out crooked ranks of home-made shelves, a drift of cans and broken bottles across the narrow floor.

"Who's there?" I called inanely. Something moved in the darkness at the back of the room. Cans clattered as I kicked them aside. A thick sour stink of rotted food penetrated my respirator mask. I stepped on broken ketchup bottles and smashed cans, went past a festering display of lunch meat, a freezer with raised lid jumped and almost fired when a foot-long rat darted out.

"Come on out," I called. My voice sounded as confident as a rookie cop bracing Public Enemy

Number One. There was the sound of a shuddering breath.

I went toward it, saw the dim rectangle of a dust-coated window set in a rear door. The door was locked, but a kick slammed it open, let in a roil of sun-bright haze. A man was sitting on the floor, his back against the wall, his lap full of plaster fragments and broken glass. A massive double laundry sink rested across his legs below the knees, trailing a festoon of twisted pipes. His face was oily-pale, with eyes as round as half-dollars, and there was a quarter-inch stubble across across hollow cheeks. Mud was caked in a ring around each nostril, his eyes, his mouth. Something was wrong with his nose and ears—they were lumped with thick, whitish scar tissue—and there were patches of keloid on his cheekbones. Joints were missing from several of the fingers of his clawlike left hand, which was holding a .45 automatic, propped up, aimed approximately at my left knee. I swung a foot and kicked the gun off into the shadows.

"Didn't need . . . do that," he mumbled. His voice was as thin as lost hope.

I got a grip on the weight across his legs, heaved at it. Water sloshed, and he gave a wail as his head fell sideways.

It took five minutes to get him free, drag him up front where the light was better, settle him in comparative comfort on the floor with his head propped up on broken flour sacks covered with newspaper. He snored with his mouth slackly open. He smelled as though he had been dead for a week. Outside, the sun was glaring low through drifting smoke and dust layers, shaping up for another spectacular sunset.

I used my Boy Scout knife to cut away stiff cloth, examined his legs. They were both badly broken, but the bruises were several days old, at least. The last tremor had not been the one that caught him.

He opened his eyes. "You're not one of them," he said, faintly but clearly.

"How long have you been here?"

He shook his head, a barely perceptible movement. "Don't know. Maybe a week."

"I'll get you some water."

"Had plenty . . . water," he said. "Cans, too . . . but no opener. Rats were the worst."

"Take it easy. How about some food?"

"Never mind that. Better get moving. Bad here. Tremors every few hours. Last one was bad. Woke me up . . ."

"You need food. Then I'll get you to my car."

"No use, mister, I've got . . . internal injuries. Hurts too much to move. You cut out now . . . while you can."

I sorted through the strewn cans, found a couple that seemed sound, cut the tops out. The odor of kidney beans and applesauce made my jaws ache. He shook his head. "You've got . . . get clear. Leave me my gun."

"You won't need a gun—"

"I need it, mister." His whispering voice had taken on a harsh note. "I'd have used it on myself—but I was hoping they'd find me. I could take a couple of them along."

"Forget it, old-timer. You're—"

"No time for talk. They're here—in the town. I saw them, before. They won't give up." His eyes got worried. "You've got a car?"

I nodded.

"They'll spot it. Maybe already have. Get . . . going . . ."

I used the knife blade to spoon beans into his mouth. He turned his face away.

"Eat it, sailor—it's good for you."

His eyes were on my face. "How'd you know I was Navy?"

I nodded toward his hand. He lifted it half an inch, let it fall back.

"The ring. I should have gotten rid of it, but . . ."

"Now take your beans like an old campaigner."

He gritted his teeth, twisted his face. "Can't eat," he protested. "God, the pain . . ."

I tossed the can aside. "I'm going out and check the car," I said. "Then I'll be back for you."

"Listen," he croaked. "You think I'm raving, but I know what I'm saying. Get clear of this town—now. Got no time to explain. Just move out."

I grunted at him, went out into the street, recovered may plank, propped it with its end resting on the upper edge of the ravine that split the pavement. It was a shaky bridge; I went up it on all fours. As I was about to rise and step clear, I saw a movement ahead. My car sat ten yards away where I had left it, thickly coated now with new-fallen pumice. A man was circling it warily. He stepped in close, wiped a hand across the canopy, peered into the interior. I stayed where I was, kneeling on the plank over the dark fissure, just the top of my head above ground level.

The man went around to the driver's side, flipped the lever that opened the hatch, thrust his head inside. I shifted position, eased my gun out. I could not afford to be robbed of the car—not here, not now.

Instead of climbing in, he stepped away from the car, stood looking intently around at the ruined storefronts. He took a step my way, abruptly stopped dead, reached inside his coat, snatched out a small revolver, brought it up and in the same movement fired. The bullet threw dust in my face, sang off across the street and struck wood with a dull smack. Two more shots cracked before the first had stopped echoing—all this in perhaps three-quarters of a second. I hugged the board under me, dragged my gun clear as another shot scored concrete inches from my face. I squinted through haze, centered my sights on the black necktie of the man as he stood with his feet planted wide apart, frowning down the length of his outstretched arm. His small automatic flashed bright in the same instant that my shot boomed. He leaped back, bounced against the side of the car, went down on his back in the dust.

My breath went out in a long sigh, I holstered the .38, scrambled up to stand on the side of the riven street. He was lying on his side like a tired bum curled up for a nap, his face resting in a black paste of bloodied dust, lots of dustcaked blood on his shirt front. He was wearing a neat, dark suit, now dusty, new-looking shoes with almost unscratched soles. His age might have been anything from thirty-five to fifty. His eyes were open and a film of dust had already dimmed their shine.

One hand was outflung, still holding the gun. I picked it up, looked it over absently. My head was still ringing from the gunfire. It was a Spanish automatic, nickel-plated. I tossed it aside, went through his coat pockets, found nothing except a small rectangle of paper stating that the garment had been checked by Inspector 13. Maybe that had been a bad omen. But then maybe he had not believed in omens.

His pants pockets were as empty: no wallet, no identification. He was as anonymous as a store-window dummy. And he had tried, without warning and without reason, to kill me on sight.

Back inside the store, the man with the broken legs lay where I had left him, staring toward me with glass eyes in a skull face.

"I met your friend," I said. My voice sounded strange in my ears, like an announcement beyond the grave.

"You're all right," he gasped.

"He wasn't very smart," I said. "Perfect target. He shot at me. I didn't have much choice." I felt my voice start to shake. I was not used to killing men.

"Listen," the skull-face said. "Get out now—while you can. There'll be more of them—"

"I killed him," I said. "One shot, one dead man." I looked down at the gun at my hip. "The world is coming apart and I'm killing men with a gun." I looked at him. "Who was he?"

"Forget him! Run! Get away!"

I squatted at his side. "Forget him, huh? Just like that. Get in my car and tootle off, whistling a merry tune." I reached out, grabbed his shoulder, not gently. "Who was he?" I was snarling between my teeth now, letting the shock work itself out in good healthy anger.

"You . . . wouldn't understand. Wouldn't believe—"

"Try me!" I gripped harder. "Spit it out, sailor! What's it all about? Who are you? What were you doing here? Why was he after you? Why did he shoot at me? Who was he?"

"All right," he was gasping, showing his teeth. His face was that of a mummy who had died in agony. "I'll tell you. But you won't believe me."

"It was almost a year ago," he said. "The fall of '90. I was on satellite duty on Sheppard Platform when the first quakes hit. We saw it all from up there—the smoke on the day side and the thousand-mile fires at night. They gave the order to evacuate the station—I never knew why."

"Pressure from Moscow," I told him. "They thought we were doing it."

"Sure. Everybody panicked. I guess we did, too. Our shuttle made a bad landing southwest of Havana. I was one of three survivors. Spent a few days at Key West; then they flew me in to Washington. Hell of a sight. Ruins, fires, the Potomac out of its banks, meandering across Pennsylvania, the Washington Monument sticking up out of twenty feet of water, the capitol dome down, a baby volcano building up where Mount Vernon used to be—"

"I know all that. Who was the man I shot?"

He ignored me. "I gave my testimony. No signs

of enemy activity. Just nature busting loose like nineteen hells. There was some professor there—he had all the facts. A hell of an uproar when he sprang his punch line, senators jumping up and yelling, M.P.'s everywhere, old Admiral Conaghy red in the face—"

"You're wandering," I reminded him. "Get to the point."

"The crust of the earth was slipping, he told them. Polnac, that was his name. Some kind of big shot from Free Hungary. The South Polar ice cap building up, throwing the machinery out of kilter. Eccentric thrust started the lithosphere sliding. He said it had slipped more than four miles then. Estimated it would hit an equilibrium at about a thousand. Take about two years—"

"I read the papers—or I did while there were any papers to read."

"Conaghy got the floor. Hit the South Pole with everything we had, he said; bust up the icecap. He scribbled on the back of an envelope and said fifty super-H's would do the job."

"They'd have loaded the atmosphere with enough radio activity to sterilize the planet."

"No, might've worked. Propaganda. Scared of the Russkis, what they'd do. I missed out on the rest. They cleared the hearing room then. But I heard rumors later they'd put it to Koprovin and he said that at the first sign of a nuclear launch he'd hit us with his whole menagerie." The hollow eyes closed; a dry-looking tongue touched blackish lips. He swallowed hard. Then his eyes flew open again and he went on: "That's when Hayle came up with his plan. Secret force to be despatched to the Pole, loaded with modified nuclear generator plant gear. There was a lot of resistance, but they bought it. He picked me to go with him."

I narrowed my eyes at him. "Vice-Admiral Hayle was lost on a routine orbital mission early in '90," I told him. "I never heard of any polar expedition."

"That's right—that was the covery story. Cosmic Top Secret. Operation Defrost, we called it."

"Sounds as though you were on the inside."

He nodded, a weak twitch. All his strength was going into his story. "We sailed from San Juan on Christmas Day. Two deep-water battlewagons, *Maine* and *Pearl*."

"They were lost with the submarine station at Guam."

"No. We had 'em. A dozen smaller ships, three thousand men. This was a major effort. New York was already gone, Boston, Philly, most of the East Coast, San Diego, Corpus—you remember how it was. Blue water over Panama. Hell, we spotted bodies floating a thousand miles at sea after the tornadoes. Surface covered with floating pumice as far south as Tierra del Fuego; new volcanoes there that made a glow in the sky six hundred miles east.

"Ice everywhere; a two-hundred-mile field of bergs broken loose from the cap. Looked like a lot of ice, but it was just crumbs. I saw those blue ice cliffs, rising two miles sheer out of the sea, peaks covered with black dust. That's a sight, mister . . ." His voice trailed off; his eyes wandered from me, staring into the past—or into a pipedream.

"The man with the gun," I brought him back. "Where does he come in?"

"We made our landfall: lost our first men scaling the ice cliffs. Never even found the bodies. Treacherous footing. Used the new model laser-type handguns to melt a path up, then blasted. Took two weeks to get our gear ashore. Funny, wasn't too cold. Big yellow sun shining down on the ice, balmy breeze blowing. Gorgeous sunsets, but not much dust that far south. Ice looked fairly clean. We started inland in heavy assault and landing craft. Made two hundred miles a day. Our target was a spot Hayle had picked in Queen Maud Land—the Pensacola Mountains, under the ice. The plan was to cut the glacier at the ridge and free a couple of hundred square miles of it to move off toward the sea, with a little help from us. We were to bore sinks to the rock, and pump hot air down. Theory was we'd create a lubricating fluid layer at the interface.

"We reached our site, set up a base camp, and started in. I had the north complex—six drill sites stretched out over forty miles of glare ice. Things went pretty well. We were sinking our shafts at the rate of about two hundred feet a day. Couldn't go faster because of melt disposal. On the thirty-first day, I had a hurry-up call from Station Four. I went out on a snowcat. Trench—he was in command there—was excited. They'd spotted dark shapes down in the ice, lying off some yards from the shaft. Bad visibility, he said; the ice was as clear as water, but light did strange tricks down there. I went down to see for myself.

"It was a regulation-type mine lift, open-work sides. I watched the ice slid up past me—lots of dirt in it at places, strata two and three inches thick as black as your hat. We reached bottom. Trench had widened out a chamber down there, thirty feet wide, walls like black glass, damp, cold. Water dripping from the shaft above, puddling up underfoot, pumps whining, the stink of decay. He took me over to where they'd smoothed off a flat place, like a picture window. It was opaque—like polished marble—until we put the big lights on it. Then I saw what the excitement was all about.

"Rocks, bits of broken stone, tufts of grass, twigs. Looked as if they were floating in water, frozen. Swirls of mud here and there, all petrified in the ice. And way back—maybe fifty yards—you could see other things—bigger things."

"What kind of things?" I asked him, but he did not see me any longer.

"I told Trench to go ahead," the whispering voice went on. "Cut a side tunnel back. Sent word to the admiral to come down. By the time he got there we were sixty feet into the side wall. I'd had them steer for the nearest big object. He came down that tunnel swearing, wanting to know who the damned sightseers were who were diverting our resources into jaunts off into the countryside. I didn't answer him—just pointed.

"There, about forty feet away, a creature slumped a little sideways as though he'd leaned against a wall for a rest. His trunk was curled back against his chest and his tusks sort of glowed in the searchlight. Looked just like the old elephant they had back in the zoo at home, when I was a kid, except he had a coat of two-foot-long hair, reddish-black, plastered to his body as if he was wet.

"Hayle damn near fell down. He stood there and gaped, then yelled at the crew to work in closer. We cleared the way, and they went at it. Water was sloshing around our feet, ankle deep; the pumps weren't keeping up. Air smelled bad. Lots of small items melting out; small animals, vegetation, black mud. He called a halt at ten feet. You could see old Jumbo now as if you were standing just beyond a glass cage. There was dirt caked on his flanks, and you could see mud still adhering to his feet. His eyes were open, and they caught the light and threw it back. His mouth was half open and the inside was dull red, and his tongue poked out at one corner. One of his tusks had the tip broken and splintered. They were yellower than elephant ivory, long and thin, and they curved out . . ."

"I know what a mammoth looks like," I said, "So you found one frozen; it's happened before. What makes it important?"

He moved his eyes to look at me. "Not like this one, they haven't. It wasn't a mammoth! It was a mastodon. And he was buckled into a harness like a circus pony."

CHAPTER TWO

"A mastadon in harness," I snorted, I was humoring him. "I suppose that implies that Antarctica was warmer once than it is now, that it was inhabited, and that the natives had tamed elephants. If the world weren't in the process of shaking itself to pieces, I'd find that pretty interesting, I guess—but still nothing to do murder over."

He lay there, his eyes shut, his chest rising and falling unevenly. His wrist was like a dry stick when I checked it; the pulse was fast and light. I did not know whether he was asleep or in a coma. Then his eyes opened suddenly. They were the only part of him that moved now.

"That was only the beginning," he said. His voice was fainter now, as though it were coming from somewhere far away. "We went on down with the main shaft. At seventy-three hundred feet, we came into a layer filled with artifacts like the Field Museum in Chicago before the lake got it. Wood, vegetation, planks, pieces of structures, paper, cloth items. Clothing in vivid colors, woven of heavy wool. Leather shoes, furniture, broken dishes—and some that weren't broken. Then we found the man." He stopped, and his face twitched. I waited and he went on.

"Short—not over five six, thick in the body, arms like a wrestler. Covered with hair—like Jumbo; pale, dirty-blond hair, and a face like your bad dreams. Big square teeth, and he was showing 'em. Thin lips, pulled back. He looked mad—plenty mad. He was wearing clothes—mostly straps and bits of brass, but well made. And there was a gun in his hand—a mean-looking weapon, short, like a riot gun, with a big chamber. We tested it later. It blew a forty-foot crater in the ice on the shortest burst I could fire. Never did figure out how it worked.

"It was all pay dirt from then on. More of these ape men, more animals; then we saw the peak of what we thought was a mountain, rising up from below. It wasn't a mountain. It was a building. We melted our way down to it, forced a door. There was no ice inside. We wondered about that; then we decided that snowfalls had buried the buildings; and the inhabitants had evacuated, set up temporary camps on the top of the snow. But it kept snowing. In time the weight compressed the snow into clear ice. Probably there was some tunneling down to the city; we found what looked like old bores, flooded and frozen.

"I was in the advance party that broke into the tower. Terrible odor. Strange-looking furniture, mostly rotted, rotted rugs and wall hanging, some bones—men and animals. And one skeleton of a modern type man with a broken skull. We got the idea the Neanderthal types were slaves. Maybe one of them paid off a grudge.

"There were plenty of metal and ceramic items around—not primitive. We were all pretty excited. Then—things started to happen. We heard noises, saw signs that somebody had been there ahead of us. Then men started disappearing. Found one man dead, with a hole in him. Hayle called topside for reinforcements. No answer. He figured the cable was broken. He sent me up with a couple of men to check on things, report what we'd run into. He was worried—plenty worried.

"At the top, Bachman and the other sailor stepped off. I stayed in the lift to run a test on the telephone. I got Hayle: he yelled something at me, but I couldn't make it out. Sounded like shots; then nothing.

"I started out to join the men—and it blew. I saw a flash; ice hit me in the face, and the car started to fall . . .

"When I came to, I was still in the car, in the dark. It was canted sideways, hall full of pulverized ice. I wasn't hurt much—a few bruises, but my left glove was gone, and my faceplate.

"I could see a dim glow up above. I went to work on the ice. It was like loose gravel. Maybe I should have gone down to check on the Admiral—but I didn't. I got to the surface the quickest way I could. The car had jammed in the shaft about ten feet down. There was nothing in sight but ice. No sign of the camp, or of Bachman or the other men. And no signs of a big quake, either. Just a sort of crater where the tunnel mouth had been.

"It was eight miles to Station Three. My snowcat was gone with the rest. I took a bearing on the sun and started walking. Made it in just under five hours. Nothing there. Just a lot of broken ice.

"I took a break, rested, ate part of my suit rations. The coverall was keeping me warm enough. The batteries were good for another couple of hundred hours. I headed for Station Four. Half a mile out from it I found a motor sledge, loaded and fueled and footprints leading off to a ridge of ice, blood on the snow. I followed. It was Hansen, dead.

"I took the sledge, went on in. It was the same—just a stretch of ice. No trace of the huts, the equipment—or the men. The shaft was closed, obliterated. I used the radio on the sledge to try to raise Base Camp. No answer.

"It took me four days to check out the camps and get back to the coast. We'd left the squadron at anchor, sub-surface. I made it out to a tender—it was the closest to shore, and in shallow water. I got in and found her flooded. We'd left a skeleton complement behind. Three of them were there, dead, no marks on their bodies. I could have pumped her out, but I couldn't handle a two-thousand-tonner alone. I took a motorized lifeboat, stocked it with canned goods, and headed north.

"Seven days at sea; then I made port at a small Argentine town that had been a plantation village halfway up a mountain. It was a port now; a couple of hundred boats tied up to makeshift wharves, refugees everywhere. I tried to find a doctor for my hand and face—frostbite. There weren't any. No communications, either. I tried to pull rank on an Argentine gunboat skipper and nearly got myself shot.

"That night I went down to my boat with an armful of fresh fruit I'd gotten for my wristwatch. They jumped me as I was untying the dinghy to row out to her. I was lucky. The light was bad and the first one missed with his knife and I nailed him with a boathook. I shot the other one, and pushed off. Lots of lights on the beach by the time I headed out of the harbor, but nobody chased me.

"I made landfall south of Baton Rouge in four days. Played it cagy, brought her into a bayou mouth at night, kept out of sight behind flooded-out houses. Left the boat hidden and got into town. Tried to get a message off to a contact in Washington, but no luck. Chaos in the town. Famine was beginning to pinch then. All the refugees from the coast and from the fault areas farther west. Air like a foundry, soot everywhere, and more tremors every day.

"I took a car and headed east. Near Vicksburg a car tried to force me off the road. I fooled 'em; they hit instead. I went back and looked them over. Two men, dressed in plain suits, no identification. Looked about forty, fifty, might have been Americans, maybe not.

"Towns in bad shape all the way. Big buildings down, smaller places looted clean, not many cars on the road, and those playing it safe. I kept my pistol up on the dash, in plain sight.

"Reached here on the third day—maybe a week ago. Saw food in here; then a quake caught me. Thought it was them, at first—like the ice shaft." He twitched his face in a ghastly grin.

"You think the polar expedition was wiped out

by—whoever is chasing you?"

"You can stake your life on it!" His whisper was fierce. "And they're in the town now. They're out there—looking for me. I was shrewd. I parked the car blocks away, meant to walk back . . ."

"They're not there now," I reminded him, trying to speak gently.

"Searching the town," he said. "Won't give up. Find me in the end. And I'll be ready . . ." He lifted his hand an inch, looked puzzled. "Where's my gun?"

"You won't need it," I started. "I'm going to take you—"

"They got it," he said. A tear leaked from the corner of his eye, ran down his scarred face. "Must have . . . gone to sleep . . ."

I got to my feet, fitted my mask back on. "Come on," I said. "Time to go." I got an arm under his back, started to lift him. He gave a thin cry like a stepped-on kitten. His eyes blinked, settled on my face.

"You take it," he said. "Show it . . . them. Make . . . listen . . ."

"Sure, old-timer. Come on, now; got to pick you up—"

"Pocket," he gasped out. "Take it. Show . . ." His jaw dropped and his eyes glazed over like hardening solder. I checked his wrist again. The last feeble flutter was gone.

For a minute, in the total silence, I looked at him, wondering how much, if any, of the wild story he had told had been true, and how much delirium. His pocket, he had said. I tried two, found only dust. There was an old-fashioned watch pocket under his belt that I almost missed. I stuck a finger in, felt something smooth and cool. I eased it out—a big, thick, round coin, just smaller than a silver dollar, with the tawdry yellow shine of pure gold. There was a stylized representation of a bird on one side; the obverse was covered with an elaborate pattern of curlicues that didn't quite seem to be writing.

I pocketed it, stood up—and heard a sound from the street.

Below the level of the glass- and plaster-littered sill where the front window had been was a scatter of glass chips and broken brick. I went flat on them, the gun in my hand without a conscious move on my part. The sound came again; the rattle of my plank bridge under the weight of feet. It was thirty feet to the back of the shop, through an obstacle course of fallen cans and broken bottles. I made it with no more sound than smoke makes going up a chimney, got to my feet in an alley half choked with flood-washed rubbish over-sprinkled with fallen stucco and drifted dust. It was almost dark now; the sun had sunk behind the dust clouds. I moved along silent-footed in the dust carpet, keeping near the wall to make my prints a little less obvious to anyone who might try to follow.

The street at the end was empty. I went along it to the corner, risked a look, saw a man in a dark suit come out of the store. He went to the plank, climbed up. The street was dark except for long shafts of blood red light striking across through gaps in the buildings. there were no birdcalls, no hum of insects, just the creaking from the man on the bridge, going carefully on all fours. He reached the top, stepped off. He must have found the dead sailor; that would satisfy him. Now he would be on his way. I watched him move off out of sight; then I stepped out, hugging the building fronts. I was not thinking—just reacting. It seemed suddenly important to keep him in sight, get the license number of his car, maybe trail him . . .

I heard the click of metal and dived, hit hard on cracked concrete, rolled, came up among the folds of a dangling awning, heard the flat *crack!* of a gun. I could not tell what direction the shot had come from; the dust muffled everything, killing echoes. Feet were hurrying toward me. I heard a shout, an answer from above. The steps were slower now, passing by mere feet from me—

They halted, and I crouched, almost feeling the bullet crashing through my brain. It was not a time for indecision. I doubled my legs, launched myself from my hideaway in a driving tackle, hit him just below the knees—face-first. I saw a blinding shower of stars, and he was down, and I lunged, caught a swinging arm, drove a fist into what felt like his throat. He made a noise like broken pipes, kicked out, but I was across his chest now, my right hand on his throat. He pounded my back like a pal trying to clear my windpipe, then quit and lay back. I got to my knees, breathing hard. Blood was running down into my mouth, I squinted up at the higher section of the street, saw a head moving along away from me. He had not heard the skirmish—or had not interpreted it correctly. He thought his partner was still padding along the street, following whatever it was he had fired at.

Kneeling, I checked the dead man's pockets. They were clean. He wore no watch, no ring, nothing personal.

Steps were coming back. I saw, not thirty feet away, a silhouette against the streak of red sky under the smoke layer. The man looked at the plank, swung round, started down, twisting his head to look over his shoulder; dim light from below cast a ruddy highlight on his cheek. Then he saw me. His mouth opened and I jumped, caught the edge of the two-by-six, heaved it up. He went over without a sound, caught himself with one hand, held on, dangling, his feet working like a bicycle rider. I jerked the board hard, and he went down. It seemed like a long time before he hit.

Ten minutes later, not rested and not fed, operating on pure adrenalin, I was headed east along a dirt road with the autodrive on ninety.

CHAPTER THREE

An hour after full dark I pulled into a one-pump motel-cum-cafe where a long-legged fellow with thin blondish hair and a mouth like a torn pocket met me at the door with a shotgun. He fueled me up, sold me coffee and a moon pie with a texture like vinyl tile, and accepted a well-worn twenty as payment. I felt him smiling craftily at his business acumen; the habits of a lifetime of penny-pinching are hard to break.

The beach came into view an hour later—a dark mirrorgleam reflecting the dirty clouds boiling along above. Trees and rooftops showed above the surface for a mile or two out; it had been gently sloping farmland before the ocean reclaimed it. The pavement slid off under the water without a ripple; I boosted my revs, rode my air cushion out onto it. It was not recommended practice—if you lost power you sank, but I was in no mood to go boat hunting. I poured on the coal and headed south.

It was a nice three-hour run on still water under a moon the color and shape of a rotten grapefruit. Once a patrol boat hailed me, but I doused my lights and outran him. Once I passed over a town that had installed one of the new floodproof all-automatic power systems. The lights gleamed up at me through green water like something from a fairy tale.

Just before dawn I hit a stretch of treetops clogged with floating wild life. I threaded a twisting path through them, reached dry land as the sun came up reddish-black and flat on the bottom.

Tampa was a reeking ruin, a seaport town miles from the sea, surrounded by a bog of gray mud, left high and dry by the freakish withdrawal of the Gulf. Nothing there for me.

Early afternoon brought me into Miami. The beach was wiped clean—a bare sandbar, but the city proper still gleamed white beside a shore stained black by pumice and scum oil, and heaped with the jetsam of a drowned continent. Conditions were better here. There had been no major quakes to judge from the still-standing towers of coral and chartreuse and turquoise; maybe their hurricane-proof construction had helped when the ground shook under them. There was even a semblance of normal commerce. Police were much in evidence, along with squads of nervous-looking Guard recruits weighted down with combat gear. Lights were on in shops and restaurants, and the polyarcs along Biscayne were shedding their baleful light on an orderly traffic of cars, trucks and buses. There were fewer people on the streets than in normal times, but that suited me.

I checked into the Gulfstream—a lavish hundred and fifty-story hostelry that had known my custom in happier times. The desk man was a former Las Vegas man named Sal Anzio; he gave a two-handed shake and the twitch of the left check that passed with him for smile.

"Mal Irish," he stated in the tone of one answering questions under duress. "What brings you into town?"

"Things went a little sour down south," I told him. "The Mexicans have a tendency to get over-excited when things go wrong, and blame it all on the gringos. Anything doing here?"

"Sure. Plenty of action. We had most of the regular spring crowd down here when the word went out. Most of 'em stayed on. A few tourists pulled out, but what the hell. We're doing OK. We got power, water, plenty of reserve food. Every hotel in town had their freezers stocked for a big summer trade. We're all right—for another six months, anyway. After that—well, I got a boat staked out. For a grand I can fix you with a spot."

I told him I would let him know later, took the key to a suite on the hundred and twelfth, and took the high-speed lift up.

It was a nice room, spacious, tastefully decorated, with a big doubled bed and a bath big enough to water a pet hippo in. I soaked off the dust of five days' travel, called room service for a change of clothes. I had a drink in the room, then, prompted by a vague yearning for human companionship, went down to the tenth floor terrace for dinner.

The best of the sunset was just past. Coal-black clouds rimmed with melted gold hung over the ink-colored sea like a threat. The sky was glowing yellow green, and it shed an eerie, enchanted light over the tables, the potted palms, the couples at the tables.

Off to the north you could see a dull glow in the sky—a reflection from the red-hot lava that was building a new mountain range across Georgia. The surface of the Gulf was a little odd too. The normal wave pattern was disturbed by an overlay of ripples set up by the constant minor trembling of the sea bottom. But the band murmured of love and the diners smiled and lifted glasses and to hell with tomorrow.

After a nice dinner of fresh scampi and Honduras shrimp accented with an Anjou rose, I went down to the pleasure rooms on the third floor. Anzio was there, wearing his pale lavender tux and overlooking the tables with his version of a look of benign efficiency—an expression like Caesar's favorite executioner picking out his next client.

"Howzit, Mal," he checked me over with his quick glance that could estimate the size of a bankroll to the last half cee. "Care to try your luck tonight?"

"Maybe later, Sal," I told him. "Who's in town?"

He reeled off a roster of familiar ne'er-do-wells and the parasites who preyed off them. I found my attention wandering. It was a nice night, a nice crowd, but something was worrying me. I kept remembering the man with the broken legs, and the silent, not overly bright boys who had come gunning for him—and for me. Three of them. All dead. Killed by me, a peaceful man who'd never fired a shot in anger until yesterday. But what else could I have done? They were out to kill—and I had beaten them to the prize. It was that simple. And yet it was not simple at all.

"... people in town," Sal was saying. "Some strange cats, true, but rolled, Mal, rolled."

"Who's that fellow?" A slim chap was moving past in black tails and white tie, almost but not quite conservative enough to look a little odd in the fashionable crowd.

"Huh? I dunno." Sal lifted his chin in a gesture of dismissal. "One of those kooks in here for this convention, I guess."

"What convention?" I did not know quite what it was about the man's look that bothered me. He was bland-faced, fortyish, well groomed, quiet, wearing about as much expression as an omelet.

"This noomismatics bunch, or whatever you call it. Got the twenty-eighth and twenty-ninth floors. Biggest bunch of creeps you ever saw, if you ask me. No action there, Mal."

"Numismatics, huh?" Coin collectors. I had a coin upstairs—a heavy gold coin, handed me by a dying man with as wild a tale as ever curled a kid's hair at bedtime. He had wanted me to take it—somewhere, tell someone his story. Some story. I would wind up either kicked down a couple of flights of official stairs, or locked up until the birdies stopped singing in my ears. Mammoths under ice. Cave men in fancy pants, packing ray guns. The poor fellow had been raving, blowing his top in his final delirium, that was all. Nothing for me to get emotional about. The coin was probably a novelty piece, solid lead with a gold wash, issued to commemorate a tie for third in basketball scored by good old Pawtucket High in the hot season of '87.

And then again, maybe not.

Numismatics. They would know about coins. It would not take ten minutes to show it to one of them, get an opinion. That would settle the question once and for all, and leave me to get on undisturbed with the important business of providing for the needs of one Malcome Irish, late of the U.S. Navy and later still of the army of the unemployed, a healthy eater with a burning desire to experience the best his era had to offer—such as it was—with the least possible discomfort.

"Thanks, Sal," I said, and headed for the elevators.

The twenty-eighth floor was silent, somber under rose-toned glare strips set in the ceiling in a geometric pattern. Through wide double glass doors at the end of the corridor I could see a bright room where people stood in the static poses of cocktail-party conversation. I went along the pale, immaculate carpet, pushed through into a dull mutter of talk. Faces turned my way—bland, ordinary faces, calm to the point of boredom. A waiter eased over, offered a small tray of sweet-smelling drinks in flimsy glasses. I lifted one, let my eyes drift over the crowd.

They were all men, none very old, none very young, mostly in neat, dull-colored evening clothes, a few wearing sportier tartans or pastels. Eyes followed my progress as I moved across the room. A tall fellow with slicked-back gray hair drifted in from offside, edged casually into my path. It was either talk to him or knock him down—a smooth intercept. I gave him a crafty smile.

"I'm not party-crashing," I confided. "I'm not one of your group here, but I do have an interest in coins—"

"Certainly, sir," he purred; the corners of his mouth lifted the required amount, no more. "An amateur coin fancier, perhaps?"

"Yes, in a small way. Actually, I wanted an opinion on a piece I picked up a while back . . ." I fished the big coin from an inner pocket. Light gleamed on it as I turned it over in my fingers.

"Probably a phony," I said lightly, "but maybe you can tell me for sure." I held it out to him. He did not take it. He was looking at the coin, the protocol smile gone now, lines showing tight in his neck.

"Don't get the wrong impression," I said quickly. "I'm not asking for free service. I realize that an expert opinion is worth a reasonable fee . . ."

"Yes," he said. "I wonder, sir, if you would be so kind as to step this way for one moment. I will ask Mr. Zablun to have a look at your, ah, find." He had a trace of accent, I thought, a barely discernible oddness of intonation. He turned away and I followed him across to a limed-oak slab door, through it and down a step into a lounge with a look of institutional intimacy, like a corporation waiting room.

"If you'll have a seat for a moment . . ." He waved a neat hand at a too-low chair done in fuzzy gray polyon, disappeared through a door across the room. I stood where I was, holding the coin on my palm. It was heavy enough, but so were all properly made gold bricks. In a minute I would probably get a withering smile from some old geezer with a pince-nez who would tell me my prize was inscribed in pig latin meaning "there's a sucker born every minute." I put it between my teeth, bit down gently, felt the metal yield. If it was gold, it was the pure article.

A door opened behind me and I jumped. I was as tense as a second-story man waiting for the down car. The bouncer was back with a short, plumpish fellow with artificial-looking black hair and a darting eye.

"May I present Mr. Zablun," the gray-haired smoothie waved a hand in a prestidigitator's gesture. "He will be happy to have a look at the piece, Mr. ummm . . ."

"Philbert," I supplied. "Jimmy Philbert, from Butte, Montana."

Mr. Zablun's head bobbed on his short neck in a Prussian-type nod. He came across and held out a cluster of fingers. I poked the coin at them and he thrust it up under his eye as though he were wearing a jeweler's lens. Then he held it in front of the other eye, giving it a crack at the find.

He and Gray Hair exchanged a quick glance. I started to reach for the coin, but Zablun had turned for the side door.

"If you'll just follow along, Mr. Philbert," Gray Hair said. He waved that graceful hand again and I trailed the short man along a narrow passage into a low-ceilinged room with a plain desk with a draftsman's lamp shedding a cold light on a green show blotter. Zablun went briskly behind the desk, pulled open a drawer, got out a black cloth, a small electronic-looking gadget, a set of lenses like measuring spoons, began fussing over my trophy. If it was a hog-calling award, at least it was not obvious at a glance.

Gray Hair stood by, not saying anything, no expression on his face. There was a small window at the side of the office; through it I could see a red glare on the water from the rising moon.

Zablun was putting things back in the drawer now, being very precise about their arrangement. He placed the coin back on the desktop at the exact center of the pool of light, stood.

"The coin is genuine," he said indifferently. "Gold, twenty-four point nine fine. Mint specimen."

"You've seen one like it before?"

"It is not a great rarity."

"Where's it from?"

"A number have come to light at Crete in recent years. Not so fine, you understand. Not uncirculated."

"A Greek coin, eh?"

"The actual origin is unknown. Where did you secure the piece?" His tone was as cool as a detective lieutenant running through his list of routine questions; it had that same quality of impeccable politeness, as impersonal as a traffic light.

"I picked it up in a poker game at Potosi a couple of weeks back," I confided. "I was afraid I'd been suckered. Ah, by the way, what's it worth?"

"I can offer you fifty cees, Mr. Philbert." Gray Hair stepped into the conversation.

"I don't think I want to sell right now," I said. "Makes a nice pocket piece." I reached, lifted the thick coin from the desk. "Just wanted to be sure I hadn't been taken."

"Perhaps an offer of one hundred cees—"

"It's not a matter of price." I showed them a breezy smile. "I took it for a ten-cee bet. I think I'll just hang onto it. Maybe it brings me luck. I've stayed alive lately; that takes luck today." I turned to the door. Gray Hair beat me to it, slipped past me, led the way back to a door that opened into the wide hall with the cream-colored carpet.

"How much do I owe you?" I reached for my wallet, still beaming the happy smile of a fellow who has lucked into something.

"Please." Gray Hair waved the idea of payment away. "If you should change your mind, Mr. Philbert . . ."

"I'll let you know first thing," I assured him. He inclined his head; I sauntered off toward the lift. At the end of the hall I looked back. The lights were just going off in the big room. In the elevator I took out the coin, studied it carefully under the dome light. The metal was bright, smooth, unscarred. The little mark I had made biting it was gone.

Zablun had switched coins on me.

CHAPTER FOUR

Anzio was the kind of man who never let curiosity interfere with business arrangements. The fifty-cee note I passed him assured me free access to an empty suite on the twenty-ninth floor of the unused north wing, commanding a view of the full length of the main east-west block, with a set of 8x40 binoculars from the lost-and-found room thrown in. Another ten cees covered the services of an off-duty hop to loiter near the side entrance and report to me when and if the gray-haired gent—who was registered as R. Sethys—chose that route to leave the building.

Room service brought me a midnight snack. I ate it in the dark, watching the activities of the money men behind the dozen lighted windows on their two floors. Mr. Zablun appeared half an hour after I started my vigil, talking to a group who seemed to listen with monumental indifference. Men came and went, moving with unhurried gravity. They did not seem to be doing any drinking; no women were in evidence; no one even lit a cigar. They were an abstemious bunch, these numismatists. For that matter, they did not seem much interested in coins. I had a fine, clear view of their activities through the glass and steelprod walls, and not a glint of gold or silver did I see.

After a few hours of this sport, I left my post and went down to bed. I did not know what it was I was looking for, but my instincts told me to play a concealed hand, to lie low and watch. Mr. Zablun had not lifted my souvenir for nothing. Raising a howl when I discovered the switch would not have bought me anything, but a little judicious spying might net me something solid to work on. The theft of the gold piece did not lend any specific support to the sailor's story—Zablun might have palmed it for the gold in it—but on the other hand it had not been the nice, clean dismissal I had expected. Whatever the coin was, it had not come in a Cracker Jack box—and I had had ample evidence that there were men loose in the land who would kill to get it—

Or would they? There was no necessary connection between the dead man's story and the real reason for the hunters on his trail. For all I knew, he might have been an escaped maniac, and the men in the unmarked suits might have been CBI boys, with orders to shoot on sight. The shots they had fired at me might have been a simple case of mistaken identity; maybe they were not expecting anyone but Jack the Ripper in the ruined streets of Greenleaf.

And maybe I was Shirley Temple. No CBI man that ever packed a badge was as lousy a shot as the clowns I had gunned down, or as unschooled in the basics of alley fighting. They might, for reasons known to the inner circles of bureaucracy, wander around in suits with empty pockets and no labels—but even a Federal man moving in for a hot pinch would not blaze away at a stranger on sight.

It was a futile argument, and I was losing both sides of it. I switched off the light, punched the pillow into shape, and made myself a promise that first thing in the morning I would scale the coin out over the breakers and channel my efforts to matters of more immediate concern to my future—such as locating a serious poker game to replenish my reduced resources. I was picturing a succession of inside straights and four-card flushes when the phone rang.

"Mal—funny thing. Your stamp collectors—they're stirred up like an Elk's smoker tipped off to a vice raid. Your friend Sethys left by the front door two minutes ago; he's standing out on the drive in the rain giving the garageman a hard time about bringing out his car. Now, he says. Hell, it's probably buried in the stacks somewhere down on level four—"

"I'll be down," I told him. "Get me a car—any car—before he has his."

Six minutes later by my cuff-link Omega I slid into the seat of a low-built foreign job that Anzio had pulled around to the side in the shelter of a screen of hibiscus.

"For cripe's sake get it back in one piece, Mal," he hissed at me, squinting against the drizzle. "It belongs to some big oil bid in the tower suite—"

"If they nab me, I stole it." Another fifty cees changed hands. At this rate that game had better be soon—preferably with a couple of Maharajahs with just enough IQ to raise into a pat hand.

The turbos hummed at me when I touched the go pedal; there was plenty of power under the squat black hood. I eased her out, watched Sethys get into the back of a heavy maroon Monojag with three other coin collectors. They gunned off down the drive and I let them take a hundred-yard lead, then slid out behind them.

Old Miami was a town I had known well once, a lot of years ago. It had not changed much in the decade since I had last seen it—except for the recent scars of storm and flood. The high tides set up by the tremors that rocked the Gulf floor had swept it, east to west, half a dozen times, scoured away topsoil, lawns, shrubbery, felling twenty-year-old royal palms, sweeping to well-deserved oblivion the older, flimsier construction that dated back to post-boom times. But the main portion of the city—the famous two-hundred-story luxury hotels, the downtown streets of high-priced shops, the walled and remote residences, each on its manicured acre that made up the wealthiest suburbs north of Rio—they were unchanged.

I followed the Monojag along Flagler under the multiple spans of Interstate 509, west into a section of massive concrete warehouses and gaunt steel food-processing plants, the ugly spawn of the South American import trade that had been building to boom proportions before the onset of the catastrophies. Now they were run-down, rust-streaked, their yards grown high with rank weeds sprouted since the last high water a few weeks before. There were few polyarcs here; the Jag's headlights cut diamond-white swathes through flat black shadow.

My quarry was moving slowly now, creeping along at ten miles per hour. Once or twice the wan beam of a hand-flash probed furtively at a dark side street, flicked over a sign post. I kept well back, showing no lights, my turbos flicking over at minimum—just enough to keep my bumper rails off the blacktop. Ahead, the car stopped; I slid to the curb and grounded. Two men hopped out briskly, casting long, awkward shadows in the light of a block-distant pole. They ducked to confer briefly with their driver, shot a look my way which missed me in the shadows, then stepped off into an alley mouth. The Jag started up, moved quickly to the next corner, swung left. By the time I reached the corner—hanging back a little to give the ground troops time to put distance between themselves and the street—it was making another left turn ahead. I pulled to the curb halfway up the block.

I cracked the canopy, listened hard, heard nothing but the ancient song of the frogs, sounding complacent about the changes that had come to the area—their tribe had seen it all before, a hundred times. Out on the sidewalk I listened some more, heard car doors clack. It was a short sprint to the corner. Fifty yards along I saw the Monojag parked, doors open, a dim courtesy light from inside spilling out on the legs of two men, one of whom might have been my gray-haired acquaintance. They turned away, disappeared into what looked like a blank wall.

I did some mental estimating; their position was roughly opposite the alley mouth the first pair had entered. They were setting up a cordon—closing in on something—or someone.

But they had missed a bet—maybe. Back around the corner, where I had parked my borrowed Humber there had been a narrow air space cutting back into the monolothic Portland facades. I did not know where the alleys my friends had entered joined, but there was at least a chance that the side way I had seen intersected them. If so, their rabbit had a bolt hole. I dropped back and ran.

At the car, all was quiet. No hunted fugitives had dashed out from the dark crack in the wall; no shots and yells indicated a successful snatch somewhere back in the lightless recesses of the warehouse complex. There was not even a cheery drunk caroling his way home after a long evening with the daughter of the vine. There was just me, feeling a little fuzzy at three A.M., standing in the rain and wearing a trench coat over pajamas, and shoes without socks, looking from my borrowed car to the silent, faceless wall before me, and wondering just what it was that had seemed so important a few minutes earlier. For all I knew, Gray Hair owned the warehouse. Maybe he was a big importer, down checking on a report of mice. Maybe he was a member of the volunteer firemen, hot on the trail of an incipient blaze. If I was really interested in what he was doing, the small, shy voice of common sense was suggesting, why not walk up to him and ask him.

"Hi, there, Mr. Sethys," I would say. "Just noticed you taking a drive in the middle of the night, and thought I'd trail along and ask why . . ."

There was a sound from the two-foot wide air space—a rustle, as of someone moving quickly, stealthily. I moved over against the wall, one hand on the butt of my .38 like a good churchman fingering his crucifix for luck. I could hear breathing now—short, gasping breaths, noises made by someone who had run a long way and was about played out. Then I caught another sound—the hard clack of feet, running without much concern for who might be listening; confident feet, closing the gap.

I waited. Sound would carry in the confined space; the chaser and the chased were close, but it was hard to estimate—

There was a grunt, a muffled yelp, noises that indicated blows, lots of heavy breathing. The chasee had been caught yards from where I stood. Whoever it was, he was in the hands of Sethys' legmen now. I had poked my nose in—or tried to—but so far I was clean. I could slide back into my black leather seat and drift off into the night, and no one the wiser. Tomorrow I could get started on recouping my fortunes, and by this time next week the whole thing would seem like a bout of delirium. It was none of my business and if I was smart, it never would be.

I took two steps and slid into the narrow alley.

Ten feet away, a man stood, his arms clamped around a little slim fellow wrapped in a too-long coat. It was three jumps to where the tableau showed as a contorted black silhouette against the light from behind; I made it in two, caught the big boy by the collar, laid the flat of the gun across the side of his head. He kicked out, hit the wall as I pivoted behind him. My second swing caught him on the jaw. He lost his grip, slipped down into a half crouch, and I hit him again, putting plenty of power behind it, saw him sprawl out flat. Then I looked up—just in time to meet a big steel ball somebody had brought in to wreck the building with.

Fireworks were showering, pretty colors whirling around and round, round and round, and I was whirling with them, feeling ghostly bricks grinding into my face. I was remotely aware of a thin scream, the crunch of heavy feet across me, the impact of a mule kick in my side. Then I was clawing at a coarse-textured wall, blinking through haze at two figures who swayed above me in a strange and violent dance, swinging first this way, then that, locked in a close embrace. One of the dancers slipped, almost went down. I was on my knees now, creeping up the wall like a human fly tackling the Blue Tower in Manhattan, game, but a little discouraged by the long trip ahead.

There was another cry—a chocked-off sob—and somehow I was standing, watching the close walls sway, under my hands. My mouth was open and drums beat behind my eyes; something hot and wet was running down over my chin. The back of a man before me was big, broad in a dark coat; the head was bent down, only the mussed hair on the back of the neck visible. I could not see the other dancer now.

I moved and my foot hit the gun. I grabbed it, went up on my toes, swung it down in a stiff-armed blow that had all my weight behind it. The impact was solid and unyielding, like kicking a watermelon. The big wide back twisted, fell away, and I was looking into a thin, frightened face, coal-dark eyes as big as black pansies—a woman's face.

A fan of light from a dropped torch gleamed on the rain-wet wall. I stamped on it, grabbed for her arm that was thrust out as if to push me away.

"Come on," I said blurrily. "Got a car—down here."

A trickle of blood was running down the high-cheek-boned face. She did not look much better than I felt. I yanked her arm, and she came, reluctantly.

"Let's go—fast." I set off at a ragged run. There might have been a shout from along the alley behind me; I was not sure, and I did not care. The object of the game was to get to the car before my legs quit on me, before the rocketing pains back of my eyes blew their way to the surface and took a piece of skull with them. That was enough for me to think about at the moment.

It seemed like a long way before I came out onto the street, still holding her damp sleeve in one hand, the gun in the other, thinking about Mr. Sethys and his chums waiting there to greet me, but the shining, dark pavement was empty. I groped my way to the canopy release, popped it, half lifted my new friend in, swung aboard and kicked the car away from the curb before the hatch dropped. The Humber howled up to speed, bounced her side bumpers twice on the guide rail as I swung her into a well-lit cross avenue, then settled down to outrun whatever might be chewing up the pavement behind her.

They were waiting for me at the Gulfstream, three men in a cosy group by the waterless fountain beside the entrance to the big main drive, standing hatless in the rain. I slid the Humber on past, whipped to the right at the corner, gunned it back to sixty.

Six blocks from the hotel I parked in a half empty lot littered with fallen palm fronds. The woman on the seat beside me looked around quickly, then at me.

"We walk from here," I said. My tongue was too thick for my mouth. The pain in my head had abated to a dull throbbing, but I was dizzy as a week-end sailor in a sixty-mile gale. The hatch lifted and cold rain spattered in. I helped her out, took a minute to wipe blood from my chin from a cut lip, started off at a fast walk toward the lights of an all-night bar shining a cheerful mortuary blue through the smoke-tasting mist.

Inside, we took a table at the back near a door that ought to open onto an alley. I did not check it; I was not doing anything until I had downed a bracing dram. A thin, sunscarred man with small eyes in nests of pale wrinkles came over, took an order for two double Scotches. So far, my lady fair had not said a word.

"Sethys must have a phone in his car," I told her. "Must have called in, told them what to look for. Or maybe he didn't. Maybe I spooked. Those three might have been off-duty waiters sweating out the last bus to the suburbs. Just as well. Don't know what I stuck my neck into. Good idea to fade out of sight anyway."

The waiter brought the drinks; I took half of

mine without coming up for air. My drinking partner had hers in both hands swallowing. Then she choked, almost dropped the glass. From her expression I guessed that she had just discovered you do not chugalug hard liquor.

"Take it easy," I suggested. There was a glass of water beside her; I picked it up, offered it. She grabbed at it, sniffed, then drank, stuck her tongue into the glass to get the last drop.

"You're hungry," I said. The waiter was there again, holding out a folded towel.

"You missed a spot on the side of your jaw, buddy," he said in a voice like wind on hot sand. "Got a nice mouse working there, too." He flicked his eyes to my table mate, took in the wet hair, the oversized coat, the hungry look. I took the towel. It was cold and wet.

"Thanks. How about something to eat—hot soup, maybe?"

"Yeah, I can fetch you something." He went away without asking the questions; if you are lucky, you meet a few like that in a lifetime. I waited until the fat man getting up from the next booth had wheezed his way to the cashier, then I leaned across the table. The big dark eyes looked at me, still wary.

"Who are you, miss?" I kept my voice at a confidential pitch. "What was it all about back there?"

Her expression tightened a bit. She had nice teeth, even and white; they were set together like a soldier biting a bullet.

"I'm the fellow who butted in on your side, remember?" I tried out a small smile. "Any enemy of Sethys is a friend of mine."

She shivered. Her fingers were locked together like two arthritics shaking hands. I put my hand over them. They were as cold as marble.

"You've had a hell of an experience, but it's over now. Relax. I think we've got enough now to take to the police. Even in these times attempted murder's enough to interrupt the chief's nap for."

The waiter was back with two big plates of fish chowder on a tray, a couple of sandwiches on the side. The girl watched him put hers down in front of her, eyed the big spoon, then grabbed it with a ping-pong player's grip and dug in. She did not slow down until the bowl was dry. Then she looked at my bowl, I was watching her with my mouth open—a favorite expression of mine lately.

"Slow down, kid," I advised. "Here, try a sandwich." I picked up one of them—thick slabs of bread with a generous pile of ham between them—and offered it. She put it in her bowl, lifted the top bread slice, sniffed, then proceeded to clean out the ham with her fingers. When she finished, she licked them carefully, like a cat.

"Well," I commented, "maybe now we can get on with our talk. You haven't told me who you are."

She gave me an appealing look, flashed what might have been the hint of a smile, and said something that sounded like: "*Ithat ottoc otacu.*"

"Swell," I said. "That helps. The one person in this nutty world that might be able to tell me what's going on, and you speak Low Zulese—or is it Choctaw?"

"*Ottoc oll thitassa,*" she agreed.

"*como se llamo?*? I tried. "*Comment vous*

appelez-vous? Vie heissen Sie? Vad Heter du?" . .

"*Ithat oll uttruk mapala yo,*" she said. "*Mrack.*"

I gnawed the inside of my lip and stared at her. My head was throbbing; I could feel my eyelids wince with each pulse beat.

"We'll have to find a quiet place to hole up," I said, talking to myself now. "It might be a good idea to leave Miami, but to hell with that. I like it here. Mr. Sethys isn't going to run me out of town before I've had my plan."

A medium-sized man in a dark suit had left his bar stool, sauntered over near our table. He stood six feet away, shaking a cigaret from a flip-top box, looking over the selections on the tape-screen box. He was thirty-five, give or take a couple of years, ordinary-looking, with sandy hair and a slightly receding chin. He seemed to be taking a long time with the cigaret.

"Wait right here," I said to the girl in what I hoped was a soothing tone. I stood, pushed the chair back. The man shot a quick glance my way, turned and went across to the door. I followed him through into the misty rain. He was already twenty feet away, walking fast, head down. I closed the gap, caught him by one shoulder, spun him around.

"All right, spill it," I said. "If you've got a gun, don't try it; mine's aimed at your second coat button."

His jaw dropped. He backed away, his hand up chest-high as if to fend me off. I followed him.

"Tell it fast, Mister. Make it good. This headache I've got puts me in a nasty temper."

He shot a look up and down the street. "Listen," he said in a choked voice, "don't shoot, see? You can have the wallet, and the watch—I got a pretty good watch . . ." He fumbled at his wrist.

"Skip the act," I put plenty of snarl into it. "Who's Sethys? What did the coin mean to him? Who were the men tracking the sailor? And what was the idea of mugging the girl?"

"Hah?" He got the watch off, fumbled it, dropped it on the sidewalk. He was against the wall now, leaning away from me. His face was slack and yellowish.

"Last chance." I rammed the gun against him; he made a bleating sound and grabbed for it. I jerked it back and hit him on the side of the jaw. He covered his head with both arms and made broken noises.

"The wallet," I ordered. "Let's see it."

He lowered an arm to fumble it out of his hip pocket; I grabbed it, flipped it open. Stained cards told me this was Jim Ezzard, of 319 S. Tulip Way, insured by Eterna Mutual, accredited to the nation's Standard Oil dealers, a member in arrears of the Jolly Boys Social and Sporting Club, with a draft status of 4-G.

I dropped the wallet on the pavement. "Where were you headed in such a hurry, Ezzard—or whatever your name is? What were you going to tell your boss?"

He was looking at the wallet, lying open at his feet, the few well-worn bills still in it. I could see an idea struggling for birth behind his face.

"You . . . some kind of a cop?" he got out. "I—"

"Never mind what I am. We'll talk about you—"

"You got nothing on me." He was making a fast recovery, jerking his lapels back into line, working his jaw with his hand. "I'm clean as a cue ball all evening, you can check with the bar girls at Simon's—"

"Skip the bar girl at Simon's," I cut him off. "Turn your pockets out." He did, grumbling. They were full of the usual assortment of small change, paperclips, lint and canceled movie tickets.

"You guys are getting too big for your britches," he told me. "Getting where a guy can't stick his nose outside without some flattie—"

"Can it, Jim," I told him, "or I'll turn back into a bad guy."

I walked away, listening to his muttering get louder in inverse ratio to the distance between us.

Back inside the beanery, the girl waited where I had left her.

"Nothing," I said. "False alarm. I guess I'm getting hypersensitive to ordinary-looking men. They all look like they're carrying a hand-filled shiv and cyanide in a back tooth." She gave me her smile again—this time I was sure of it. She was nice to talk to, no back-talk, just a smile.

"Let's go," I took her hand, urged her to her feet. "We'll pick a second-rate house near here. We both need rest. In the morning . . ."

Our waiter caught my eye, tipped his head. I went over. He went on arranging salt and pepper shakers on a tray, spoke from the corner of his mouth.

"I don't know if it's got anything to do with you folks," he said very softly. "But there's a couple fellers got this place staked out, front and rear."

The back door let onto a service passage, very old, very dark, very choked with overflowing garbage cans, heaped plastic cartons, weeds, and less savory reminders of the collapse of the municipal refuse collection system. I was getting pretty familiar with the back alleys of the city. This seemed like one of the less appealing in which to be cornered.

The girl stayed close beside me, scanning the dark path in both directions, even without words she seemed to understand the situation. She was nervous, but there was no panic in the way she watched me and followed my lead.

I kept to the wall, moved off easy-footed. The boy at the back door had been posted down near the street, according to my waiter friend. We might be stealing a march on him—or walking right into his arms, if he had changed position. The first warning I had was a gasp from the girl. She stopped, pointed. I saw him then—flattened against the wall a good twenty feet from the end of the alley. I pulled at her, and she resumed walking, keeping on my left, half a pace behind. My hope was that he had not noticed the momentary hesitation.

Ten feet from him, I started talking—something about the weather—which gave me an excuse to look away from him as the gap closed. Five feet, a yard, one more pace—

I spun, swung my fist backhanded, caught him just under the ribs in the same instant that he lifted a foot to swing in behind us. He doubled over and I kneed him, felt his nose go against my shin. Then he was down, twisting over on his back, one arm groping. I stamped on his wrist, saw the glint of metal as a small gun spun away, clattered against the wall. He lunged, tried to bite my leg. I got a grip on his coat, jerked him half to his feet, yanked the coat down off his shoulders, then held him by his arms.

"Get his tie," I hissed at the girl. I made meaningless motions with my head. She pulled the belt from her oversized coat, went to one knee, took two turns around his wrists and cinched it up as efficiently as a head nurse changing a diaper.

"Tell me about it, mister," I said into his ear. He kicked out, squirmed, spat at me. His mouth was working like someone's who had just gotten a big bite of a bad apple. Then his face tried to stretch itself around to the back of his head. The tendons of his neck stood out like lift cables; his legs straightened, thrust hard. Suddenly there was foam on his mouth. Then he went slack. His wrist when I grabbed it had as much pulse as a leg of lamb.

"I guess I wasn't kidding about the cyanide in the back tooth," I said to the balmy night air. The girl watched with eyes that seemed bigger than ever, while I checked his pockets. Nothing.

I stood up. "The Case of the Inept Asassins," I said aloud. "I don't know what the game is that's afoot, but I've got a feeling we're not winning, in spite of the impressive score we're racking up. They must have manpower to burn."

"*Im allak otturu*," the girl said. She was pointing at a rotted door standing six inches ajar, its lock broken by the frenzy of the man who lay dead at my feet. I pushed it open; across a littered room filled with dark shapes, faint predawn light glowed through dusty windows.

"It looks too easy," I said. "But let's try it anyway."

Ten minutes later, five blocks east of the scene of the skirmish, we found a sagging three-story house with a sign that read ROOMS—DAY, WEEK, MONTH, and a light on in a front window. The old rooster dozing at the desk looked us over like a sorority housemother checking for whiskey breath.

"Ten cees, advance," he challenged. I paid him, added a five.

"That's for that million-dollar smile, Pop," I told him. "Forget you ever saw us, and there'll be another one to keep it warm these cold nights."

"Cops looking for you?" he came back.

"Heck, no," I looked sheepish. "Her brother. Wants to keep her on the farm all her life. I plan to marry her and raise Scottie dogs."

He blinked at me. Then he blinked at her. His cheeks cracked and he showed pink gums in a sly grin.

"None o' my business," he said. He handed over two worn aluminum keys chained to rubber rings the size of airplane tires. "How long you folks staying?"

"A few days," I said, working my eyebrows to imply deep meaning behind the words. "You know."

"That'll be payment in advance every morning." The stern, businesslike look was back—we might be co-conspirators, but I need not get any big ideas about pulling any fast ones.

"I knew we could count on you," I said. We went around a louvered trellis set in a dry planting box, started up the stairs. At the landing I looked back to see him peering after us through a loose slat.

CHAPTER FIVE

The rooms were not much more than do-it-yourself partitions dividing what had once been somebody's grandmother's sewing room into two airless cubicles with built-in closets like up-ended coffins. The floors no longer lay as flat as might have been desired, and the faded wallpaper had not been an asset when new. There was a tiny bathroom between them with a rust-edged shower stall, a toilet with a cracked plastic seat, a sink big enough to wash out your socks in—just barely.

I took the cell nearest the stairs, just in case of funny noises during the night. It had a concave mattress on a steel frame, a chest of drawers with one drawer missing and a machine-knitted doily on top, a chair made of metal tubing with a red plastic seat with cigaret burns, a bedside table with a glass ashtray containing a cigar butt, and a Gideon Bible. There was an air conditioner unevenly mounted in the big double-hung window. I switched it on and it woke to life with a clatter like a broken fan belt.

"Luxury quarters," I told my lady friend. "And we seem to have the place to ourselves." I escorted her past the water closet into her chamber, appointed at least as handsomely as mine. She went to the bed, sat on it. Under the tan, her face looked greenish-pale. She was at the ragged edge of exhaustion.

"Here, get the wet coat off," I said. I took a stiff, yellowish towel from the bar in the bath, brought it over to her. She was sitting, watching me, fighting to hold her eyes open.

"Get out of the coat," I said. "You'll have a nice case of pneumonia in the morning." She did not lift a hand when I reached down, unbuttoned the collar that was turned up under her chin. I pulled her to her feet, undid the coat; she swayed against me.

"Another two minutes and you're tucked in," I soothed her. I flipped the coat back, hauled it free from her limp arms. It was an old trench coat, black with grease around the collar, torn and stained. She might have found it in a garbage can. I turned back to her with a snappy comment ready and found myself gaping at a skin-tight outfit of metallic blackish-green that reached from her neck to her feet, hugging a figure that would have graced a *premiere danseuse* at the Follies Bergere. She reached up, pulled the scarf off her head; coils of lustrous dark hair cascaded down. Then her knees let go and she folded onto the bed.

I straightened her out, used the towel to dry her face, then mopped my own. Looking down at her, I wondered if she were a Polynesian—or maybe a Mexican, or an Arab. None of them seemed to fit. She was a type I had never seen before. And she was young—not over twenty-five. Asleep, she looked helpless, innocent. But I remembered her in the dark alley where I had found her, battling the man who had sapped me, giving me time to get back on my feet. I had saved her neck—and she had saved mine. That was enough of a bond to keep me sleeping at her bedroom door for as long as she needed a watchdog.

I stumbled back into my own room, and do not even remember my face touching the pillow.

The rain was still coming down next morning. I lay for a few minutes, watching it drop from the eaves, feeling the ache along the side of my head beat at me as it had beat all night through exhausting dreams of running through knee-deep, blood-red water, with a pack of dead-pan commuter types trailing me. My neck was stiff, the right eye was swollen and tender, and my upper lip felt as though I had a German sausage stuffed under it. I was not sure, but I thought I had a couple of loose teeth to complete the composition.

The bedsprings groaned when I sat up and swung my legs down, and I groaned right along with them. Now my hand was hurting; I looked at it. The knuckles were skinned raw. I had no idea where I had done that.

The connecting door to the bathroom swung back and I grabbed, came up with the .38 aimed at a slim female shape in lizard-skin tights. She did not jump; she gave me a hesitant smile, came on into the room, ignoring the gun. I had a strange feeling that she did not know what it was.

"Good morning." I put the pistol on the bed and stood. "Gamoning." She smiled a little wider. Her hair was pulled back, tied with a piece of string.

The hunted expression was gone. She still looked like someone who had not eaten for three days, but in her own exotic way she was rather pretty.

Then what she had said registered. "You speak English after all!" The grin on my face made it ache in three new places. "Thank God for that. Now maybe we can get somewhere. I don't know what you did to get Sethys mad at you, but whatever it was, I'm on your side. Now tell me about it."

"*Ot ottroc atahru,*" she said diffidently.

"Back to that, huh? What's the idea? I heard you say 'good morning' like a little lady—"

"Gamoning," she said. "Liddalady."

"Oh," I felt the smile go sour on my face. "Like a parrot."

"Likaparot," she mimicked.

"Maybe it's a start at that." I put a hand on her arm. "Listen, kid, I've never even taught a pup to fetch newspapers, but if we work at it, maybe you can learn enough American to shed a little light on this farce." I pointed to my chest. "Malcome Irish."

"Akmalcomiriss," she repeated.

"Leave off the *akk* part; it's Malcome—Mal, if you prefer."

"Akmal." She looked confused—or maybe stubborn.

"OK; have it your way." I pointed at her. "What's your name?"

"Akricia," she said promptly, and inclined her head in a sort of formal gesture.

"Akricia," I said, and her face lit up in a real smile. "Suppose I call you 'Ricia for short.

Ricia—nice name."

She looked flustered; two or three expressions tried themselves out on her face. Then she ducked her head again. "Ricia," she whispered. "Mal . . ." She nibbled her lip, then slipped a silver ring from her finger, held it out to me shyly, like a child offering candy. I took it; it was thick, heavy. "Very pretty," I said.

She seemed to be expecting something to happen. I thought of handing the ring back, but that did not seem to be indicated. I put it on my little finger and held it up. She smiled, took my hand between hers, and said something. I had a feeling we were now officially friends.

"Thanks, kid," I said. "It's a very nice present. Now let's get on with the lesson." I patted her hand—and suddenly noticed the grimy knuckles, the broken nails.

"Ricia, you need a bath. You slept in that leotard; it's time you got out of it and cleaned yourself up." I went into the bathroom, found a bar of green soap with hair stuck to it glued to a soap dish in the shower stall.

"You go ahead and take a shower," I suggested. "I'll get you some clothes, and I could use a change of socks myself." I pointed. "Take a bath," I turned the water on, pantomined scrubbing my neck. Ricia nodded, looking eager. As I closed the door she was reaching for some kind of invisible fastener on the front of her outfit.

Downstairs, I explained my needs to our host, gave him money and added a five-cee note, the sight of which seemed to delight him just as much as if the bottom had not dropped out of the fiscal system. He pulled on a jacket that looked like something salvaged from a drowned man, made a big thing of locking the sheet-metal safe, set off at a fast dodder.

In half an hour he was back, rapping at the door with an armload of groceries, toiletries, and drygoods. He gave the room a sharp once-over, checking for rumpled bedding or other signs of dissipation, hovered as though ready to start a long conversation. I eased him out, hinting at more heavy tips in the offing.

Small sounds were coming from next door. I tapped, pushed the door open six inches and reached in with a paper bag containing soap with pink perfume, a comb, a toothbrush, a fingernail kit, a washcloth, odds and ends of cosmetics."

"Hurry it up," I called. "My hide is beginning to crawl around on me."

I set the food out on the lace doily: bread, bottled cheese, canned meat, some fruit, coffee, a fifth of brandy with a blurry label. Ten minutes crawled past. There was a creak from the connecting door; it swung back and Ricia stepped through, looking as fresh and scrubbed as a baby on its first birthday—and dressed about the same. Her hair was done up in a striking composition on top of her head, tied with a red plastic ribbon from one of the cosmetic boxes. Her nails that had been gray crescents were pink and shiny. She was wearing just enough cologne to give me a faint whiff of florist shop—nothing else.

"Nice," I commented, trying to look as calm as she did. "A little unconventional, but very nice.

Still, I think you'd better slip into something before I come down with hot flashes." I fumbled packages, dug out a little nylon nothings I had gotten for her, added a one-piece thing with a tag on it that said it was a playsuit. She accepted them with a wondering expression. I went through some ludicrous antics intended to show her what to do with them. She laughed at me. I could see a bruise along the side of her throat now that the dirt was gone.

Then she saw the food, tossed the clothes on the end of my bed, and went past me with a glint in her eye. The closed containers seemed to puzzle her, she picked up an orange, sniffed it, took a bite. She seemed to like it, peel and all. I just stood, gazing at the orange juice running down that fine, olive-hued figure, wondering just who—and what—the little creature was I had taken under my wing.

Ricia had an amazing ability to remember the words I taught her—and an equally amazing ignorance of the customs and appurtenances of society. The coffee made her wrinkle her nose; the potted meat made her gag. She liked the bread—once she accepted the idea that it was something to eat. Only the fruit seemed in any measure familiar to her.

In an hour she was talking to me—using sentences like "Ricia eat, Mal eat, good, no. Today, tomorrow, walk."

"We have to stay where we are until dark," I told her. "It's known as waiting till the heat's off. I'm sorry about the food, but there's not much available in the neighborhood. Miami's beginning to feel the pinch now. Even with nineteenths of the population gone, the town can't run forever on what was on the shelves when the storms hit."

She nodded as though she understood. Maybe she did, maybe she was picking up more than I thought, the same way a child does—by listening and watching. She was sitting in front of the oval mirror over her dresser now, trying out different elaborate hair-do's.

Meanwhile, I was thinking over my plan of action—what to do when the time came to venture out from our hole. Going to the police was out now; there were too many bodies lying around town—to say nothing of the shambles at Greenlead, Georgia—to invite close inquiry. Martial law was no joke. The looters and ghouls had seen to it that old-fashioned ideas regarding the innocence of the accused did not get in the way of quick and final disposition—usually by a firing squad. There was no time or temper to bother pampering criminals—or suspects—in cosy jail cells. I paced up and down explaining it all to Ricia.

"There are plenty of boats here, it's not like the foothills of Georgia. I can get something—a thirty-foot cabin cruiser would be about right. This fellow Sethys plays for keeps. Well, he can keep it. Maybe the sailor was telling the truth: maybe there are trained elephants under the ice. OK, they can stay there. My curiosity isn't satisfied, I'll admit—but it's cured. We'll head north and find a nice town in high country and weather this out."

"Sethys, no. Mal and Ricia, walk, today." She looked scared—or maybe just concerned, trying to understand what I was talking about, not able to express her own ideas.

"I wish you could talk to me, Ricia." I told her. "Who is Sethys? Why did he send his boys out after you? How did you get into that part of town in the first place? Where you come from?"

She shook her head, gave me a stubborn look. She understood all right—she just was not talking. I let it go. Maybe I did not really want to hear the answers.

It was twilight now, an eerie red and green time when the glare of the dusty sun lit up the room like a stage light, casting shadows across the crimsoned floor.

"I'm going out to see about picking up a boat," I told Ricia. "Don't let anybody in until I get back. And don't forget the gun." I laid the .38 in her hand; I had shown her how to aim and pull the trigger.

"Don't hesitate to use it. Anybody who breaks through that door is asking for it."

She gave me her second-best game smile. She did not like my leaving her alone, did not like the sight of the gun, but she was game, whatever happened.

Downstairs, old Bob, our landlord watched me cross the ten-by-twelve lobby.

"I see you're growing a beard," he snapped, as if he had caught me sneaking something out in a paper bag.

"You're a very perceptive fellow, Bob," I conceded.

"That what you come here for, figgered it was a good place to grow a beard?"

"As good as any."

"A disguise, like hey?" He was squinting at me, his voice lowered to a confidential tone.

"No, it's so my old friends will know me, Bob. Used to have a beard and shaved it off. Tried to hit one of them up for a small loan a few days back and he cut me dead."

"Hah?" Bob snapped his gallus at me. "Meant to tell you, raising the rates first of the week." He pushed his lips in and out, estimating what the traffic would bear. "Cost you fifteen a day, starting Monday."

"Fifteen a day," I nodded.

"That's day after tomorrow," he clarified. "You can have one more day at the ten cees."

"Hey Bob"—I leaned on the counter—"I should have told you sooner, maybe, but I wasn't sure I could trust you not to panic." I looked carefully around the room, frowned at the old-fashioned breakfront with glass-doored shelves loaded with bundled papers, stepped back a pace to peer behind the rubber plant. Bob followed every move.

"I'm with Greater Miami Bomb Disposal," I told him in the tone of a turf accountant imparting a hot tip. "The little lady's a medium-psychic, you know. Great help in our work. Lots of nuts loose in the city these days—couldn't make the readjustment when their farms went under, mother-in-law drowned, the whole bit—you know how it is. Not tough like you and me.

"What's that about a bomb?" Bob's Adam's apple was vibrating like a cello string.

I nodded. "Figured you knew what was up. You don't miss much, Bob. You've got enemies. Comes of being sharp, successful—like you. The word is it's one of those Chinese jobs—on bigger than a one-shot VD capsule but power enough to lift the roof off this place and dump the contents all over Biscayne Bay. I think we've got it pinpointed in the third-floor john; don't pull any chains until you hear from me."

"Here, you mean—"

"Keep it under your hairpiece. Bob. We're with you all the way. Should be able to let you know something by sundown tomorrow."

"Tomorrow? Me sit here with a bomb ticking someplace—"

"You're a cool one, Bob. Nerve like cast iron." I looked rueful. "I have to admit sometimes I get a little peckish, myself."

"Here, where you going? You're not leaving here without finding the thing?"

"Just stepping out for another pound or two of Indian cheese wax and a spare framitizer. Won't take long." I pushed on out the door, feeling a little lightheaded, aware of the stink of death and ruin and decay as the world shook civilization to pieces—and still, among the ruins, the little green weed of avarice grew and flourished. The emperors of the world were all dead, but the Bobs we have with us always.

It was a street that had once—maybe twenty years before—been a moderately prosperous avenue of not quite fashionable shops of the kind that catered to the middle-class tourist trade, offering lines of shoddy goods with mass-produced Miami labels to impress the folks back home. Its hour of respectability had passed long ago. Even before the disasters the cheap, bright cardboard and plastic had disappeared from the shop windows, the false elegance of the shop fronts had faded into the cracked pastels of neglect. Now, with the unswept debris of wind and flood and the litter of hasty departure drifted at the curbs and around the broken sidewalk benches and the rusting light poles, the muddy light of late twilight showed a dreary parade of boarded windows, hand-lettered signs tacked furtively on door frames, tall weeds fighting their way up between the jumbled hexagonal tiles that had once seemed gay. It was a poor address, but Mr. Sethys could look a long time and not find us here—if he was looking.

The coast looked clear. I turned up the collar of Ricia's grimy coat and set off toward a cross street on which a little traffic was moving.

It was a ten-block walk to the waterfront. I moved along at a moderate shamble, keeping a weather eye out for ordinary-looking men in conservative suits. There was little traffic, few cars parked at the curb. Miami had had plenty of warning, plenty of time for the citizenry to pack and head north in time to meet disaster head-on in the floods and eruptions that had wiped out the upper half of the state.

Most of the marinas were dark, heavily fenced and padlocked. I walked north, toward the run-down portion of the bay shore that had had its flush of popularity fifty years ago. Here there were rotting board fences, rusted wire mesh, a jungle of abandoned hot-dog and beer stands, bait stalls, faded signs offering fresh fish and shrimp, plenty of tall weeds, and an astonishing abundance of lean, wary cats who looked as though they had run out of mice and were living off each other.

About every third polyarc was still burning along this stretch; inbetween, the shadows lay across the street as black as powdered coal. Off to the right a light surf slapped at the beach; there was a heavy odor of decaying sea things, salt water and soot. I sniffed, caught the hot-iron odor of volcanic activity—even here, a thousand miles from the eruptions in Georgia.

A big concrete shed loomed up ahead; I made out the words NORTH BAY MARINE SALES in flaked paint along the side. The big main doors were shut, locked tight. Beside them a small personnel entrance swung idly in the fitful wind. Inside, the office was a mess. Papers were scattered on the two desks, on the chairs, on the floor. The drawers of the filing cabinet hung open, empty. An ashtray on a stand lay on its side, its contents spilled. Even the girlie calendar on the wall hung crooked on its nail. The odor of rot and dead meat was strong here.

An unlocked glass door lead through into the back. My feet echoed on gritty concrete; the sound rang back from corrugated metal and oily water. Three boats were moored in the dock—a pair of bright-colored sixteen-footers with lots of shiny fittings, one sunk to the gunwales, and a big, sullen-looking catamaran-hulled job, use-scarred, built for blue-water cruising. Aboard, I found a pair of Rolls-Royce Arthurs, a megahorse each, shipshape and ready to turn. Half a dozen heavy cartons were stacked in the stern—Air Force field rations, type Y, enough to feed a battalion for a week. A long, canvas-wrapped bundle was shoved down behind the cartons. I hauled it out, found a leather gun case. Inside were a .375 Weatherby and an evil-looking automatic rifle, about .25 caliber, with a spare magazine. I had never seen one before, but I knew it by reputation. It was the latest military model, and it could empty its thousand-round drum in one two-second burst on full automatic—a hail of steel that would cut a rhino in two. Someone had made some careful preparations for a getaway.

The cabin door was locked tight. I used a rusted fish knife I found on deck to pry the latch open. The door swung in, and the odor hit me in the face like a shovel. On the floor between the bunks, what had been a man lay on his back, his face a fright mask of empty eye sockets and a ragged mouth hole with yellow teeth showing in a snarl, the claw hands outspread. He was not so much decomposed as mummified in the intense heat of the closed room. The lean, blackened neck disappeared into a shirt collar, neatly buttoned but badly discolored. His blazer was well cut, expensive-looking; his deck shoes new. There were two large black stains on his chest, on the left side, above and below the heart. The artillery stowed aft had not done him much good.

He was amazingly light; I hauled him up the three steps, tilted him sideways to get him through the hatch, put him over the side. He slid down smoothly, disappeared. Then I went back to the stern and lost my lunch.

His preparations had been complete: there was

a compact sea-water converter, spare clothes, foul-weather gear, a well-stocked bar, even a rack filled with books. I had made a lucky find. Now to see if I could open the sea doors.

They were heavy metal panels, power-operated. I followed the leads, tried the switch. Nothing. There was a master switch below the junction box. I threw it, tried again. Still nothing.

Outside, the water slammed and gurgled against the door, wanting in. I kept looking. It took me ten minutes to find the hand crank, folded back into a recess beside the left-hand door. I turned the crank; the doors groaned, started up. I cranked them back down, checked the boat's lines to be sure I could cast off in a hurry, then went back through the rifled office, stepped out into the dark street. There was an odd smell in the air—not just the stink of decay and volcanic dust, but a new scent—a choking odor like a pot boiled dry. Far away, thunder rolled and rumbled. There was a glow to the west, over beyond the city. I started walking.

A car came toward me, howling along at eighty or better, rocketed past, streaking north. Half a minute later another one shot by, then two more, neck and neck, like a chariot race. An instant later I felt the shock—a slow, inevitable sinking of the pavement under my feet, a pause, then a thrust upward. A ripple had passed over the city as if over a pond.

I broke into a run, fell flat when the next ripple hit, got up, ran on. Another car came into view, weaving across the road, turbos screaming. The next wave caught the car as it swerved wildly, going too fast for the narrow, rubble-strewn streets. The heaving pavement picked up the car as a breaker lifts a surfer, hurled it ahead in its long diagonal path. The car struck a brick warehouse, flipped on its back, hurtled along that way for fifty yards, then bounded high, exploded twenty feet above the street as I dived for a doorway. The shock brought bricks and shingles down in a long surf roar that seemed to echo long after the last shard of broken glass had tinkled from its frame. I stepped out, gave the boiling inferno one quick glance, ran on.

There were people in sight now, all running. Some ran toward me, others sprinted beside me. A wild-eyed woman darted aimlessly from one doorway to another. There were a lot of sounds: screams, yells, distant smashings and thumpings. The next tremor spilled people off their feet like a machine gun mowing down infantry. I rode it, jumped a drift of bricks that poured out across my path like a slot machine disgorging quarters.

A steady rain of debris was falling all around me. Ahead, a knot of half a dozen men darted toward me like comedians in a silent film, their footfalls and the yells from their open mouths lost in the background roar. I saw a man lying on his back in dusty rubble, the back of his head caved in, a woman tugging at his arm. A wrecked car lay on its side, its headlights still burning. Smoke churned from windows, backed by bright flames.

The next shock was worse. I went sprawling, came up to see building fronts toppling outward, crazily canted roofs sliding down into the street, truckloads of rubbish dropping like bombs among people—more and more of them running out now like excited ants, falling, jumping up and running, disappearing under clouds of brick and dust. There was a continuous crashing now like tanks battering through walls. A light pole ahead bounced twice, danced free of its mounting, hopped away ten feet before it fell with a back-breaking smash.

I saw my hotel ahead, a glimpse of dirty white stucco through wind-whipped dust and smoke, stained a dull orange by hundred-foot flames from a burning building across the street. Something blew up, and I felt the shock wave, the blast of heat against my face as small objects hissed past. Something ponderously heavy crashed down behind me close enough to send a hail of stinging concrete particles against the back of my neck. A length of wood, burning cheerfully, came arcing down, bounced away ahead of me.

The front door was gone. I took the broken steps in one jump, groped through dust past a tangle of fallen rafters. The breakfront lay across the counter, its papers spilled among broken glass. A thin arm poked out from under its edge; Bob had died at his post.

The stairs were gone, collapsed into shattered boards linked by a rope of worn carpet. Water was gushing down, staining bricks and plaster black in the gloom; pipes sagged in a graceless festoon. I went over a jumble of smashed furniture, pushed through the swinging door into a hall where the aroma of cabbage was still detectable through the smoke reek, went across a cramped, greasy kitchen full of broken crockery and dented pots. The service stair was there, at the back, almost hidden by the bulk of a toppled refrigerator. I climbed over it and went up.

On the second floor, things didn't look good: the passage was blocked by a jumble of two by fours and shattered plaster board. I pushed through a gap in the wall, ducked under cascading plaster dust, kicked the jammed door open, re-emerged into the hall ten feet from the open door to my room. Inside I found fallen plaster, toppled furniture, broken glass. A quarter-inch of water on the bathroom floor, trapped by the thresholds, danced with an intricate geometric pattern of ripples. I splashed through, calling Ricia's name.

She did not answer. The bed had collapsed; the mattress was spilled half off it, littered with plaster fragments. The chest of drawers still stood upright, its empty drawers pulled out. The patched Venetian blind at the window bulged with the weight of broken glass. The bottles and clothes that the late Bob had brought up a few hours earlier were scattered across the floor. I yelled for Ricia again over the roar of disintegration, jerked the closet door open, lifted the broken bed aside, found nothing but dust devils and worn linoleum.

Back in the other room, I shouted again, dug through the ruins of a fallen partition; nothing. Ricia was gone.

I stood in the middle of the room, trying to think in an orderly fashion, a neat trick in the best of times. I had told her to stay in the room; she had not done so. At least she had not died here. She was somewhere out in the street—and it was time for me to join her. I wove my way across the swaying floor, stepped into the hall and was looking down the barrel of a gun in the hand of the gray-haired man named Sethys.

CHAPTER SIX

He was standing ten feet away, looking as unmoved as an undertaker figuring how much to mark up the florist's bill. There was a liberal sprinkling of plaster dust on his shoulders, a streak of something dark along his jaw; the slicked-back hair was a trifle ruffled, like a bird in a high wind. But the gun held steady as a tombstone. I saw his finger start to tighten—and the floor picked that moment to rock sideways.

Sethys staggered, put out a hand to catch himself; the gun went off, and the iron radiator beside me rang like a bell. Dust was spurting from the cracks between the dark-varnished floorboards. Sethys backed, braced himself with his feet apart, took careful aim at my second shirt button—

A section of the ceiling sagged, dropped suddenly, obscuring his view. He stepped sideways, started between the obstruction and the wall. There was a sound of tearing metal. Part of the fallen framing swung around, and a projecting stub of a broken joist stabbed out, caught him low in the stomach, thrust him back against the wall. He stood there, still neat, still unhurried; then his arms went out. The gun fell, bounced away and disappeared through a gap in the floor. He made a sound like a rusted nail being drawn from an oak plank. Then the rusting bulk of a radiator dropped out of the hole in the ceiling. When the dust cleared, Sethys lay face down, half under the radiator, with six inches of splintered timber projecting from his back.

It was no fun checking his pockets, but I did the best I could, brought out a much-folded map from inside his coat. A colorful spread published by the Oceanographic Institute at Woods Hole, the map showed the oceans of the world complete with bottom contours and the locations of ancient wrecks—as out of date now as last year's almanac. A mark on it caught my eye—a loose circle drawn around the island of Crete. It was a place that had been named earlier, by Zablun, the little man with the disappearing coin trick. It was an interesting thought, but just then another section of ceiling fell, close enough to seem personal. Research would have to wait; it was time to get out. I tossed the map aside and headed for the open air.

The house was coming apart fast. I picked a path through broken walls to the stair well, jumped down bare seconds before the ceiling let go with a sound like Golden Gate Bridge falling into the bay. The front of the building had fallen outward; I climbed across ruins toward the red glow of the fire across the way. The remains of the front door frame blocked the way; I started around, and a glint of green caught my eye. Something fluttered in the draft—a strip of cloth caught on the broken timber. I pulled it free, recognized the strange metallic fabric of Ricia's garment. It had been cut, not torn.

I wanted to think she had dissolved our partnership—run out on me when the going got rough, but a little voice back of my left ear said it was not so—and the strip of cloth proved it. She had waited—until Sethy's showed up. His goons had taken her, while he waited around to clean me up when I arrived. For all my efforts, the girl was back where she had started.

I tossed the scrap of cloth aside and went on out into the roar of doomsday.

The boathouse was still standing; inside, my boat was floating high, looking ready and efficient. I got the doors open, saw strange, choppy whitecaps sliding across the black water—moving away from shore. The engines caught immediately; I backed the big cat out, brought her about, gunned toward open water. The big bow lights trained on the water dead ahead illuminated floating trees, half submerged roofs with shingles awash, the bodies of cows, a dead man. I rode out three big waves that overtook me, traveling fast from the west. The sluiced down over my deck like Niagaras, left me half drowned but still aboard. The boat did not seem to mind; she kept her transoms to the wind, came up purring smoothly as an outboard on a fresh-water pond. The white crests of the big waves rushed on ahead into darkness. Behind me, the lights of Miami gradually sank down, winked out. I did not know whether I was losing the city over the horizon, or if it was sliding down under the waves. I hoped Ricia was clear—free or captive. Drowning is a bad way to go. I was remembering the scared, hopeful, trusting look on her face when I had left her alone the last time. She had put herself in my hands—and I was running out.

But damn it—what could a man do when the town was falling to pieces around him? I had myself to keep alive, too. I thought of the ring she had given me—some kind of token of trust. To hell with rings. I tugged at it; it seemed to tingle on my finger like a reminder of duties undone, faith betrayed. The harder I pulled, the harder it jammed itself against my knuckle. All right, I would get rid of it later, and forget the waif who had given it to me.

Meanwhile I had a course to chart. I could swing north, cruise the coast until I found a suitable harbor, rejoin the main stream of human society—such as it was. Somewhere in the mountains I would find a nice town built on rock that had been stable for a few hundred million years where I could ride out the cataclysm until the smoke cleared and the glow went out of the night sky and life picked up where it had left off . . .

I was thinking about the girl again, about the cold-eyed men closing in on her, breaking down the door, dragging her away; hurting her—

Damn them! Damn her, too! Where would they be by now? Not in Miami—not if I was any judge of survivorship. Sethys had had a bad break, but his boys would be in the clear. As to where they would go . . .

Crete, the name popped into my mind. Sethys

had marked it on his map. Zablun had mentioned it; the coin came from there. I took it out, held it in the binnacle light. The dull gold winked at me; the figure of the bird with spread wings seemed to be poised, ready to leap off into flight to unkown lands.

Crete. It was not much to go on—maybe nothing at all; but the named seemed to tug at me. It was a long haul, but barring typhoons at sea, I could circle the globe on the supplies I had aboard. And it was not as though I had a destination . . .

I flicked on the North Atlantic chart, checked the compass, and plugged in a course three points north of east. I was laughing at myself; I felt like a fool. But in an odd way, I felt better, too.

The route I had charted through the channel north of Great Abaco Island turned out to be a sloping ridge of black mud from which a salty ocean breeze blew an odor of broken drains. It was down before I found a clear passage north of Great Bahama, now a mountain range on a new subcontinent, a series of green peaks raised above rolling plains of stinking gray sands, shining in the ominous dawn. Far away on my port beam I saw shapes resting on the former sea bottom: the rusted hulks of drowned steamers, the gaunt ribs of wooden sailing vessels, sunk long ago.

Long, businesslike swells were passing in under my stern at fifteen-second intervals, rolling in on the long beaches with a sustained hiss like a forest fire. I quartered across them, holding my easterly course again. Four hours' run took me past the position from which Bermuda should have been a dark smudge on the port horizon. I could not sight it—either my navigation was off or another nice piece of real estate had gone to the bottom.

It was a long haul then, booming along at high speed across open water under skies that were as near clear as any on the planet. The sun was filtered to a flat red disc by a high stratum of stringy smog; a low haze layer carried the familiar hot-stone and sulphur odor. Five hundred miles at sea I was still brushing cinders off the map screen and picking them out of my mouth and eyes. The deck was crunchy with a drift of tiny black fragments of lava. I sighted drifting trees, boxes, rubbish of every description. It was like sailing on and on through an endless scene of shipwreck, but still it was the same sea I had always known. It had weathered other eras of planet-wide disaster, and when this was over, man and his cities might be gone, but the ocean would endure.

My rations were not bad—a big improvement over the cans I had been opening lately. There was smoked turkey, artichoke hearts, fresh-water prawns, plenty of Scottish wheat bread, a variety of fresh-frozen vegetables, even some irradiated apples. The small freezer yielded an ample supply of ice cubes to chill my whiskey, and my unknown benefactor's taste in wines left nothing to be desired: I had a chilled Dom Perignon with my gammon and eggs, a Spanish rose for lunch, a Chateau Lafitte-Rothschilde with the evening's rare beef and crepes suzettes. The diet kept me in a mild alcoholic fog, a state that had my full approval.

The boat's radio produced nothing but a crackle

like New Year's Day in Chinatown, but there was a tape system aboard that boomed out Wagner and Sibelius and the jeweled sounds of deFalla and Borodin while the sun burned red across the sky, sank in a blaze like a continent afire.

The steady wind blowing through open windows had cleared the odor of death and decay from the cabin, but I brought up a folding bunk, clamped it to the roof of the deckhouse and slept under the open sky the first night. In the morning the drift of soot that covered me sent me below again.

On the third day the wind shifted to the south; the sky darkened with big black rain clouds; then the downpour started. It seemed to clear the air, though. By late afternoon the sun was out, looking more like its old self than I had seen it for months.

An hour before sunset I sighted Madeira, a misty rise of green far to the north of my course. At dusk the African coast was in view, looking normal except for an expanse of glistening mud flats that the charts did not show.

I sailed north during the night, passed lights that I identified as Casablanca and Rabat, reached Gibraltar at dawn. The famous rock was gone, and a new channel that I estimated at twenty miles wide stretched ahead into the open water of the Mediterranean. A fifteen-knot current poured out through the strait; I bucked it for more than two hours before I made still water under the cap above Tetuan.

The town looked peaceful—after four days at sea, I needed a drink ashore. There was a rough-and-ready wharf scabbed to heaped rock by the shore. I tied up to it, waved at a lean Moroccan who came down to stare at me.

"I need fresh water," I told him. He nodded, led me up the slope to a collapsing shed largely supported by a chipped Pepsi Cola sign. Inside, a fat woman with bracelets to the elbow gave me a warm Spanish beer across a bar made from a boat's mahogony foredeck, stood by warding off flies with a red plastic swatter. She talked to me in bad Spanish while I drank, telling me her troubles. She had plenty, but no worse than mine.

The man came in with two boys.

"Eesa nice boat, Senor," one of the lads told me. "Where you go een eet?"

"I'm headed for Crete," I told him.

They gabbled together for a while, using their hands to help them over the rough spots. I heard "Kreta" several times, and "Sicilia." Then the boy wagged his head at me.

"No sail to Kreta, Senor. No ees passage. Ees all"—he made lifting motions—"dry land between."

I quizzed them a little further, got a reasonably coherent story. Sicily was no longer an island; its southern tip now joined Cape Bon, and its northern extremity was one with the mainland of Italy. So much for an uneventful boat ride. I gave them a fistful of worthless money, went back down and cast off. At the last minute the old man hurried down with a jug of vin ordinaire; I tossed him a package of cigarets and pushed off.

They were right. I made it through the strait south of Sardinia dragging my keels, while the air grew fouler with every mile. Another half day's run over shoal water brought me into Naples harbor, still solidly at sea level under a blanket of smoke through which the glare of Vesuvius was only a bright haze. Wearing my respirator now, I tied up at three P.M. in darkness like an eclipse, within half an hour had sold my rig—no questions asked—to a quick-eyed man who looked like a Martian in an antique gas mask and the filthiest white suit on the planet. The deal was not good, but I got what I needed—a fairly sound-looking late model Turino ground car. I would have preferred to store the boat, but property not under armed guard was an ephemeral thing in Naples in the best of times.

I transferred two cases of rations from the boat to the car. The buyer got ready to protest when I took the cased guns, but I cut him off short; he chose not to argue the point. An hour later I was through the city, on the road leading east to Taranto. From there, my new business contact had assured me, I could ride the air cushion across some seventy miles of former sea bottom to the Greek mainland. He did not know about Crete, but his guess was I could make it all the way dry-shod.

The striking feature of the country—aside from the midnight pall from the line of volcanos linking Vesuvius and Etna—was the absence of people. Even in Naples, they had been sparse; here there were none. It was easy to see why: even with the car closed and the filters going full blast, the air was as thick as a London pea-souper. I ploughed ahead, holding my new acquisition at fifty through the mountains, opened her up to a shaky ninety-five across the plains.

At a little town called Lecce on what had been Italy's east coast my Neapolitan friend's guess was confirmed: the Strait of Otranto was a rolling sun-hardened expanse of rock-dotted clay. The light was better here; the hills seemed to be holding back some of the smoke from the volcanoes. The crossing took two hours of eye straining through the murky twilight; then on higher ground I headed south, threaded a precarious route among broken hills. At sunset I reached a swampy stretch on the far side of which the island of Crete was a dim line of light. I found a sheltered stretch of former beach under a line of giant weed-covered rocks, pulled the car over and slept until dawn.

The Cretan shore was rocky, dry, parched, a landscape in Hell under the garish colors of sunrise seen through smoke. I found a road a mile inland, followed it to a town marked Khania on my map. It was an impoverished cluster of handmade hovels packed close along a cobbled street that led by a circuituous route up a hill from which I caught a sudden dramatic view of the modern city below, most of its church spires still intact, its streets busy with commerce.

There was a town square, a raised block, walled and turfed, where twisted dark trees brooded over benches and a small fountain from which no water flowed. I followed the imperative gestures of a small policeman in tan shorts, parked before a veranda-like promenade with chipped stone columns held upright by timber truss work. Small merchants hawked dubious wares on the cracked pavement, and busy pigeons, unconcerned by the unnatural darkness of the morning sky, flapped under the high overhang, or pecked among the hurrying feet of the shoppers. There was an air of hectic activity, like a beach town before a hurricane. The wind, from the north now, had a chill edge to it not native to these latitudes. The atmospheric dust was making its presence felt, now that fall was coming on.

There was a glowing neon rectangle suspended over the walk half a block from where I left the car. Inside, the long bar looked calm and dignified, like a judicial bench. A short, dark-faced man in a neat white jacket gave the polished top a swipe as I took a stool.

"Brandy," I said.

He stooped, brought a squat brown bottle up from under the bar, poured. I raised it to him, took a solid belt. It went down like cool smoke.

"That's Metaxa, Mac," the barman said. "You don't take that from the neck."

"My mistake. Join me."

He got out another glass, filled it. We clicked glasses and sipped.

"Just in from down south?" he asked me.

I shook my head. He didn't press the point. The door opened, let in baleful light, closed again. Someone slid onto the next stool. I glanced his way in the mirror, saw a square, sun-blackened face, pale hair in a Kennedy bang, a neck like a concrete piling. I felt my face breaking into a grin; I nodded to the Brooklyn Greek.

"A drink for Mr. Carmody," I said.

The man beside me swung around quickly; then a smile lit up his face like a floodlight. A hand the size of a catcher's mitt grabbed mine, tried to tear it off at the wrist.

We spent ten minutes remembering our past; then I shot a look at the bartender, busy at the far end of the bar. What I had to say next was private.

"I'm not here on a pleasure cruise, Carmody," I told him. "I'm doing a little amateur investigative work."

"Must be something big, to bring you this far from the joy circuit."

"Big enough. A friend of mine's been killed—or kidnapped."

"Know who did it?"

"Yes and no. I know who, I think—but not why."

"And you think you'll find out in Crete?"

I got out the gold piece, slid it across to him. He picked it up, frowned at it, flipped it over to look at the reverse. The barman was coming back.

"Nick's all right," Carmody said so softly I was not sure I heard him. He was squinting at the engraved bird. "This come from around here?"

"That's the story."

"How does this tie to your friend?"

"I'm not sure. But it's all I have to go on."

"Where'd you get it?"

"If you've got a few free minutes, I'll tell you."

He finished his drink with a flip of the wrist, stood. "Where you're concerned, pal, it's all free. Let's grab a table."

He picked a quiet position in the corner with a good view of both doors. Carmody had always been a man who liked to know who was coming and going. The barman brought refills. While we worked on them, I told the whole story, from

Greenleaf to Sethys' last big scene in the collapsing hotel at Miami.

"I don't know whether she got out, or was nabbed by Sethys' boys," I finished. "If they got her, I'm pretty sure she's dead; that's the way they operate. But maybe not."

"This sailor," Carmody said, "you get his name, or rank?"

"No, but he must have been pretty well up the ladder—commander or better, I'd guess."

"Any holes in this story of his—holes you're sure about?"

"Aside from the idea of a Heidelberg man sporting a ray gun, no. The official story was that Admiral Hayle was lost in space, that the two ships he mentioned had been sunk in one of the early eruptions—but that could have been just a cover for the operation."

"What about his getaway in a lifeboat—possible?"

"No worse than my crossing the Atlantic in a thirty-foot cat."

"You knocked off three of these birds in the hick town; any reason to think there might have been more of them around?"

"I don't know. I didn't see anybody, no signs of a tail."

"Seems like this guy Sethys wised to you pretty quick; you think he was tipped?"

"Maybe."

"Could the girl have been a plant?"

I thought about it. "She could have been—but she wasn't."

"Any idea why they high-graded your gold piece

and gave you one just like it?"

"Maybe this one's counterfeit." I clinked it on the table. Carmody picked it up, weighed it on his palm, fingered it, tried a fingernail on it. "That's gold," he said. He studied the design, frowning at it in the subdued light.

"I don't think I've seen one just like this before, Mal, but I think I can tell you what that bird is. A wild goose."

"Probably," I took the coin back. Nick came up behind him, soft-footed as a hungry lynx.

"How about it, Nick?" Carmody said. "Who's the man to see about old gold?"

"Hurous. Lives in a shack a couple miles east. He might know."

"Yeah, he might at that." Carmody looked at me. "Come on, Mal. Let's go pay a call before cocktail hour rolls around."

The road came to an end a quarter of a mile from the spot we were headed for; it was a stiff climb up a goat trail to the hut perched on a cliff edge under a lone olive tree. Hurous was home, lying on an iron cot in the shade of a one-vine grape arbor. He was sixtyish, unshaven, with small black eyes, a round, bald head, a roll of fat bulging a soiled undershirt packed with hair like a burst mattress. He sat up on one elbow when he saw us coming, reached under the cot for a nicke-plated .44 revolver as big as a tomahawk.

"Put the hog leg back where it was, Hurous," Carmody said easily. "It's a friendly call. A friendly business call."

"Yeah?" The man's voice was thick as a clogged

drain.

"This is Mr. Smith. He wants to know where he could pick up some souvenirs. Old coins, for example."

"What you think, I run a souvenir stand?" Hurous lowered the gun.

"He likes big ones—the size of a five-drachma piece, say," Carmody amplified.

Hurous was looking me over like a skeptical buyer studying a second-hand slave. "Who's this fella?" He had the heavy accent of a tri-D spy.

"Mr. Smith, remember? He's a big man in the chicken business. Likes money with birds on it. He heard you might put him line for some."

"Birds. What kind money got birds, hah? You try to pull my foot?"

"Show him a sample, Mr. Smith." Carmody flicked his eyelid in a wink. I got out my lucky piece, passed it over. Hurous let it lie on his fat palm; I thought maybe his puffed face stiffened a little.

"I don't see nothing like this before," he said. "Take it. You come to the wrong place. You waste my time."

Carmody reached for the gold piece, tossed it and caught it; the fat man's eyes followed.

"Mr. Smith is prepared to pay well for another like this, Hurous. Enough to set you up for the year."

Hurous's eyes darted a look at the blackened sky. "What year?" he growled. "Tomorrow maybe the whole island fall in the sea. What's a year to me?" He flopped back on the dirty cot, thrust the big gun under it. "You get off my place now, leave me be. I got nothing for you."

Carmody stepped forward, got a grip on the side of the bed's metal frame, heaved it over on its side. Hurous yelled, hit the ground with a heavy thump, came up reaching for his boot. Carmody scooped up the .44 with his left hand, dangled it negligently by the trigger guard.

"Let's not horse around, Hurous," he said genially. "Let's do business."

The fat man had snatched a slim-bladed dirk from its sheath on the inside of his shin. He held it point outward toward Carmody, the other hand spread as if it were a shield.

"I cut your heart out." He started around the end of the cot. Carmody did not move; he watched the man come, smiling lazily.

"You make a pass at me with that hatpin and I'll carve my initials on your jaw," he said gently.

Hurous stopped, stood, legs apart, his face a dull purplish shade. "You get offa my land." Then he said something in Greek. I had the impression it was uncomplimentary.

"Why get yourself roughed up?" Carmody inquired reasonably. "I didn't come up here for the view."

Hurous gathered in the bubbles at the corners of his mouth with a blackish tongue, spat at my feet. "Take this snooper with you."

There was a sudden move, a *pow!* like a cracked whip, and Hurous was lying on his back while Carmody stood over him, rubbing his palm on his thigh.

"Give, Hurous," he said.

The Greek rolled quickly, came to his feet, charged the big man head down. Carmody bounced him back with a casual swing of his right arm, followed up, twisted the man's arm behind him.

"We're wasting time," he said briskly. "Let's cut short the preliminaries. You spill or I break it. Clear?" He jerked the arm. Hurous yelped.

"Check around, Mr. Smith," Carmody said.

I gave him a look that felt stiff on my face, went inside the shack, looked around at stacked rubbish, broken odds and ends of furniture. The place smelled like the locker room at the Railroad Men's Y. I poked at a chipped teapot, lifted the lid on a cigar box filled with scraps of paper and pencil stubs, went back out.

"If there's anything in there it will have to stay there," I said. "Let's go, Carmody."

"Last chance before the fracture," Carmody twisted Hurous's arm another three degrees. The Greek went to his knees, made a noise like a rusty hinge.

"Rassias," he squealed. "Fishermen."

Carmody pushed him away, watched the man pick himself up painfully.

"What's his address?"

Hurous was working his arm experimentally. "Ten cees," he said.

I got out my wallet, handed over the paper money.

"He got a place out west of town," Hurous said. "Ask the fishermen, they tell you. You know you almost bust my arm?"

Carmody broke the .44, took out the chunky cartridges, tossed them away, dropped the gun on the ground.

"Let's go, Mr. Smith," he said.

Back at the car, I gave him a sideways look.

"You're a hard man, Carmody."

He gave me a one-sided grin. "Hurous and I are old pals. He sold me to the mainland police once. He didn't even get a good price. I was clean as a hound's tooth, as it happened. He's been waiting around for me to call ever since. Expected me to cut his throat. Old Greek custom. They can't figure us foreigners out. Right now he's counting his money and laughing. I had to bend him a little; he figures this squares things."

"Swell," I said. "If there's anything I don't need it's a new enemy."

CHAPTER SEVEN

Down by the shore that curved away west of town there were wooden shacks, strung nets, beached boats, weather-beatened docks that seemed to sway with each wave that splashed up around the barnacle-ringed pilings. We left the car up on the road, walked down across gray sand to a group of men gathered around on overturned boat. They watched us come up; none of them showed any signs of joy at our arrival. Carmody greeted them in Greek, made what I judged were a few remarks about the weather which netted him reluctant nods. Then I caught the name Rassias. The silence that fell made their previous taciturnity seem noisy. One man crossed himself when he thought no one was looking.

"Maybe the smell of money would help their memories, Mr. Smith," he suggested. I took out my usual ten-cee note; nobody reached for it. Carmody talked some more. The men looked at each other, at their feet, out to sea. Then one of them waved an arm; another plucked the note from my fingers. They closed ranks, moved off toward what I suspected was the nearest bar.

Carmody nodded toward a lone shack, almost

out of sight around a curve of the beach.

"That must be it."

"I got the feeling Rassias isn't a big favorite with them."

"They're afraid of him. They didn't say why."

I pulled the car along the road, turned off on a track that led down through the dunes, pulled up behind the house. It looked a little more substantial than the others; there were some new boards across the back, and a meter on a pole attested to the presence of electric power. We walked around to the front; a wharf led out across the mud, projected fifty feet into the water. A solid-looking thirty-foot boat was tied up beyond it.

"Looks like Rassias is in the chips," Carmody noted. He rapped on the door. Nobody answered. He tried the knob, pushed it open, looked inside.

"He's out."

"Not very far out," I said. He followed my look. A thin, wiry man with a cloth tied around his head had appeared on the dock. He wore a black turtleneck sweater, vague-colored pants that fitted tightly from the knee down to bare feet. He was smoking a brown cigaret in a long black holder.

"What you want?" he said in a low, husky voice.

"You Rassias?" Carmody called.

"That's right."

"My name's Carmody—"

"I know you, mister."

"OK. This is my friend Smith. He's looking for something; maybe you can help him."

"He lose something?"

"I understand you might be able to tell me where to get a gold coin of a certain type," I said. Rassias thought that over, came along the dock, jumped down to face us. He studied my face, wrinkling his nose at the smoke from the cigaret.

"Come inside." He walked away and we followed.

The cabin was fitted up with a neatly-made bunk, wall shelves, a newspaper-covered table. chairs. A big shiny tri-D set occupied a place of prominence at one end of the single room; a two-tube flourescent fixture hung from weathered ceiling beams. Rassias motioned us to chairs, sat down across the table from us. He crushed out the cigaret in a sea-shell ashtray, blew through the holder, tucked it away.

"You been talking to them . . ." He motioned with his head to indicate the town.

"They don't talk much," I said. "I'm hoping maybe you can be of a little more help."

"Help how?"

I got out my magic gold piece, the sight of which struck people dumb. "Ever see one like this before?"

Rassias glanced at it.

"What's in it, mister?"

"I'll pay for whatever you can tell me."

"Why?"

"I'm paying for information," I pointed out. "Not selling."

"You could take a walk," Rassias said. He spoke English with a unique mixture of Greek and Cockney accents.

"I've had my walk," I said. "This is the end of the line."

Rassias nodded. "Always me," he said. "Always it's me they come to with their dirty work. Why me?" He leaned forward. "I'll tell you why me.

Because I'm Rassias, and Rassias is not afraid." He leaned back, looking unafraid.

"Good, then you're not too shy to tell me what you know about the coin."

"I've seen a few like it," he said flatly. I waited.

"Talk it up, Rassias," Carmody said. "Mr. Smith hasn't got time to sit here and play twenty questions."

"Mr. Smith can get in his car and tootle off," Rassias told him.

"Where did you see these coins?" I cut in. I had an idea Carmody's weight tactics would not buy anything here.

"Right here." Rassias held out a hand lumpy with callouses.

"Where did you get them?"

"They was paid to me."

"Who paid them to you?"

"A number of gentlemen." Rassias smiled crookedly. He had good teeth except for a gap at the side where a left hook might have landed once.

"What were they paying for?"

"My services."

"What kind of services?"

Rassias pointed with his chin in the general direction of the Mediterranean. "I own a boat. A good boat. Fast. Reliable. I know these waters—even now."

"You took them somewhere?"

"Sure."

"Where?"

Rassias frowned. "Out there," he said, and pointed again with his chin.

"How about getting a little more specific, Mr. Rassias?" I suggested. "I told you I'd pay for information; so far I haven't gotten any."

Rassias laughed; I thought I detected just a faint note of nervousness. "I answer everything you ask, Mister. Maybe you don't ask the right questions."

"I want to know where the coin came from."

"All I know is, they pay me. I don't ask no questions." Rassias wasn't laughing now; he wasn't even smiling.

"You know where you took them."

"That's right. I know."

"So?"

"I tell you, maybe you don't believe." His English was getting worse. He sounded worried now.

"Why wouldn't I believe you—if you're telling the truth?"

Rassias shifted in his chair. He wiped the back of his hand across his mouth.

"OK," he said, speaking in a flat, businesslike tone now. "They come here, say can I take them out, twenty kilometers, twenty-five kilometers. I say sure. Why not? They nice-looking gentlemen, dress good, speak good. From Athens, maybe, businessmen. They want to go then, same night.

"An hour out, one fellow, he comes back to the wheelhouse, stands by me, tells me steer right, steer left. I don't know where he goes, but what's that to me?

"Another half hour, he says 'Stop here.' OK I stop. This man says to me, go below, in the cabin. I argue, but I go. You say why? I say why not? They pay me plenty, OK. But I know something they don't. Sometimes out working deep for scampi, I set the automatic steering, I go below, get a little rest. But I want to know what is up ahead. I don't want no collision. So I rig up the mirrors. I can lie on the bunk and I can see the foredeck and the sea off the bow.

"So I watch the mirror. Down below I got also a gun, you know? Maybe I have to use it, if these nice gentlemen start some monkey business. But I see them go forward, and I see them go over the side. In their nice suits. All of them. Four men, all go over the side.

"I come up on deck quick. In those clothes they drown. I got a life preserver. I put on the big deck light. But it's nothing. I don't see nothing. All I see is black water, a light sea running, good moon, stars. But no passengers. They go over the side. And they don't come back."

Carmody whistled. "What is it, some kind of crazy suicide club?"

"You tell me the name, I don't know. They hire me, they pay me, I take them out. They want to go over the side, that's their business."

"How long ago was this?"

Rassias looked wary. "I forgot."

"In the last month, say?"

"Maybe. Maybe longer."

"And you never saw them before?"

"No—not before."

"What does that mean?"

"I saw one—after."

"What did he do, wash up on the beach?" Carmody wrinkled his forehead.

Rassias pointed at the door. "He came there and knocked. I let him in."

"This was after you took him out and he jumped overboard?"

"A month later."

"They must have had a boat out there—"

"No boat. Nothing. A man in those clothes, he couldn't swim ten yards. I stayed half an hour that night, working the deck light. Nothing."

"But he came back."

"He came back."

"What for?"

"To rent my boat. He had two friends with him. He paid in advance." Rassias grinned. "For this kind of business, it is always the pay in advance, you understand."

"You took them out too?"

"Sure. It's what they pay for. To the same place."

"How do you know it was the same place. You said—"

"I know. By the smell of the sea, by the wind, by the ripples on the water, by something here"—he pointed at his chest—"that makes me the true sailor. I know."

"And what did they do this time?"

"It was the same. I go below, and they throw themselves into the sea. But quietly. This time I waste no time with the decklight. I have a quiet smoke below; then I come back."

"And they paid you in coins like this?" I picked up my trophy.

"I tell them no paper money. For this work, gold! But the second time, I raise the price. I told him, if the police hear about it, finish! I don't tell them, but—word gets out. You know—" Rassias twitched his mouth in a half-smile. "They all know about my cargoes that go out and never come back. They too don't talk to the police. What for?

Who are the police? Who knows the police? Pouf! He dismissed the police with a downward sweep of his hand.

"Some tale," Carmody said. "Wonder how much of it's true."

The sailor looked at him from the corners of his eyes.

"You think a little bit, mister," he said softly, "before you call Rassias a liar."

"I haven't called you anything—yet," Carmody grunted. "You have any proof you didn't dream the whole thing?"

Rassias smiled a quick smile, got up and went to a box on the shelf, came back and spread half a dozen bright gold discs on the newspaper that covered the tabletop. I leaned over to study them, picked one up, there was a tiny depression in the gold, just to the left of the bird's beak: the mark of my tooth. It was the coin the sailor had given me—the one Mr. Zablun had switched in his neat little office on the twenty-eighth floor at the Gulfstream, a week earlier.

"I had more," Rassias was saying. "I sold a couple."

"A month ago, huh, that last run?"

"Sure."

I swung from the floor, caught him on the cheekbone; he went down hard, came up with a knife ready. I yanked my .38 up, held it on him. Carmody started a move, checked it.

"Forget it, Rassias," I cut him off. "Can you find that spot again?"

"Sure." He looked at the gun, rubbed his face. "Inside a hundred meters, same spot." His eyes probed at me like scalpels. "Why?"

"I'm going out."

He laughed. "Maybe I was a little off on the date, OK. My boat's for hire. You pay, I take you out." He got to his feet, put the knife away.

"We won't need your boat," Carmody said. "My boat. You pilot her."

Rassias thought about it. "Cost you one hundred cees," he said. Carmody looked at me. I nodded.

"OK." Rassias showed me his teeth. "Your boat, my boat, what's the difference? I go."

"Tonight?"

"Sure, tonight."

"Meet us at nine o'clock at Stavros' Bar, Rassias," Carmody said. "That sound all right to you, Mr. Smith?"

I said it did; Rassias said he would be there. Outside, Carmody gave me his sideways look. "You got a little rough yourself."

"Yeah. A hundred cees is a nice tab for a look at a piece of sea water."

"Money's free, where I come from."

"What do you expect to find out there, a bottle with a clue in it?"

"I'd settle for that."

"Face it, Mal, this kid you found in the alley is dead."

"Probably."

"OK, it's your game." We went back to the car and drove into town.

Carmody's boat was a handsome thirty-eight-footer, equipped with more electronic gear than a Navy picket. Rassias followed us aboard, prowled it from one end to the other while I stowed my gun case. He came back, grinning at Carmody in the yellow light of a carbide lantern set on a pole on the wharf.

"She's nice, mister. When you die, you leave her to me, OK?"

"You know how to make sail?"

"Sure, what you think, I'm one of these gasoline sailors?"

"We'll take her out on the diesels. When we're half a mile from target, we'll shut down and ride the breeze in."

We cast loose and edged across the bar, then Carmody threw power to her and the big boat put her stern down and headed out.

"You know this is a nutty idea, don't you?" he said over the thrum of the big engines and the shrill of the air stream. "You ever used scuba gear before?"

"A few times."

"A swell way to drown."

"As good as any."

"You sound bitter, pal."

"What's there to be bitter about? Half the world is under water and most of the rest is choking to death on volcanic gas. Every building on earth over two stories high is piled in what's left of the street. The only government still operating is what a few towns here and there have managed to keep alive at gunpoint—and just to liven things up, a pack of madmen are running around loose picking victims out of a hat. But I'm still breathing, so what do I care?"

"The girl must have meant a lot to you."

"I hardly knew her."

A stiff westerly breeze was blowing cool salt mist against my face; underfoot the deck trembled and thudded like something alive. Out here, at night, it was almost possible to imagine that back on shore life went on, music played, people laughed, sang, went for walks in the woods, took picnic lunches to the park secure in the knowledge that the ground would not break apart under their feet, that the worst natural disaster they were likely to encounter was an unexpected shower.

But that dream was gone forever—or for my lifetime, at least. Man, the bright young primate, had had it lucky for his first million years. There had been a few brief eras of planetary upheavel in his time; the legends of flood and hellfire attested to their impact on the race memory. But, by and large, he had had a long vacation in which to evolve, build cities, invent culture.

And now the vacation was over.

It was nothing abnormal, as events in the life of a planet went; you had to expect an age of mountain raising, sea draining, continent breaking now and then. It was only the egotism of man that had made him imagine it could not happen to him. Now it was happening—and when it was over, future generations would tell the story to their surviving young down through the centuries, and graybeards would sort through the rock strata chipping out coffee pots and fossilized spare tires and make beautiful theories to account for it all.

But we were here; we knew: A planet is a strange and fearful place for fragile living creatures.

Forty minutes' run nearly due east, Rassias came back from the prow where he had been standing straddle-legged in the blue glow of the bow lights watching the water.

"Time to break out the sail, Captain." He was smiling as if he were pleased with the whole thing, happy to be here, eager for the fun.

Carmody cut the throttles back. "You sure?"

Rassias shrugged. "If you got no confidence, why you pay me?" He went forward, set to work hauling the tarpaulin clear of the sail locker. He finished, gave a wave; Carmody pushed a button. The telescoping mast rose up, pivoted into position; the sail shook itself out, took the wind, came taut with a soft boom. The sound of the engines died and I could hear the hiss of water, the sigh of air through the rigging. We rode in darkness now, running lights off.

"I'll go below and dress out," I told Carmody. In the cabin I stripped, pulled on cotton longjohns, then the cold-suit; rigged harness straps so that the air tanks would ride comfortably. The mask was one of the new all-in-one type—a flexible plastic helmet with a 180-degree glass window. I got it on, adjusted the air flow.

Up above, a whine started up; a moment later Carmody came down, checked me over.

"We're in position, according to Rassias," he said. "I've set the gyro anchor to hold us on the spot." His voice sounded tinny through the inductance pickups. "The bottom's at thirty-five fathoms out here," he added.

"Fine. I'm ready."

Up on deck, Carmody showed me the controls—a few simple knobs that regulated the breathing mixture, a bigger one that controlled the power unit.

"Remember this one." He tapped a flat lever set in the small panel above my right knee. "It's a wake-up shot if you begin to go woozy down there."

"I've got plenty to keep me awake."

"Sure. Remember it anyway." He took a small canvas case from a locker, clipped it to my belt.

"Tools," he said. "There's a little cutting torch, pry bars, special stuff. Maybe you'll want it."

"I'm not going down to crack a safe."

"Why are you going down, Mal? What do you expect to find down there?"

"If I knew, I might not have to go."

"I ought to go with you, but I have to keep an eye on our boy. Embarrassing if he pulled out and left us."

"It's all right."

"You don't have to go, you know. You could forget the whole thing. I need a partner."

"Thanks. I've got to play the hand I drew."

"This is no card game, pal—but every man to his own kick."

It was a fine night, as nights went nowadays. The sea was flat, moving in slow swells; there was no moon, no stars. The odor of volcano was a little thicker than it had been ashore. Carmody pushed another button and a chrome-plated ladder ran out astern. I climbed the rail and felt the tug of the water at my legs.

"Say something every now and then, old buddy," Carmody's voice sounded in my ear. "Keep in touch."

"I will. Don't go 'way."

"We'll be here, pal."

The surface closed over my head and I let go and sank down into utter blackness.

CHAPTER EIGHT

There were sounds: the wheeze of my breathing, the tiny hum of the recycler, the creak of the belt against the foam suit. I touched the power switch, felt the instant thrust from the water jet mounted under my back tanks. The glow of the depth meter and attitude indicator on my wrist was barely visible through the cloudy water. I held them close to my eyes, maneuvered into the recommended face-down position by working my ankle fins.

There was a stiff current flowing. Carmody had told me that the Mediterranean was still falling by half an inch a week, pouring out through Gibraltar to equalize the difference in levels created by the upthrust of the Sicilian bridge. The land-locked eastern portion in which I was now having my dip was feeding the flow through subterranean channels. I faced myself upstream, assumed a forty-five-degree downward angle, and concentrated on holding my stance.

At seventy-five feet I eased off power, studied the depths under me. It was like looking at the back of your eyelids in a dark room. The water was cold here; my bare hands ached. I thrust them into the heated pockets on the sides of the suit, twisted over on my back to look up. There was a barely peceptible lightening of the darkness there—or maybe it was my imagination.

My position indicator said I had drifted a hundred yards from the boat; I swam level for five minutes to get back on target, then started down again. The pressure was beginning to bother me a little now; I ignored the pins-and-needles sensation back of my eyes, bored on down to a hundred and fifty feet.

This time I needed a longer rest. Breathing against the pressure of the sea was hard work at this depth. There was still nothing in sight. A lot of unwelcome thoughts were running through my head: sharks, a plugged air conduit, seasickness . . .

That was not buying me anything. I blanked off the nagging instinct that told me I was a land animal a long way from the open air, oriented myself, and went on down.

The glowing needle on my left wrist quivered past the hundred-and-seventy-foot mark—the deepest I had ever dived, back in the clear water off Bermuda under a tropical sun shining out of a sky full of fluffy little clouds like freshly scrubbed lambs. It was a nice thought; I held on to it, rode it down past the two-hundred-foot mark.

Time for another short break. I was breathing hard, listening to a roaring in my head like a fast freight making up lost time in the Channel tunnel. The water seemed warmer now—or maybe my hands were getting numb. It was hard than ever to see my instrument faces; I had to hold them against my nose.

I started below. Thirty-five fathoms, Carmody had said; my faceplate should be scraping bottom now. I waggled my feet swam down another yard—

Something moved and I shied; it was a waving frond of weed, glowing faintly with marine phosphorescence. I was on the bottom.

I drifted down, felt my legs touch yielding ooze. The tall stand of kelp held its position; there seemed to be no current here. Standing upright, I did a slow three-sixty, staring through blackness, saw nothing but the ghostly weeds. They moved with a pleasing grace, disturbed by my intrusion among them. I had the thought that if I relaxed, hung absolutely still, they would forget I was here. I would sink slowly to the soft muck of the sea floor, and there I could rest, and watch the slow dance of the glowing ribbons, and—

A phrase popped into my head: "The rapture of the deep." I tried to move, almost gave it up as too much effort, then kicked out, beat at the water with my arms to shake off the lethargy that was wrapping around me like a warm blanket. I kept it up for what seemed like a long time, then hung in the water, breathing hard.

My depth gauge read two hundred and twelve feet. A high, singing sound had joined the other noises in my ears. The glow of the instrument face seemed to be sliding away from me, a tiny light glowing in the big dark, and in a moment more it would be gone. It did not seem important. I let it go, and suddenly in its place were colors, flowing around me like a molten rainbow, and as they flowed they sang in a high sweet voice, and I was flying through space at a fantastic speed and the singing voices were all around me, escorting me through pillars of cool fire toward that attainable place seen only in dreams where the soul would dance naked in golden sunshine—

But first, there was something—something that had been important, once; something I was supposed to do.

I groped for my knee, felt a square button against my fingers, pushed at it. It moved. I felt a sense of relief at a tiresome chore done; now I could turn back to the colors and the song—

There was a sharp pang in my throat, a sensation like hot wires jammed up my nose. My head jerked and I took a deep breath to yell, choked instead. I kicked out, flapped my arms, got my feet under me, looked at my watch. I had been floating head down, blacked-out for nearly fifteen minutes.

The singing was gone but the thud of my heart was loud enough to make up for it. Darkness was all around me; even the weed was gone now. It had been a wild venture to start with, and nothing I had seen down here made it look any more promising. It was time to go up, shake hands all around, and head back to Stavros' for a couple of stirrup cups. Carmody was a good lad in spite of his informal methods of making a living. I could throw in with him; we could head for the South Seas where the living was easy, and forget this forlorn chase.

I reached for the power control to start my ascent and found myself looking at the soft, green glow of a light shining steadily through the murk.

My depth gauge said I was at two hundred and one feet now. I stroked with my feet, moved toward the glow, found myself sliding past; I was back in the current. The water was clearer here. A school of small silvery darts hovered nearby; light glinted on their sides as they shot away. I used the water jet to work back upstream to the source of the light.

It came from a round cave mouth like a four-foot-high section of sewer pipe lying in a trough in the mud. Ten feet inside its mouth a baffle stood half open; the light came from beyond it. I swam into the opening; beyond the disc that half blocked the passage I could see the tunnel fading away, light reflecting along its sides. There was room at the side of the baffle for me to pass; I turned on my side and eased through into the passage.

A slight current thrust me back through the barrier; I used more power to push upstream. I could feel a heavy thumping through the water, like a whale's heartbeat. The tunnel curved gently, leading off to the left and trending downward. I thought about Carmody, slouching in a canvas chair on a deck two hundred feet above and an unknown number of feet west, chewing on his pipestem and checking the watch on his thick, hairy wrist. I had forgotten all about calling in; by now he had probably decided the sharks had me. I checked my watch; it had been thirty-five minutes since I went over the side.

The current seemed stronger now. I put the jet control knob all the way over, made headway against turbulent currents that slammed me against first one side of the tunnel and then the other. Ahead, the light was brighter; I made out vertical lines silhouetted against a brilliant glare.

Up close, the lines resolved into a set of louvers, each a foot wide, standing half open. I got a grip on one, held on against a stiff flow that tugged at me hard enough to make my shoulder ache. The pressure was increasing by the second. Inside my helmet, a fine sweat prickled on my forehead. If I let go now, I would be tossed downstream like a chip in a millrace—with the baffle waiting at the end of the line to break my back. If I held on until my arms gave out, I would hit even harder. I felt like a blimp's ground crewman who has forgotten to let go of the rope.

There was one other possibility: I got a grip with the other hand, hauled hard, pulled myself forward between the louvers. The tunnel curved upward sharply ahead. Working hard, I got my shoulders through, then my chest. The water pounded at me, as heavy as falling pianos. My legs came through, and I braced them, stood up, reached for the rim of a circular port above through which the water sluiced down in a cascade that broke, turned to churning white, fell away abruptly to a splash, then a trickle. Under my feet, the heavy metal slats rotated suddenly, came together with a solid snap that sounded as final as dirt hitting a coffin. If I had been thirty seconds slower getting through, I would have been sliced like a salami.

I hauled myself up and through the manhole, looked around at a room the size of the main roulette salon at Monte Carlo, ringed with stumpy spiral-carved columns. The walls looked like ancient, discolored stone, broken by half a dozen rectangular openings that might have been windows once, blocked up now with rough masonry and black mortar.

I looked for the source of the light, saw strips set into recesses in the ceiling, glowing a cold blue. There were massive items of furniture here and there—stone benches, a stone table, what looked like a birdbath with a pipe projecting from it. Through a coating of black on the floor, I could make out traces of a mosaic pattern.

The thumping had stopped now. My faceplate was frosting over. I pulled the helmet off, snorted at a stink of decay thick enough to shovel. Still, it was air. I went across the room, found a flight of slimy steps leading up. At the top a heavy door swung open when I pushed on it, and I stepped through into what looked like a junk dealer's attic.

It was a big, square room, stacked, heaped, packed with statues, pots, tall clay vases, wooden chests, bundles, bulging sacks of scuffed leather, odds and ends of spidery chairs, massive benches, carved screens. There was a slim statuette that must have been brass, lying on its side nearby, next to it a dark red bown with black designs of women and sheep, beyond that a carved cat with a long body like a rail fence and bits of stone for eyes. Under everything there was a drift of broken potsherd, rotted wood fragments, the glint of small bright objects half buried in the rubbish. Where the floor was visible, it looked wet.

A path of sorts led through the collection to an alcove in the opposite wall where water trickled down steps leading up to a massive door made of wide planks bound with brass straps. I had my foot on the bottom step when the door rattled, swung open.

I stepped back into a recess between a statue of a squatting diety and an upturned two-wheeled cart. The legs of a man came into view, moving awkwardly under the weight of a wooden chest the size of a foot locker. He reached the floor, paused, looked around, then turned and shoved the box back on top of the nearest heap. He turned my way then, stood wiping his hands on a piece of brown cloth with beads along the edge. I held my breath and pretended to be a shadow.

Ten slow seconds ticked by; then he took a step my way. My disguise had not worked. I put a hand on the grip of the spear pistol at my right hip and waited for him. He stopped a few feet away, looked me over, then said something in what might have been Greek.

I shook my head. "No kapisch," I told him. "I was just waiting for the cross-town car."

His expression did not change; it looked like something carved on a wooden Indian. He was dressed in thick, olive-drab trouses and a tan shirt with shoulder straps, both badly worn and dirt-stained.

"Who ordered you to this section?" he asked in a tone like a tired cop making a routine license check.

"I came here on my own," I told him.

"Where is your leader?" He had some kind of accent, but I could not place it.

"I'm the leader," I came back. He was a little too far away to reach without taking a step. I debated whether to try him now, or wait for him to move in a little closer.

"I was not informed," he said. He dropped the cloth he had been using on his hands and made some sort of gesture with his fingers.

"Never mind the excuses," I said. "You can go now."

"Those instructions are not explicit," he commented. "To where am I instructed to go?"

"Where would you like to go?" My upper lip was getting sweaty now; the nutty conversation was getting on my nerves. I wished he would either flash his badge, let out a yell or make his play. Instead, he stood there, looking thoughtful.

"I would like to return to my room and sleep," he stated.

"Swell. You do that."

He turned his back and headed for the steps. I watched him go, then stepped out after him.

"Maybe before you go to sleep you'd better show me around a little," I called after him. "I'm new here."

He was on the steps, looking back at me. "What do you wish to see?"

"Everything."

"Your instructions are not clear," he stated.

"Just show me around, I'll decide what to look at."

He hesitated. "I know," I said, cutting him off before he said anything, "that's not explicit. Just start showing me things as we come to them."

The door opened into a hallway better lit than the room below. It smelled of moldy cucumbers and iodine, with an overlay of river mud. The floor was made of large stone slabs, between the joints of which water oozed. There were discolored cracks in the rough-plastered walls, and more water trickled from them. We passed doorways, blocked with tarred brickword, likewise damp-looking. It appeared the place had sprung a number of leaks.

The passage made an abrupt righturn, ended at a metal wall with a circular door that looked as massive as a bank vault. My guide gripped a two-handed lever, pulled it out, turned it to the left; the port swung in. He ducked, stepped through, with me close behind.

We were in a wide corridor, brightly lit, with smooth walls, a polished floor, fresh-smelling air. A few yards along, we turned into a spacious room with a mosaic floor as bright as neon, and mural-covered walls showing men and women in short white kilts throwing sticks at birds rising from a swamp. In the far corner of the room, near a wide doorway with a gold lintel, a man sat behind a long marble-slab table, working over papers. We went across to him.

"I require your help," my guide said. The man looked at him, past him at me, got to his feet. My guide stepped back, waited for him to come around the table.

"Seize him," he said in an unexcited tone and lunged for my arm. I gave him the back of my hand, spun around in time to meet his partner with a wild swing that connected somewhere in the vicinity of his right ear, knocked him over the table as the other man landed on my back. We went down together and I twisted as I fell, heard his head hit hard. I rolled clear and he slid off on his face, out cold. The man behind the table was on his knees, fumbling with a little gold whistle hanging on a cord around his neck; I grabbed for it, yanked his head hard. It hit marble with a dull sound and he went down bubbling.

I was breathing hard, listening to surf booming way back in my skull. I still had not gotten my wind back from the swim up the sewer pipe. The place was silent now, except for two sets of hoarse breathing; then I heard footsteps coming along the hall—more than one man. Various ideas ran through my head, none of them good; two bleeding bodies are too much of a burden for any bluff to carry.

The gold-ornamented door caught my eye. I jumped the secretarial type lying half under it, tried the big handle. It turned, and the door opened with a squeal as I pushed through and closed it behind me.

This time the passage was wider, higher, floored with red flagstones, lit by chandeliers hanging at five-yard intervals. Along one side were columns supporting arches, like a Gothic cloister; all the openings had been smoothly cemented in. There was a wide, open door on the right ahead. I went along to it, turned in to a roomy apartment fitted out with modern factory-built furnishings, rugs, framed pictures. The place was in a state of chaotic disarray: papers and odd garments were heaped on tables, scattered over the floor; dirty dishes were stacked on the arms of chairs, on a wide buffet, on two carpeted steps that led down to an open archway. There were dark stains on the rug, the glisten of water along a crack in the patterned wallpaper.

From the corridor I heard the scrape of the big door, a mutter of voices. I was in plain sight from the apartment door. I went down the steps, through into the next room, almost choked on a reek of garlic and stale bedding. Against the left wall, a vast, bloated bulk of a man lay spread eagled on a four-poster just smaller than a handball court, propped up on a heap of gold-tasseled pillows. He stared at me fixedly with small, protruding eyes in a brown face that looked too small for the big, hairless skull. The massive jowls quivered; a voice like a rubber doll squeaked something at me.

"Keep quiet," I ordered. I yanked the spear pistol from its sheath, moved over against the wall beside the bed, out of sight from the doorway.

"If they stick their heads in here, I'll put a bolt through your neck. Do I make myself clear?"

The bulging eyes bulged at me a little harder; otherwise he made no sign that he had heard me. Maybe he was deaf; maybe he did not understand English. Either way, the weapon in my hand should have given him enough of a hint. The voices were coming from the outer room now.

"Tell them to go away," I hissed at him. "In English."

He heaved his chest—an effect like a wave rolling inshore—and shrilled, "Go away!"

Steps approached the door, soft on the carpet. Someone spoke, no more than six feet from where I stood flattened against the wall. I measured the distance to the rolls of fat around the reclining beauty's neck.

"Go away!" the Minnie Mouse voice squealed. "Go away instantly."

The voice outside made a final comment and the steps retreated. I waited until the silence had stretched out to breaking point, then let out a breath I did not realize I had been holding. The big man was watching me as if he expected me to do something astonishing at any moment and he did not want to miss it.

"You are not of us," he piped suddenly.

"Who is us?"

"How did you come here?" he came back.

"I followed a trail; this is where it ended."

"That is impossible," the hairless head wobbled in agitation.

"It's happening. Talk it up, big boy. I'm a long way from home and my nerves are shot. I could get violent at any moment."

"I have a great deal of money," the tiny voice stated, sounding calm now.

"In gold pieces?"

"Whatever you wish. I will summon one who—"

"You won't summon anybody. Who were the lads who paid Rassias to bring them out here?"

The purse mouth worked. "I can give you power—"

"I've got all the power I need." I took a step, poked the triangular point of the foot-long harpoon against his throat. "Who are you? What is this place? Who are the silent lads with the quick guns?"

He squeaked and flapped his hands against the dirty silken sheet.

"Ever met a man named Sethys?" If the name startled him, he did not show it. He kept the eyes glued on me like gold stars on a stripper. I stepped back, looked around the room. It was like the sitting room outside—an unwholesome combination of luxury and dirty socks. There was a closed door across the room; I tried it, found it locked. Beside it was a tall wardrobe, it opened and I looked in at suits, coats, hats, shoes, all on the same gargantuan scale as my new chum on the bed. A table beside the wardrobe was stacked with newspapers, soiled clothes, scattered coins—none gold—more gravy-stained dishes. I dumped them off, checked the drawer, found bits of paper, a gold fountain pen of antique design, envelopes, a bottle of purple pills. The chest of drawers yielded folded underwear, chicken bones, an expensive-looking wrist watch, an empty bottle. I did not know what I was looking for, but I was not finding it.

Fatty was watching every move. The sheet was thrown back from his chest, exposing an expanse of tough-looking brown skin like a hairless walrus. He had one hand out, fingering the top of a carved chest beside the bed; he pulled it back when I looked his way. I went over and lifted the lid. A heap of metallic green cloth lay on top of folded linens. I was reaching for it when he made a noise like a strangled chicken and lunged for me.

I jumped, but not quickly enough. One fat hand caught my gun hand below the wrist with a grip like a hydraulic vise, yanked me to him. I twisted far enough to get a hip into his belly, put my elbow in his eye, and socked him on the ear as hard as circumstances permitted. It was not enough. He screeched like an insulted elephant, made a grab for my neck, got a handful of shoulder instead. I brought a hard chop down on the bridge of his nose, hit him across his well-padded throat, got a thumb into the other eye. He dropped the grip on my shoulder, heaved himself up for another try at my throat. This time he made it. Fingers like bolt cutters dug in. I braced myself, picked a spot just behind the corner of his mouth, put everything I had into a right-handed chop that snapped his head sideways hard enough to bounce it off his shoulder. His eyes went dull; he shuddered and went limp.

I dragged myself to my feet, checked my major bones and joints. I was a little surprised to find them all intact. When Big Boy got started, he was full of surprises.

I picked up the green garment, shook it out. It was an overall, cut to fit a medium-sized female. There was a tear down the back, and another on the right sleeve. I laid it out flat on the side of the bed, smoothed it. A piece was missing from the torn sleeve—a piece that would be some six inches long and half an inch wide—just the size of the strip I had found at the door of the collapsing hotel.

CHAPTER NINE

He came to five minutes later, made a couple of convulsive flops, steadied down when I touched his side with the razor-sharp spear point.

"Where is she?"

He looked at the garment in my hand. His face worked like fudge about to come to a boil.

"I cannot tell you."

"Too bad." I rammed the spear medium hard; blood started from the cut. He jerked away and I prodded him again.

"You used up all your good will with me when you put your thumb in my neck," I told him. "Get her here or I'll pin you to the mattress and go looking for her myself."

"You must not kill me," he chirped. He seemed very serious about this. "I must not be touched, damaged, or caused pain."

"That's understandable—but life is full of disappointments. I can give you five minutes."

"I will give you other women—as many as you like—"

"Just the one, thanks."

"I need this woman," he insisted.

"For what? Why did you bring her here?"

"I require a mistress—many mistresses—"

"All the way from Miami?"

"She caught my eye; I desired her."

"Let's have the truth. It's less taxing on the brain."

"I have told you—"

I poked him; he jumped, made a half-hearted grab for the pistol. I shifted position, caught him on on the hand with the point. He gave a squeal like a stepped-on rat, jammed the hand in his mouth and made sucking sounds.

"Call one of your boys and have her brought here; then tell them to go away. You know just how to do it—nice and easy."

He made gobbling noises, pointed to a large button set in the carved headboard.

"I must use this," he choked out.

"Go ahead. You know the rules."

I watched while he thumbed the call button; faint crackling sounds started up. "Yes," a voice said from across the room. I looked across at a small tri-D screen from which a face was staring.

"He cannot see us," the fat man whispered in a hoarse yelp.

The man on the screen said something in a strange, staccato language. My host replied in kind. I kept a little pressure on the spear point to remind him of our arrangement. The face went away and the screen winked off. Fatty whined and flopped his hands on the bed. There was quite a bit of blackish blood spattered around on the sheets now from the punctures in his hide. I must have been pushing harder than I thought.

"When the woman is brought here, you must go

away," he piped.

"Get her here; I'll take it from there."

He lay on the bed, looking at me. From time to time his chest heaved in a shuddery sob. I checked my watch. It had been five minutes since the call.

Suddenly, there were footsteps in the outer room. I moved back against the wall.

"Just the girl," I whispered through my teeth. Fatty chirped orders. There were sounds of a scuffle; then Ricia stumbled through the doorway. She was dressed in a shapeless gray sack, barefooted.There was a small cut on her forehead. Her hands were trussed behind her. She looked at the man on the bed with an expression of mild distaste, said something haughty in the same language she had used on me. He flopped his hands, pointed at me. Ricia took a step forward, saw me and stiffened—then smiled like the sun breaking through clouds.

"Akmal!" She took a step my way, then faltered, looked at the fat man. He spoke to her in what sounded like he own tongue.

"Tell her I'm getting her out of here," I snapped. Then, to her: "It's all right now, Ricia. We're leaving." I went to her, cut the tough cords binding her wrists. There were deep red marks where they had been. The fat man was talking—speaking persuasively, waving his hands.

"That's enough," I cut him off. "Let's go, Ricia." I took her hand. She hung back, spoke sharply to the fat man. He answered. She snapped an order at him. He rolled the bugged eyes at me.

"You will be caught," he said. "They will kill you. The woman commands me to say this to you."

"Sure." I looked into Ricia's face. She smiled again, tentatively. "It's good to see you again, kid," I told her. "Let's travel." I went to the head of Fatty's bed, used the spear point to dig the call button out of the wood and poke the connecting wires back in out of reach.

"I need one more thing of you," I told him. A diving outfit for the girl."

"I know nothing—"

"Better try." Another jab—a hearty one. He yelped.

"Perhaps—at the lock. Yes—I remember it now. It has been many years—"

"Where's the nearest exit?"

"There." He pointed at the locked door beside the wardrobe, "Follow the passage. The lock is there."

"Where's the key?"

"Press the head of the carved dragon."

I tried it. The door slid back; I looked in at wet floor stretching off into darkness. Ricia was beside me.

"Mal—no walk. Bad," she said.

"I don't like it too well myself, but if we don't find the lock I'll come back and cut him a new mouth under those chins." I gave Fatty a last smile to show him my morale was up, took Ricia's hand, and stepped through. We had gone about ten feet when the light narrowed down, went out. My dive for the closing door was a yard short and a second late.

"Mal!" Ricia's voice was a gasp.

"I'm all right, just stupid. I guess Tubby had a button I missed." I got to my feet, groped my way to her, put an arm around her shoulders. She shivered, clung to me. My hand light was still clipped to my belt; I flashed it over the door. The inner side was smooth, with no nice dragon heads to push. I leaned on it; it was like leaning against the First National Bank.

"No joy here, Ricia. I guess we keep going." She gave me a brave smile and took my free hand. Together we followed the passage. Forty feet along it turned right and ended in a cul de sac where a doorway had been walled up.

"Swell," I said. "End of the line. But maybe there's a door we missed." We went back along the route, studying the walls. They were smooth masonry, unbroken except for a few floor-to-ceiling fractures through which water seeped to add to the slosh underfoot.

"We'll never punch our way through this, kid," I said. "I think we'd better have another look at that door."

I checked it over from edge to edge, from threshold to header. There was not even a pin hole to work on. It seemed to be a slab of solid metal.

Ricia was holding the light for me. She reached out, touched the case Carmody had clipped to my belt.

"This?" she said.

"Burglar tools," I said. "They're no help if I don't have a lock or hinges to work on." I unsnapped the case, lifted out a plastic box, opened it; the light winked from polished metal. "Jimmies, pinch bars, back saws—everything the well-dressed burglar needs."

I was looking at the small cutting torch, no

bigger than a can opener. It was something special, Carmody had told me; it used a new mixtures of gases developed for working the material used to line rocket exhaust tubes. It was intended for nothing heavier than cutting cables, but this was not a time to be particular.

It took five minutes of experimentation before I got a steady white flame burning, another five minutes to find a setting that nibbled a pit in the metal.

"At this rate we won't need to make any social engagements for a while," I said over the crackle of the torch. "I'll try for a hole big enough to get my hand through. This spot should be just about opposite the dragon's left ear."

Ricia stood by me, watching as the glow spread. The pockmark in the hard metal widened to a half-inch pit. Suddenly sparks showered and molten metal welled out.

"Luck," I said. "I've cut through into a softer layer."

Ricia put a hand on my arm. "Mal, listen!"

I listened, heard nothing but the snap and pop of the flame.

"Bad men. Here." She pointed at the door. I shut down the torch and at once heard a dull pounding.

"Sounds like they're beating on the door."

Ricia looked up at me, said nothing.

"Why the hell would they pound on the door? All they have to do is push the dragon's head."

Ricia pointed to the glowing orifice in the door. "Broken," she said. "No dragon's head."

"Could be—I must have cut a wire." My lips felt as dry as blotters. "I had a wild idea they might stay away for a while, but it looks like Big Boy was a couple of jumps ahead of me all the way."

Nobody contradicted me. I stood there, watching the glow fade, feeling the glow of forlorn hope fading along with it. Ricia crept in close, put her head against my chest.

"Sorry, kid." I stroked her hair. "I guess you might have had a better chance if I'd kept out of it. They hadn't murdered you yet; maybe they didn't intend to . . ."

"Better here, Mal."

"Yeah, if you're lucky, they get the door open and take you back; if not, you starve where you are." My fingers touched the smooth skin of her throat. Before I would let her starve, I would have to kill her myself—choke her or break her neck. She would understand what I was doing, and smile at me as I touched her.

"No!" I slammed a fist against the door. "Come and get her, you lousy killers! Tear that door down—"

"Mal . . ." Ricia's hands were on my face, around my neck, her lips against mine. Slowly the roaring died down in my head. I leaned against the wall while she talked to me, soothing me like you sooth a restless animal.

"If I could rig a trap for those zombies," I said. "Something that would blow . . ." I stopped talking, feeling a thump in my chest that meant that hope, down for the count, was picking herself off the canvas for another try.

"Mal, what?"

"Nothing. An idiot idea. But it might—just might be something . . ."

She held the light again while I set to work, digging the flash metal away from the hole I had cut. The door was hollow, filled with a perforated honeycomb of light metal under the quarter-inch covering of stainless steel.

"So far so good." My fingers had developed a gross tremor, like a dipso groping for his first drink of the morning. I used the spear head to saw a strip from Ricia's cuff, wrapped it around the nozzle of the torch, fitted it into the hole; then I thumbed the control full over. The gas mixture hissed softly, pouring into the hollow interior of the door.

"This part is guesswork," I told Ricia. "These capsules at the base of the handle store the gas in liquid form; I don't know how long they'll feed. And I need to keep a little in reserve."

Ricia was sniffling. I sniffed, too, caught the sour lemon smell of the gas.

"I guess she's full." I removed the torch, plugged the hole with the scrap of cloth, then propped the torch on the floor, using the tool kit to support it in a vertical position.

"I'll light the torch and let it play on the door. When the metal gets white-hot—well, we'll see what happens."

A moment later the blue-white flame was sputtering against the metal, eight inches from the bottom edge of the door.

"Let's go," I took Ricia's hand and we ran for the end of the corridor, ducked around into the shelter of the walled-off cubicle at its end.

"This will probably be a dud," I said, talking to hear myself. "There won't be enough gas there to ignite, maybe. Or maybe it'll go *pop!* and blow the plug out."

"Yes, Mal." Ricia patted my hand.

"Or maybe nothing will happen at all. Maybe the torch will go out. Maybe—"

Ricia took my hands, placed them over her ears. I smiled a crooked smile at her. "Good idea," I said. "Just in case—"

A club struck my head, slammed me back against the stone wall like a mouse riding the clapper of a giant bell. I seemed to be flying end over end, while bright pinwheels whirled all around me like Independence Day in Texas. I groped, found rough masonry under me. I could taste blood in my mouth.

"Ricia!" I felt my throat vibrate with the yell, but all I could hear was a high, insistent singing, like a stuck siren. Then I touched her hands; I caught at it, pulled her close, felt over her face and body for wounds. She was limp, out cold, but I could feel her breath on my face; she was alive. I yelled her name again, but nothing could penetrate the siren tone that filled the darkness as water fills a well.

Something cold was washing up my side. I found my hand light, switched it on. Muddy water was swirling around the corner, foaming, bearig a litter of floating debris.

"Must have knocked a hole in the wall," I felt myself say. I groped my way to my feet, caught up Ricia, got her over my shoulder, stepped out past the angle of the short passage. At the far end, light glared through a ragged opening like a paper hoop the trick dog has just jumped through. Dirty water poured toward me in a white cataract, carrying papers, small objects, fragments of shattered wood. I waded upstream, climbed through into the room beyond.

The fat man was gone. The bed lay like a crashed balloon, the mattress split wide in a welter of soggy cotton and coil springs, the headboard collapsed over it, the canopy of dark brown silk sagging above, dirty water tugging at its corner. By the steps, a man lay half-submerged, trails of pink blood swirling away from him. Another man lay on his back across the shattered wardrobe, his face and chest torn into blackish-red jam. Major fragments of other men bumped along in the current.

"They must have been standing in front of the door when it went." I towed Ricia across through shin-deep water, up the steps into the sitting room. A wide crack had opened across the left wall, through which water jetted in a translucent sheet halfway across the room. I ducked through it, reached the outer passage, stumbled over broken stones crumbled from the walled-up arches, reached the open door into the lounge with the marble table. The two men whose heads I had cracked were gone; the bright mosaic floor was a rippling pattern under a foot of water. Through cracks in the murals, more water flowed.

"That blast must have been the last straw," I mumbled aloud, hearing the words ring deafly inside my head. "The place is breaking up."

By the time I reached the closed hatch through which I had come on the way in, the stream was knee deep, awash with feather fans, wood carvings, papers. I grabbed the big handle, yanked and twisted, then calmed down, tried to remember my guide's technique. He had pushed the level in, turned it to the left. I did the same, and the heavy metal port swung toward me pushed by a vast gush of water that knocked me off my feet, washed me twenty feet downstream. Somehow I kept my grip on the girl, got my feet under me, waded back, climbed through the hatch. The water surged and boiled, eddying around a large mahogany chest wedged in the passage.

I got a foot on it, started over, saw two men fifty feet downstream, hauling at what looked like another hatch like the one we had just passed. One of them looked my way, pointed; the other went on with what he was doing. The pointer grabbed his arm and the other fellow pushed him away, kept working. Abruptly, a red light went on above the port as it swung out. I laid Ricia out across the top of the heavy chest, vaulted over it, lifted her again, half swam, half waded along to the port. Both men had disappeared behind it now. I reached it just as it started its swing inward, got a grip on its edge, braced my feet, hauled back.

Pain exploded in my hand; one of the boys was pounding my fingers. I fumbled left-handed, freed the spear pistol from my belt, aimed it past the edge of the door, and fired. There was a grunt, then threshing sounds. The door gave a foot, and I caught a glimpse of an interior like a section of sewer main, bright-lit, with a second port dogged shut on its opposite side. A locker mounted against the wall was open, and a man, half into a leathery-looking frogman outfit, was crumpled against it, three inches of blue steel bolt projecting from a bloody patch just below his ear.

I just had time to note the purplish color of the face of the man holding the door against me when something bright flashed up, swung down at me, and I ducked, took the blow across the top of my head, felt myself going back and down. Churning water closed over my face.

For what seemed like a long time, I tumbled, feeling the burn of water in my chest, the dim, ghostly blows of the walls and floor against me as the racing water hurled me along. Then somehow I was swimming, my face above water, my ears popping from the pressure of air compressed between the rising flood and the passage walls. I yelled for Ricia, then saw her dark hair afloat on the surface, swam a few floundering strokes, caught her and lifted her face clear. Water ran from her nose and mouth. Her face was a dim yellow in the faint light.

The water swept us along, dunked us rounding a bend, then hurled us down a slope into a log jam of floating chairs, tables, statuary, paper, rubbish. I took a sharp crack on the head, a gouge in the side before I caught a big box bobbing in the flood, got my back to it to fend off the flotsam. The ceiling was no more than five feet above the water; I recognized it as a room I had seen before.

The water was rising fast. There was no more than thirty inches now between the discolored bricks of the ceiling and the roiled surface of the water. My head seemed to ring with a clear, steady note. My arms ached from the effort of holding Ricia's head above the choppy ripples. A sudden lassitude swept over me; it would be so easy to relax, slide down under the black surface and let it all go.

I thought of Ricia, the trusting squeeze of her hand just before the blast that smashed her unconscious—and pictured her waking here, choking alone before those last seconds before the long blackness.

There was an abrupt change in the flow of water around me; I felt, rather than heard, the deep-toned thud of machinery. A new current stirred, pulled me toward a newly formed eddy at the center of the chamber. Down below—submerged under ten feet of black water—the louvers would be open now. Somehow, in spite of the broached walls, the pumps were working, forcing the inrushing waters out through a hundred yards of tunnel, to the open sea bottom. How much longer they would operate was a question.

There was no time for me to weigh the alternatives. I poured the water from my breathing helmet, pulled it over my head, snapped it in place. Then, with the unconscious body of the girl tucked under my arm, I let go of my support and slid under the surface.

Finding the big drain was easy; a swift current sucked at me, swept me to it, slammed me hard against the open louvers. I twisted over on my back, lowered my feet through the narrow gap between slats, pulled Ricia after me. I could see her face, a ghostly pale blue in the murky water. All around, floating objects bobbed and whirled. I grabbed at a helmet, jammed it somehow on Ricia's head. It was going to be a long haul to the surface if we ever made it.

The flow took me down, under the curve of the tunnel's ceiling. I brought the hand light around, shone it through the water; the narrow beam faded out six feet from my face.

I cracked the jet control, slowed our motion. Water hammered at me, tore at Ricia. We crept along, past yard after yard of monotonously unvarying gray wall—and then suddenly the dark barrier of the baffle was looming up in front of me. I steered to the right, held Ricia's limp body close to me, shot past the open valve and out into the murky turbulance of freedom.

I groped over the slight body in my arms, tried to find her wrist, to check her pulse, but my hands were clumsy with cold. In the beam of the hand light, an immense and curious fish swam close, shot away as I waved an arm. At one hundred feet, I felt a twinge in my left elbow, then a sharp pain at the base of my skull. The rapid ascent was equivalent to explosive decompression—a trick that could transform a healthy man into a broken cripple in a matter of seconds. It would have been nice to spend a couple of hours in a timed ascent.

I bent my arm against the pain in the joint, read the depth gauge. Fifty-one feet, forty-six, forty, thirty-two—

Pain like a hot knife seared the back of my right leg, clamped my ankle in a vise of agony. I held on, forced my eyes open against pressure that was forcing them from their pockets.

I shot clear of the surface, fell back in a cage of pain that wrenched at every joint in my body like a farmer wringing the necks of chickens. I got a quick flash of lights bobbing across the water, then found the jet control. I steered with my legs, aiming for the glitter of the chrome-plated ladder over the boat's stern, caught it, held on, while a red haze shot with lightning closed down over my brain. Then a hand was on my arm, hauling at me.

"Ricia . . . get her—decompression chamber . . ." I could feel my tongue slurring the words. Then her weight was gone from my arm. Hands hauled me up over the rail and onto the deck. Warm air struck my face as the helmet was pulled off, all in a silence broken only by the high hum that had rung in my head since the explosion. My eyes were balls of white-hot pain, spikes driven into my brain.

I made a move to get up, and the hands lifted me. Then I was on my back, feeling a deep hammer of air against me. I groped, found the cold curve of Ricia's cheek. Quite suddenly, the pain eased, like a thorn pulled from a wound. I took a breath, tasted the metallic flavor of the air, almost laughed as I realized that for an hour I had forgotten the odor of volcanoes.

Then the smell and the lights and the pain faded, and I sank down into regions of warmth and forgetfulness.

CHAPTER TEN

Consciousness was a long time returning, like an old soldier who has forgotten the way home. I was aware of the pain in my head first, then of other pains. My eyes hurt with a burning, purple agony. I opened them against pressure, saw the light in the ceiling of the decompression tank as a blurry puffball. I tried an arm; it seemed to work all right. I used it to push myself up to a sitting position. Ricia lay on her face beside me, wrapped in a blanket. For a heart-stopping instant my hand against her lips felt nothing; then a faint breath of warm air came. She was breathing.

I got to my feet, crouched under the low curve of the tank. My right knee was swollen and numb. I put my face close to the pressure gauges on the wall, made out the shape of the long needle resting square on 14.6 PSI. It would be safe to open now. I went to the closed entry hatch, tugged at the handle; I was as weak as watered booze. I started to hammer on the wall to let Carmody know I was up and around, but something stopped me. I stood with my fist raised, wondering what it was.

Then I got it; the boat was wallowing in a cross-chop. We were still at sea. My watch said twenty minutes till five—nearly seven hours since I had started my swim. Why had Carmody not run us back into port, gotten Ricia to a medic? And why was the boat drifting, broadside to the swell?"

I tried the handle again; this time it budged. I brought it around in a full turn to release the pressure latch, and the door popped free, swung in half an inch. I looked out at gray dawn light, the bleached teak of the deck, and the lower legs and feet of a man lying face down six feet from me. I eased the door shut, reached for the spear pistol; it was gone—lost in the scramble through the sewer, no doubt.

I let five minutes go by, the slow way; then I cracked the door again, took another look at the legs. My vision was like steamed glass, but they looked like Carmody's rope-soled shoes. The boat was silent, except for the hum that was still with me. Maybe I was deaf, the thought hit me. I held my fingers to my ear and rubbed them together; I could faintly hear the sound.

I stepped out, keeping ducked behind the decomp tank, closed the hatch behind me, looked over toward the man on the deck. It was Carmody, all right, and he was very dead. Twenty miles from land, the flies had already found him.

Rassias was forward, lying on his back with his head in the scuppers, shot through the right eye. Near him there was a patch of rusty-looking blood on the scarred deck, a trail of blood leading to the rail. Someone with a hole in him had gone over the side.

I had been moving carefully, barefooted—but not carefully enough. The back of a man's head appeared just as I turned, coming up from below. I dropped to a crouch, moved in close to the deck-house, crept on back until I could risk a quick look. He was standing two feet away, looking back across the stern. In another half-second he would turn; I could tell by the set of his shoulders. Before he could move, I jumped. My bum knee gave under me and I missed his back, slammed against his hip as he jumped aside. I hit the deck hard, rolled, came up facing him. His gun was out, coming down to an aiming point six inches below my chin. He had a thoughtful, intent expression on his face, like a billiards champ lining up for a two-banker.

"No. Keep this one alive for the present." I heard the call through the hum. A second man came up from the gloom of the cabin. I blinked, trying to get a clear view of his face. I was not sure, I but I thought I had seen him before—maybe in Miami.

The fellow with the gun lowered it, tucked it away. He looked like a schoolteacher—a medium-sized, medium-aged man with thinning hair, a little plump around the middle, dressed in a rumpled tan suit. The other had the carefully mournful expression of a coffin salesman. His suit was a dusty black. They stood looking at me for a moment, then the gun handler turned away.

"I will find ropes to tie him with." He spoke flawless English with a faint foreign flavor. I had the feeling he could do the same in twelve other languages.

The man who was watching me stood like a bored commuter waiting for a bus. He did not smoke, did not scowl, did not twitch. He just stood there. He looked easy to take. I sat up slowly and his hand flicked, brought out a gun.

"Take off the belt," he said flatly. I unbuckled it, heavy with gear.

"Throw it over the side," he commanded. I was looking straight up the barrel of the gun. He must have been the one who shot Rassias; he liked eye shots. I did as he told me.

"Take off the suit," he said.

I got to my feet, moving very slowly, unzipped the cold-suit, pulled it off, not without a certain amount of groaning. My bones felt as though they had been taken out and pounded.

"Throw it away." I bundled it up and tossed it over the rail. That left me my underwear and my natural dignity.

He put the gun away; I was harmless now. The other fellow came back and told me to lie down. I did. I was in a co-operative mood this morning. It was chilly on deck; I shivered while cold, smooth hands took three turns of half-inch nylon around my ankles, cinched them up tight enough to hurt, knotted the rope. Then I rolled over on my face while they did my hands. They walked away, left me lying face down on the deck in a puddle of ice-cold water.

I flip-flopped, pulled myself aft another yard, twisted over for a look. The two men stood together by the deckhouse, staring out over the port rail. The boat wallowed, drifting with the wind. Carmody lay where they had left him, attended only by the buzzing insects, one of which flew back to check me, decided not yet, and went away.

A steel storage box was bolted to the deck two feet from my head. I hunched my way back until I could see behind it. The canvas-wrapped gun case I had brought aboard was still there. I tried the ropes on my wrists; they gave a little; nylon is no good for some jobs. I could just touch one knot with my fingertips. I teased it, got a few strands started. Half a minute later the knot bulged, flopped free. Another five minutes and I was rubbing my hands together behind me, trying to work the stiffness out of fingers as cold and insensitive as frozen fishsticks.

The boys up front were ignoring me. One was pointing, and I followed his finger, saw a big, dark-painted boat coming up fast off the port bow. Sunlight winked from a big searchlight on its foredeck, and there were bulky, tarpaulin-covered shapes that would be deck guns. It looked like a revenue cutter on a business trip. My boys did not act worried; they stood indifferently, waiting for it.

I slipped a hand over behind the box, dragged the gun case toward me, unsnapped the flap, got a grip on the butt of the nearest weapon, pulled it half out, froze when the schoolteacher looked my way. I flopped, faked a futile effort to sit up. He watched me for a moment, went back to watching the boat. It was close enough for me to hear it now; the big engines were throttled back, growling as she swung past, coming around to the upwind side. She looked bigger than ever, up close—five hundred tons at least. There were half a dozen men at the rail. One of them shouted, and the coffin salesman waved a hand in a stiff gesture.

The faint hope that the law had arrived died.

Both my keepers had their backs to me now. I snaked the gun clear of the case, brought it over into my lap. It was the Weatherby .375 repeater, a good gun for elephant. I had loaded it before the trip. Lying on my back, with the gun on my chest, I snicked off the safety, raised my head far enough to sight, lined up on the schoolteacher's back, and squeezed off a round. The recoil hit my right cheekbone like a baseball bat, and my target leaped forward, went down out of sight. The other man whirled, bringing out his gun. I swung the sights over, found his face, fired again, caught a glimpse of a red explosion where his head had been.

Men were running on the deck of the cutter. I saw a bright flash, heard a ricochet whine past me. I dumped the Weatherby, hauled the gun case out, stripped it from the chrome steel and black plastic of the big military high-speed job, jacked the lever over to full automatic and dived for the shelter of the rail.

Shots were hitting all around me now; one ploughed a dark streak in the salt-bleached deck near my face. I spat splinters, poked the snout of my gun out through a hawse hole, took aim at the gun boat's water line, and squeezed. There was a roar like a gut-shot tyrannosaurus, but my gun was a sweet weapon. Except for a mule kick straight into my shoulder, it rode as smoothly as a cap pistol, poured out its magazine in one furious burst that hammered against my dulled ears like a cotton-padded alarm clock, and was abruptly silent. I dropped it and rolled right, heard the dull spang of bullets hitting the steel spray shield by my head. Looking forward, I saw paint chip from the rail, splinters shower from the deck. They were laying down a barrage like a batallion of infantry.

I hugged the deck and waited. Shots kept hitting around me; one smacked metal an inch from my face, punched a finger-tip-sized dent, scattered paint dust in my face. I could see the Weatherby lying ten feet away; a bullet had smashed the stock. If my try with the burp gun had not done the job, the cutter would be looking up alongside in another few seconds.

I watched where the shots were hitting; I was not sure, but the fire seemed to be falling off, the gouges in the deck moving away, getting longer, as from low-angle fire. I inched back to the hawsehole, risked a look. The cutter was hove to, a hundred feet off the starboard bow. Her high, sharp prow was toward me. I could not see the side I had fired a thousand rounds of armor-piercing slugs into, but there seemed to be a slight list to starboard.

The shooting stopped suddenly. I watched as men swarmed around the forward deck gun, pulling the canvas cover from it. It was time to try for the elephant gun. I made it in a dive, rolled, scrambled for cover. Nobody fired.

I crawled along the deck to my loophole, lay flat behind it, drew a bead on the man on top of the .88 millimeter. The report was a flat crack. He went down like a blown-over scarecrow. A blown-over scarecrow. A shoulder was showing to the left of the gun. I shot at it and it went away. Someone was running across the deck, I led him two feet, fired, missed, and he ducked out of sight. Another fellow popped up, reached for the breech lever; I knocked him flying. The cutter was definitely listing now. She had swung around, showing her port side. Nobody was moving near the guns.

When the cutter was a hundred yards away, I fired my last two rounds, heard them ring off the gun's shield, then snaked across to the deckhouse and down the two steps to the cockpit. I tried the starter. The diesels groaned, fired, caught. I kept low, swung her away to port, opened the throttles and she put her nose up and dug in. I worked the wheel hard, putting her into sliding turns to left and right, but it was a full minute before the first round from the cutter's gun fountained ahead, a wide miss. She fired twice more, then gave it up. When I came up for air, the cutter was a mile astern, very low by the bow, wallowing in the swells.

The lopsided orange sun of morning was glaring across the water now, painting red streaks on the waves. I corrected course to put the sun at my back, set the automatic pilot and went aft to the decomp tank to see about Ricia.

She was awake, looking wan and thinner than ever, but she smiled when she saw me, said something in a voice too faint to hear.

"Sorry, kid," I said. My voice sounded strange in my ears, like a bad recording playing in the next apartment. "I can't hear you. Too many loud noises too close to my eardrums lately. How do you feel?"

She shook her head, pointed to her ears. She was

as deaf as I was. I put a hand against her forehead; she seemed to be about the right temperature. Her pulse felt good, strong and steady.

"I'll get you some soup." In the galley I opened a can, boiled water, fixed up a tray with toast and a glass of orange juice. She almost sat up when she saw it, but I could tell the effort hurt. I propped her up on cushions from the cabin, spoon-fed her. She ate like a starved kitten. When the soup was gone, she lifted an arm that seemed too heavy for her, touched my face. I saw her lips move, but all I caught was "Mal." Then she touched her eyes. There were dark lines around them—bruises, from blood vessels broken by the sudden pressure drop when we surfaced. I got her to move her arms and legs; they seemed all right.

We had both been lucky. Aside from a few more spots no more painful than bad sprains, we had survived the bends in good shape. I wanted to move her to the cabin, but at the moment I was not up to lifting anything heavier than a soup spoon. I tucked her in, checked to be sure the ventilator was working, went down into the cabin and collapsed on the bunk.

When I woke, I had the feeling it was late afternoon. I got my feet on the floor, tottered over to the wall mirror. The face that peered out at me looked like something they keep in a cage at second-rate carnies and feed live chickens to, four shows a day. Both eyes were purple-black, swollen almost shut. There was caked blood in my hair, in the black stubble across my jaws. What showed of the rest was a dirty gray.

I sluiced my head in cold water, then hot, got out

Carmody's razor and shaved. The shower could wait until I had checked on Ricia. She was awake, showing a little color in her cheeks now. I made more soup, brought her hot water and soap and a comb, then went back down and used up a tank of hot water on myself. Carmody's clothes were a little large for me, but I rolled the cuffs of a shirt and a pair of denim pants and went up on deck to do what had to be done.

Carmody was heavy; it took me five minutes to get him to the rail and over. I saw one arm flash for an instant above the water, as though he were waving good-by. He had been a good man, and he had died helping me, no questions asked. I hated to deal so callously with his body, but it was hot out here and Ricia would be coming on deck soon.

Rassias was easier. Afterward I used a bucket of salt water to wash down the deck. The flies seemed annoyed; they buzzed angrily around my head while I worked. I finished and the sun shone down, red and sullen, on a shipshape deck.

I checked our course and position. We were holding due west, and in another hour I would be sighting the coast of Africa south of Tunis—unless it had dropped out of sight since the last time I had passed this way. Ricia was still stretched out on the floor of the tank; it was the coolest place on the boat, and the air was clean. The same unit that pumped it up to pressure filtered and chilled it.

"We'll be in port soon," I told her. "I'll get a doctor there and in a few days you'll feel fine. Then we can head somewhere—wherever you like. We've got plenty of supplies for a long cruise." I did not say anything about the leaky palazzo on the sea bottom; it was already beginning to seem like something out of a fever dream. As far as I was concerned, the score was about even. I had gotten Ricia out and saved my own neck. I was sorry about Carmody—and Rassias. But they were dead, along with a lot of odd little men whose role in life I would never discover now—and did not want to. Ricia and I were alive. My modest ambition was to keep it that way.

An hour after noon I sighted a long brown line rising out of a sea as flat as a ballroom floor. Fifteen minutes later we were threading our way into a harbor choked with wreckage like a vacant lot filled with junked cars. One of the typhoons that had swept the area had caught a lot of shipping in port.

We tied up at a quay that showed some signs of life—stacks of red-painted fuel drums, a floating crane, piled crates, half a dozen lounging men who caught the bow line, made it fast. I had already told Ricia I would leave the boat just long enough to find a doctor. I jumped down on the pier, flashed a ten-cee note, asked who spoke English. A fellow with a mustache like a GI shoebrush pushed through, took the ten, showed me a set of teeth like broken earthenware.

"I speak, you bet. You want woman?" He was the kind of linguist who shouts to make his meaning clear, which was a break for me.

"I need a doctor," I explained.

He nodded vigorously. He had a rag tied around his head like Gunga Din. "Best doctor, fix you up good, you catch something from woman." He led me up the wharf, across a noisy street of white dust into the mouth of a narrow way that snaked around an outthrust angle of ancient masonry, narrowed still further into a covered stair between mossy walls. At the top, I caught a glimpse of him darting into a doorway across a courtyard of broken brick. Halfway to it, I realized something was wrong.

It was another fifty feet to the doorway; to the left of it was another arch like the one I had come in through. I kept going, at the last moment whirled left and ran for it. It was a nice try, but useless. A small man in a dirty brown suit stepped from my sanctuary, spread his arms. I hit him full tilt, kept my feet just long enough to see the club the fellow behind him swung at my head before all the lights went out.

Waking up this time was bad. I had not felt too well before the latest crack on the skull; now I hurt all over again, from the soles of my feet to the lump over my ear. The throbbing in my head should have been audible at fifty yards and the pain in my stomach told me I had been retching even before I came to. I seemed to be lying on a bench in a room that was hot and close.

"How do you feel?" An indifferent voice said from somewhere in the surrounding misery. I got an eyelid up, looked at a neatly dressed fellow with thin hair parted on the center line, a face like a brown prune, a scrawny neck I would have enjoyed squeezing.

"Like a pulled tooth," I said. My tongue was as thick as a pastrami sandwich, but I could hear myself a little better now. Maybe I would recover my hearing in time to listen to my own last words.

"Where is the woman?" Prune Face asked. I got the feeling he did not really care how I felt after all.

"What woman?"

Someone on the other side of me made a sudden move, was checked by a bark from Brownie.

"Now you're playing it smart," I congratulated him. "Any more rough stuff now and I'll be singing in a heavenly choir instead of into your brown, shell-like ear."

"When you have told me where you have left the woman, your wound will be attended?"

"Which one?"

"The woman whom you abducted. Do not waste our time."

"I meant which wound? I've got a variety."

"Your boat has been searched. Since she is not aboard, it is apparent that you put into port and placed her ashore. It will save us time and trouble if you will state where this took place."

"Sure. Why should I make trouble for myself over a slip of a girl? I made a high-speed run over to the mudflats off Athens and dumped her over the side. A nice walk to shore."

"You are lying."

"That's right."

"Where is the woman?"

"You're not cops?"

"That has no bearing on the question."

"Like hell. If you're cops I'm not admitting anything. You might call it murder and make trouble for me."

"You are already in trouble. But we are not police."

"OK. I dumped her."

"Why?"

"She didn't want to play."

"Play?"

"Do I have to draw you a picture?"

"You abducted the woman for this purpose?"

"Why else?"

Prune Face conferred briefly with two other voices which floated around behind me, out of sight. The language they used sounded like Chinese to me. Maybe it *was* Chinese. Whatever it was, it did not seem to be a clue.

"Let me attempt pain techniques," a new voice said in English.

"That is not practical."

"He would survive long enough to speak."

"Not this type. He will die. There is no time for experimentation."

Someone said something in the other language but Prunie cut him off short.

"No," he said in a tone of flat finality. "The decision has been made. Take him to the courtyard and cut his throat."

CHAPTER ELEVEN

Fatigue is a wonderful thing. They had to wake me up five minutes later—or maybe later than that; I did not check my watch—to get me to my feet, walk me along a white-washed galley with one side open to a stormy sky, down crooked stairs to a rectangle of hard-baked mud surrounded by lofty, cracked walls. The whole proceeding did not interest me much. As soon as they let go, I sat down hard. Somebody issued orders in a flat voice, like a bank examiner asking for the books, and businesslike hands pulled me to my feet again. It seemed that around here you only got your throat cut standing up. I wondered if the knife would be sharp, if it would hurt much; but the questions seemed academic. I had the feeling that must come to the stag at the end of a long run, an almost grateful relief that it was all over.

The hard hands on my arms bothered me. I made an effort, got my knees locked to take the weight. The walls seemed to be going around me in a smooth procession like the view from a merry-go-round. Dust choked me and I coughed. The sun was hot in the enclosed space where no breeze could move. The pleasant lassitude was wearing off while they talked, on and on. Suddenly I was shaking. I started to fall and my escort grabbed my arms again. In another second I was going to be a very sick man.

Then the hands were hauling at me, and somehow my legs were moving, and they were taking me away. It got shady and almost cool, and my feet scrabbled, trying to keep up. There was daylight again suddenly, and I hit my head on something and the pain pierced the fog long enough for me to get a glimpse of a car's interior, all gray leather and inlaid Circassian walnut. Someone shoved at me, and I was wedged in between two fattish men who smelled of sweat and curry. I felt the car start up, jolt a couple of times pulling out across rough ground. A voice that I had heard before was talking: ". . . the instruction of the Primary."

"This one is of no importance. The space—"

"That is my decision."

Then it all dissolved into a glowing fog and I let go and sank into it. . . .

. . . And awoke to the same old nightmare of hands that hauled me, made me walk with legs like broken soda straws down stairs, across pavements from which the heat of day glared, along echoing boards with the slap of water near. Then there was the smell of sea water and corruption, the lift and surge of a boat, the grumble and roar of engines, and spray that fell on my face in an irregular rhythm. Voices spoke around me, sometimes in English, sometimes in French or German or Russian, sometimes in dialects I had never heard before, weaving themselves into strange dreams of pursuit and revenge. My arms and legs and back ached with a screaming fatigue that was almost, but not quite enough, to shatter the drugged semiconsciousness that I clung to like a lost child hugging a teddy bear.

And then I was in a cool place, dim-lit, and the hands were lifting me, and I was lying on my back and cold indifferent hands were touching my face, my scalp, and there was the sting of cold steel against my arm and the sounds and sensations whirled away into a blackness filled with lights that swirled and died and I slept.

Someone was prodding my foot. I opened my eyes, saw a pale-faced man in immaculate whites standing over me. He had soft features, rimless glasses that caught the light, tufts of ginger hair over each ear.

"Your food is here," he said briskly. "You will feed yourself."

I caught a whiff of meat and vegetables from a tray on a cart by the bed. Beyond it were the plain white walls of a small room, a brown dresser with a square mirror, the corner of a narrow louvered door, another door half open on the stainless-steel bathroom fittings. I was still dizzy; the bed seemed to lift under me, pause, drop gently back.

"Where am I, in a hospital?" I was surprised to hear my voice come out in a high-pitched whisper.

"Sit up," the man in white commanded. I got my hands under me, pushed, and my attendant shoved pillows down behind me. Then he lifted the tray and placed it across my lap, supported on four wire legs. I did not wait for further urging—my stomach felt as hollow as Yorick's skull. My arm was a little heavy, but I managed to get a grip on the spoon, dip into the stew. Someone had left the salt out, but otherwise it was just what my tissues were screaming for. I ate it all, while the orderly stood by, saying nothing. When I had finished the last bite, he lifted the tray and disappeared without looking back.

I dozed some more, had another meal, watched the reddish light fade into gloom. I had a vague feeling there were things I was not doing, but I did not want to think about that just now. I had a bed, food, and solitude. For now, that was enough.

Light glared abruptly. The door thumped open and a man with a wrinkled brown face came through it, walked over to stare down at me. It was a face I had seen before, in unpleasant circumstances.

"Will you tell me where the woman is now?" he asked in the tone of a hash-house waiter taking an order.

"What woman?"

"The woman you abducted—you know quite well what I mean."

"You've got a one-track mind. I thought you were having my throat cut. What happened, lose your nerve?"

"My instructions were overruled. You are to receive special interrogation. You will save yourself from acute discomfort if you speak up now."

"Don't scare me; I'm a sick man."

"You are quite recovered from the concussion.

Your scalp wound has been dressed and drugs have been administered to hasten healing of the decompression damage. You are now able to withstand prolonged questioning."

"How long have I been here?"

"I will answer no questions."

"You want answers, don't you?"

"Yes. Where—"

"I said how long have I been here?"

He looked at me; wheels seemed to be turning behind his unremarkable face. "Three days."

"Where am I?"

"Aboard an ocean-going vessel."

"Bound where?"

"I will answer no more questions. Now, where did you land the woman?"

"What woman?"

"You implied that you would co-operate if I answered your questions."

"I'm tricky."

He turned and walked out of the room and I noticed the sharp *snick!* of the lock behind him. He had told me more than he thought. Three days had passed and they had not yet found Ricia. The decompression tank on Carmody's boat was a home-built job; at a glance it looked like what it had started life as, a five-hundred-gallon auxiliary fuel tank. If you did not know about the hatch at the aft end, you would never think to look inside for a sick woman. From what I had seen of the deadly little men who were hunting her, they were curiously lacking in the imagination department.

But even if they had not found her, that did not mean she was in the clear. She had been as weak as a new-born fawn when I left her. Assuming she had lain low, weathered the search, let herself out of the tank—then what? She had no clothes but an oversized coverall, no money, could not speak any language she would be likely to encounter in North Africa. And she was still a sick girl, lacking the cozy comforts I had been enjoying.

That was the kind of thinking that can break you out in a cold sweat, while producing no useful results. I had done my best, and it had not been good enough. At least she was not in the hands of these reptile-blooded goons. I would have to settle for that for now.

Meanwhile, I had problems of my own. Prune Face had said we were aboard ship; that was something to check. I pushed back the sheet, discovered I had no clothes. I swung my legs over the side and stood up, swaying a little, but feeling better than I had expected. The medicine was doing its job.

It was a long walk to the porthole eight feet away. I made it, looked out at swift-moving dark waves, the reflections of lights shining somewhere above. The story checked, as far as it went, and it ended right here.

I went back to bed puffing like a mountain climber. When my next meal came, just after daylight, I ate it all and asked for more. My waiter this time was a lath-thin lad of about eighteen with a pulpy complexion and the dead, unquestioning eyes of a carp. He shook his head to my question, reached for the tray. I grabbed his wrist.

"I want more food, Bright Eyes," I told him. He pulled, and I held on.

"Bring me more chow or I'll raise hell."

"You have had the meal prepared for you."

"The Big Boy wouldn't like it if I raised hell, would he? He might think you were at fault. In fact, I'll tell him you were. I'll tell him you made a deal with me and then reneged."

"That is not true." He did not seem very strong; weak as I was, I held him.

"*You* know it's not true and *I* know it's not true, but the Big Boy won't. He'll believe me. I wouldn't be surprised if he had your throat cut. That's what he does with people he doesn't need."

"I will tell him it is not true."

"Don't you care if he kills you?"

The boy thought it over. "I have not yet propagated," he said.

"Tough—and you never will—unless you bring me some more of this nice breakfast slop. You can work it; just ask for it."

"Very well. Let go of my arm."

I dropped his wrist, leaned back and watched the little bright lights whirl round and round. This was a funny bunch I was mixed up with. I had met some cold fish in my time, but never before whole schools of them.

He came back in ten minutes with the food. I ate it—not that it was good—then gave the boy a nasty smile.

"If I tell old Prune Face you brought me more rations than you were ordered to, he'll dump you overboard without waiting to cut your throat."

"You will tell him?" The kid stared at me.

"Not unless I have to. All I want is the answers to a few little questions. Like where's this tub bound?"

"I can answer no question." He reached for the tray.

"Better think it over," I said. "What will it hurt if I know where we're going?"

"I can tell you nothing." He took the tray and turned to the door.

"Think about it. I'll give you till lunch time. If you don't answer my question I'll yell for the big shot and tell him the whole story. He'll see to it you never propagate."

He hesitated, went on out. I flopped back and watched the door close behind him.

He was a little late with the lunch tray. I waited until he had placed it just so, then braced him.

"I have learned where we are bound," he said. "If I tell you, you will not report my deviation from instructions?"

"I won't tell him about the extra bowl of gruel."

"Our destination is Gonwondo."

"Where's that? somewhere in Africa?"

"No."

"Come on, don't stall me, Junior. Where is it?"

"We sail south for nine days."

"South? We've passed Suez?"

"Yes."

"Nine days south—that takes you past the Cape, out into open sea. There's nothing down there but icebergs and penguins. Unless . . ." I stopped babbling and stared at him. He stared back.

"Sure," I said. "It figures. Antarctica."

I did not push my new contact too hard. The evening meal went by with no quiz session; he watched me but did not comment. When he was gone, I climbed out of bed and paced the cabin until the singing started up in my head again, then slept like a corpse until breakfast. When I was almost finished with the mess—like a soupy oatmeal—I looked up and caught the boy's eye.

"Who runs this ship?"

He made an uncomfortable motion. "We do."

"Who are 'we'?"

"*You* are not one of us?"

"Who are you, then?"

He gave me the cold eye. I tried a new tack. "Why are they after the girl?"

"I know nothing about a girl."

"What do they expect me to tell them?"

"I cannot speak of these things."

"Ah-ah, I'll tell Prune Face all about how we're going to dock in Antarctica in nine days. He'll be annoyed with you. Your only chance to propagate is to tell me what I want to know."

He was getting a glazed, resigned look. He turned, started for the door.

"Hold it," I called after him. "Think about it before you put your head on the block. What does it matter if you answer a few questions? As soon as we get there, I'll know where we are, and I'll know how long it's taken. What's the big secret?"

He turned to look at me. "My instructions are to speak no more than is necessary."

"For you, boy, it's necessary to speak to me."

He had to think that one out. "Yes," he announced, "That is true."

"They aren't shanghaiing me halfway across the globe just to ask me where I hid the girl; they could beat that out of me and we all know it. If she's not clear of where I left her now, she never will be. So what's the real interest in me?"

"I do not know."

"Find out."

"That is not possible."

"I said find out."

The fish eyes blinked at me.

"I will try."

He had news for me at lunch. "You will be taken to the hidden place for questioning."

"About what? And why don't they question me here?"

"You will tell them how you knew the location of the Secret Place. There are machines at Gonwondo which will force you to speak."

"Machines, huh? Thumbscrews? The iron maiden?"

The boy made motions indicating large size. "Great machines. They have no name."

"All right, you're doing fine, Junior. I think you may get to propagate after all, if you keep it up. Now I want to know all about the landing procedure: where this ship will dock, what kind of country, how far inland they plan to take me—the works."

"I know nothing of these things."

"Sure, but you can learn. And, by the way, you can spread the word that I'm pretty weak. It's all I can do to make it to the head and back."

He took the tray and left. I put in another half hour of pacing, then tried a few arm-swinging exercises. The soreness was going out of my joints gradually; the right knee was the worst. Aside from a little lost weight, shaky hands and a tendency for my head to ache, I was pretty well recovered from a harrowing weekend.

At the evening feeding Junior gave me a little more data: we would drop anchor offshore and go in by landing craft. It would be a half a day's run over land to the Hidden Place.

"How big are these landing craft? How many men will they carry?"

He did not know. Junior had a lot of objectionable qualities, but curioisity wasn't one of them. When he left this time, I checked the door. The lock was not much—just a thumb latch that had had the lever removed from the inside. I pried a strip of walnut veneer from the edge of the bureau, used it to jimmy the mechanism, then jam it open. I eased the door open, took a quick look out, saw a narrow passage, red lights gleaming on polished wood paneling, closed doors. There was no sound but the thud of faraway engines. It looked like as good a time as any for a little scouting expedition. I slid out, barefooted it along to the next door, reached for the knob, then rattled my knuckles on the panel instead, ready to run at the first sound. No response. I pushed the door open and stepped inside.

It was another bare little room, with a bare mattress on the bunk, bare hangers in the closet. I ducked out, tried the next, found it locked. So were the next three.

The last cabin on the right was a big room with two beds, a wide closet with more empty hangers and a dusty felt hat on the shelf. The bedside table yielded hairpins, a pencil, some hard chewing gun.

The dresser drawers were empty. In the bathroom I looked into an empty medicine cabinet, a laundry box with one sock forgotten in the bottom, a paper carton on the floor that had once contained soap. A slot beside the sink caught my eye; I poked carefully with one of my hairpins, lifted out two reasonably rusty double-edged blades for an old-type manual razor.

I dumped my loot in the hat, made it back to my cubicle without getting caught. Finding a hiding place gave me a little trouble; I tucked it all under the mattress finally, dropped on the bed and panted like a mile runner. I was not as strong as I thought I was.

I made my next foray after midnight, had a bad moment when feet clumped past in the hall while I flattened myself against the wall of a four-man cell forty feet along the corridor from my own room. They faded out and nothing happened. I resisted the impulse to dash back and pull the covers up to my chin, checked the closet instead. The shelf and bar were empty, and in the darkness I almost missed the coat wadded into a ball and kicked into a back corner. It was a heavy, dark-blue waterproof, much worn and blotched with salt-water stains. It was a few sizes small for me, but better than nudity in a pinch. Nobody nabbed me getting to my room with it. I spread it under the mattress and went to sleep to dream of dramatic escapes in which overcoats, chewed gum and bare feet played vital roles.

Junior seemed to be even more listless than usual the next morning.

"Cheer up," I urged him. "You're a cinch to

propagate now; I'm not asking any more questions, so all you have to do is carry on in your usual light-hearted fashion."

He did not answer. I did not like the beaten look on his face. He was going to need his morale boosted to shape him up for my next demands.

"Yes, sir, Junior, you should follow my example: *you* have propagating to look forward to—that's more than *I* can say. I don't suppose I'll last long once those machines get their gears on me."

He gave me a furtive, almost puzzled look. That was better than no reaction at all. I pursued the line I had taken.

"Yep, there you'll be, propagating like mad, and I'll be feeding the fish. You'll be way ahead of me, Junior. I never propagated myself, but I'm sure that to a fellow with an interest in that sort of thing, a family is hard to beat."

"You have never propagated?"

"Not even once."

His mouth opened and closed. "You are aware that your existence will soon end," he said. He seemed to be talking to himself, not to me. "It is for that reason that you behave as you do."

"I guess you're right."

"Even now, you weaken when you should regain your strength. It is because your hope of propagation is lost."

"You've put your finger on it, Junior," I encouraged him. "Whereas you—"

"I must inform my Secondary of these conclusions," he said abruptly, and started for the door—the first time he had turned his back on the tray. I whipped the spoon under the sheet and called, "Just a minute, Junior, don't do anything hasty. You want to think this thing all the way through first."

He hesitated, with his hand on the doorknob.

"If you tell him, he'll want to know how you found out. He'll discover you've been talking to me, and the next thing you know, *skrtt!*" I made a slashing motion across my throat.

He thought that over. "That is true. But it is my duty to report this information."

"Your duty to whom?"

"I must report to my Secondary." He turned the knob.

"What about propagating?" I was just stalling now; the situation had suddenly slipped out of hand. If I could get him close enough to jump him, I might be able to brain him and then sell the Big Boys a story that he had fallen and cracked his skull. If he reported our little talks, my last hope of pulling a surprise was gone.

"Yes, I have also the duty to propagate . . ." His voice sounded a little faint; I followed up my advantage.

"Sure, it's your duty to propagate! And that's a higher duty than this other thing. You've got to do everything in your power to succeed in propagating! Spilling the beans to Big Boy right now is the worst thing you could do!"

"I must report to my Secondary—but I must also propagate." Junior's loose lower lip was working like a worm on a hook. I had a feeling his wiring would burn through any moment.

"But there's a solution," I said.

"What is the solution?"

"First, propagate; *then* tell your Secondary!"

Again the pause to consider. The lip was limp

now, catching its breath. Junior gulped hard. He was a very upset lad.

"The information will be of no value unless—"

"Details," I cut him off. "You're going to report, just as soon as you've attended to the more important duty of propagating. That's all you need to think about."

"Yes." Junior was almost brisk now. "That is all I need to think about."

That night I made a reconnoiter beyond the end of the corridor, following a fore-and-aft passage that ended in a companionway leading up. At the top, I found a small room where clothes hung on pegs. I helped myself to a wool cap, a set of formerly white dungarees, a pair of knee-high plastic boots, turned to start back down and heard voices coming closer. There was a dark corner at the end of the hanging clothes. I slid into it, much aware of my pale, bare legs showing below the garments.

Feet clumped up the stair; grunting voices spoke to each other in a strange dialect. I practiced not breathing. An outer door opened and icy, blustery wind whipped the skirts of a plastic slicker against my legs. Someone came in, stamping his feet. The closing door cut off the howl of the wind.

"There is much ice," a new voice said.

Someone answered in the gobbling language they had been speaking before the interruption.

"The Primary directs that the landing craft be brought on deck tomorrow."

More gibberish. The tone suggested a half-hearted complaint.

"It will be necessary to conduct the transfer

within the ice field. The vehicles must be available for prompt landing."

Again the reply, this time a long harangue. The Englishspeaking one cut it off with a curt order: "See that the vehicles are in place on Number Two hatch within twelve hours."

There were a few mutters, then sounds of feet thumping down the companionway. I waited five minutes, then ducked out and reached my cabin just as voices sounded at the far end of the passage. There was no time to hide my new finds. I tossed the bundle into the closet, leaped for the bunk, got the sheet up to my chin as the door banged wide. Junior was there, with a fattish, middle-aged man with wide-set pale eyes and thin lips like a chimpanzee.

"What has this one told you?" he asked me. He did not sound as though he cared much.

"Told me?" I registered the astonishment. "Nothing. He wouldn't even give me the time of day. I figured the damned fool couldn't talk."

"He did not speak to you of our destination?"

"You must be mixed up. I talked to him about our destination. I know what it is, too. You fellows can't fool me."

"What is our destination?"

"Australia," I said promptly. "Only place it could be."

"This one said nothing to you of . . . other matters?"

"How could he? He doesn't speak English."

"*Verstehen Sie Deutsch?*" he said quickly.

"Huh?"

"*Est-ce-que vous parlez francais?*"

I frowned darkly. "Don't horse around. Talk

American."

"You speak only English?"

"Why not? It's the best language there is. I—"

"And you are certain this one told you nothing?"

"Look, I tried to get him to tell me his name; he wouldn't even do that."

"Why did you wish to know this name?"

"So I could call him by it."

"Why was it necessary for you to call him by a specific name?"

"That way he'd know who I was talking to."

"But if he were alone here with you there would be no possibility of confusion."

"That's why I call him Junior."

"Explain that."

"He knows I mean him, because he's the only one here."

The wide, pale eyes blinked at me, the apelike lips twitched thoughtfully. Then both callers turned and walked out. I stared at the door after it closed, wondering what sort of idiot's conversation I had stumbled into. Then I remembered Carmody, lying on deck with his face blasted away, and Rassias, and the blank look on Sethys' face as he turned his gun on me, and the others—all the way back to Greenleaf, Georgia. If they were maniacs, they were of the homicidal variety.

My next meal was brought by a new man who looked like a CPA retired after forty years with the company.

"What happened to Junior?" I asked him. He did not seem to hear me. I let it pass, ate my bowl of mush and watched him leave. On the way out he checked the latch, seemed satisfied, went on. I had not liked him much. Maybe he was a plant, sent in to see what kind of questions I was likely to ask. Maybe Junior would be back on duty for the next meal. I hoped so; I had plans for him.

But again there was a new face. This one could have belonged to a small-town mail carrier. I did not say a word to him, and he did not break the silence. After dinner, I did my regular stint of pacing. Nobody interrupted me; no feet passed in the corridor. I had an eerie sensation that they had all left the ship, that I was here alone—but I did not stick my head out to find out. Instinct said this would be a good time to lie low and play dumb.

Sometime during the night I was flung awake by a tremendous rumbling crash that nearly pitched me out on the floor. I hit the deck expecting to see green water pouring through the door, but aside from a few running feet in the distance, there was no reaction. It was an iceberg, I decided. Half an hour later there was another impact, not as bad as the first. I listened at the door, heard a few shouts, some distant thumps, more feet. The ship seemed to be coming to life; we were arriving somewhere, two days ahead of Junior's schedule. It was time for me to make a move.

I dug out my odds and ends of garments, used the blanket from the bed to wrap my feet before putting on the boots, pulled on the coverall, the coat and the wool hat. I tucked my other things away in a pocket—the hairpins and spoon and razor blades, not forgetting the Wrigley's Triple-mint, listened at the door to be sure the coast was clear, opened it and stepped out into the muzzle of a machine pistol in the hands of Prune Face.

CHAPTER TWELVE

There were two other men with him; all three wore gold suits, snow boots and unfriendly expressions. My stomach went as hard as a wash-board, waiting for the impact of the slugs.

"Walk ahead of me," Prune Face said, and motioned with the gun. I followed instructions. We went along corridors, crossed a lounge, pushed through a vestibule, stepped out into a scarlet glare of sunlight on ice and a blast of cold air that struck me like a spiked club. The gun jabbed again, and I went along the deck toward the stern, passing up little groups of men standing silently, looking incuriously across at the ranks of giant ice towers stretching away to the shimmer of the glacier face some five miles distant.

A hatch cover was open on the fantail; a deck crane rumbled, lifted a squat, fat-tired vehicle from the hold, swung it out, over the side. Landing nets were rigged, and men were scrambling over the rail down out of sight. I watched, acutely aware of the gun aimed at my ribs. The subzero wind cut through my clothes like swinging axes. I turned to my keeper.

"You want to get me there alive, don't you?" My

face was stiff and the words came out blurred. Prune Face just looked at me.

"It must be thirty below out here. I'm practically naked."

Prune Face spoke to one of the other men; he went away, came back five minutes later with a blanket. I wrapped myself like Sitting Bull, but it did not seem to help much.

Prunie watched closely until the last of the men were over the side—ten minutes that seemed longer—then motioned me to go. I went across, detoured around a massive deck fitting like a generator housing, saw a man lying on his back with his eyes open. He was dressed in white trousers and a coat caked with frozen blood. It was Junior, and his dead eyes gazed at the sky, emptier than ever now.

"I guess he won't propagate after all," I said.

"This was a defective. He would not have been permitted to propagate in any event." Prune Face sounded almost indignant.

At the rail, I looked down at choppy, dark-blue water twenty feet below. The long, mud-gray shape of a landing craft wallowed against the side of the ship. Eight or ten men were huddled in rows in the bow; three of the large-wheeled snowcats occupied the center of the boat. One man stood in the stern, looking up expectantly.

"Descend," my guardian angel ordered.

"My hands and feet are too numb for climbing," I pointed out.

The gun jabbed me hard enough to bruise a rib. I went over the rail.

The landing net rigged to the side was coated

with ice. My hands were like a couple of iron hooks. I groped my way down, fell the last few feet, hit hard, was shoved to the bench by the fellow I landed on. Prune Face and his two boys squeezed in beside me, and we pushed off. The big, ugly machine pistol was lying across the knees of the man next to me with its snout pointing at my hip bone, but it did not interest me any more. I was wrapped up in my arms like lovers meeting, while the chill cut into me like butchers' knives.

Someone was going to be very upset with Prune Face, because long before we picked our way across five miles of iceberg-filled water, I would be dead of exposure. I turned to tell him so, and my elbow accidently struck the gun. It fell off on the floor, skidded away. The fellow who had been holding it jumped up, went after it. Prune Face whirled my way, came half to his feet—

There was an ominous grinding sound, and the boat trembled, lurched sideways, riding up on a submerged ice shelf. The man reaching for the gun took an extra step, went over head first into the water without a sound. Prunie had started a lunge in my direction; I leaned back, palmed him hard as he fell past; he made a nice splash. The third man went for the gun, got it, thrust it out over the side to Prune Face.

The boat shuddered, slid down off the ice shelf it had struck, sent a soaking surge of water over the side and the man with the gun. He went back on his haunches, sputtering. The same shock knocked me off the perch, sent me flat on my face in the sluice of ice water surging in the bottom of the boat, up against the side of the nearest snowcat. I scraped floorboards, worked my knees, reached the cat's door handle, pulled myself up and in, then caught the door, slammed it behind me. A glow of warmth started up from a perforated panel a foot from my face: an automatic heating system, activated when anyone entered the car. It was a good thing. I could not have crawled to the driver's seat to push a button.

For a long time I just lay, hoping they would not haul me back out into the cold until they had picked up the men overboard. Some feeling was coming back into my hands. My ears and nose felt as though little men with pliers were working on them; I sat up, the stiff clothing scraped me like sheet metal. My toes were thawing now, a sensation like a claw hammer pulling at them. I wrung out the thawing clothing as well as I could, began chipping melting ice from the blanket. The flow of hot air from the register was as dry as only supercooled and reheated air can be; in ten minutes it had sucked the moisture from the coverall. They still hadn't come for me. They thought I had gone over the side with the others.

I risked a look out the driver's window. No one was in sight in the stern except a man I had not seen before, standing by the bench looking back toward the ship, which was half-hidden behind ice floes now. Keeping low, I slid forward to the driver's compartment, looked over the controls. It was a standard Navy Grumman VIT model, with a couple of megahorsepower and a thousand-mile range, fueled and ready to go. Nothing but the best for Prune Face and his chums. I went back to my heater, huddled up against it to soak up all the warmth I could before they found me.

An hour later the landing craft scraped bottom and the engines growled to a stop—and still nobody had yanked the door open and hauled me out into the cold. I eased back up beside the driver's padded bucket seat, looked out through the clear patch on the fogged double-glass window. A crew was working at the side of the boat, undogging the cable releases that locked the side panel in place. It went down with a heavy clang that I heard even through the insulated car. Two men in cold-suits splashed over it, waded a few feet to a pitted surface of rotten ice that shelved away toward the cliffs, looming close now. There was vibration through the floor; the snow-cat at the end on the right of the line-up moved forward, tilted down across the ramp, wallowed forward and up onto the ice, streaming water that froze in crusted stalactites. The one beside me started up, sat puffing fumes from a tall stack on its side, then lurched forward. Not until then did the idea hit me.

I swung around, flipped the door locking lever down, then climbed into the seat, looked over the panel, flipped switches, pushed the starter button. The diesels churned, popped, then caught and roared unevenly before they settled down to a smooth rumble. The second car was having difficulty; it seemed to be jammed between the ramp and the ice shelf. I threw in the drive lever just as the door handle clattered. Fists were hammering the side of the car; I steered it down past the stuck cat. I gunned it when I hit the water; and a big bow wave came up and over the glass, started the automatic wipers racing. There was a heavy shock as the clawing front wheels hit the ice, hauled the car up, a forward surge as the rear pair got traction.

Visibility ahead was not good. I could see a stretch of uneven ice, a dim streak that might have been a trail across the foothills of tumbled bergs. Someone was still pounding at the door. A man ran out from somewhere, cut across in front of me waving his arms. His face rushed toward me and I felt a slight jar and he disappeared and I gunned my engines and steered for the pass.

The track that led up through the broken ice twisted and doubled back, threading a route among slabs of transparent blue ice the size of apartment houses. I tried to keep one eye ahead, one on the rear-view mirror, a trick that produced two calls in the first hundred yards. On a badly banked curve, the car skidded, slammed stern first against an ice wall, rocked as fragments rained down on it; then it churned free and kept going. Behind me, a minor avalanche started up, blocking the route—a nice break for our side, I thought, until I saw the prow of a snowcat appear through the clod of ice chips less than fifty yards behind me and coming up fast. I kicked the throttle to the floor, and devoted my full attention to steering.

The road mounted swiftly toward the blue-black ice faced rearing up to an unbelievable height—two miles, the sailor had told me, a lifetime ago. My road turned hard to the right, paralleled the foot of that impossible cliff, then veered left and I was in purple gloom that deepened into blackness, howling upward along a ridged tunnel that threw back a million flashing reflections in the beam of my single headlight. The sailor had said that Hayle's expedition had melted a path to the cliff top. Unless my guess was no better than my luck, this was it.

The going was a little better here. The speedometer said I was doing sixty-five, but it seemed faster. The cat bounded and hammered across the uneven surface, and I held on and rode her. The headlight of the car on my tail splashed in my mirror; he was sticking to me like a California driver. Then a pinpoint of red light danced ahead, swelled into concentric rings that raced toward me, expanding into a glare of purple twilight and I was out of the tunnel, racing across a red-stained emptiness stretching to the far horizon.

My first concern was to put distance between myself and the landing party down on the beach; the second was to shake the eager party on my tail. For an hour I held the cat at the best speed I could manage without flipping her on the ridges that the wind had cut into the surface of the snow like oversized sand ripples on a beach.

The boy behind me was moving up, careless of the rough ground, closing the half-mile gap I had built up. He swung wide to the left, came up abreast, then cut in to ram me. I swung hard right, gunned the cat, swerved left again. He barreled past my stern, came around in a shower of ice, over hauling me on the right now. We were both doing eighty now, over ice rough enough to jar the fillings out of a back tooth. He swung in behind me, closing in. Now he was giving me a choice: I could either break my neck racing him on the broken ground, or let him ram me from the rear. Or maybe, if I timed it just right, there was a third choice. I gauged the distance—fifty feet, twenty-five, ten . . .

I hit the accelerator for everything it had. The cat lunged forward, and when it hit eighty-five, I hit the brakes and cut the wheel hard to the right, held on as she spun end-for-end, hit the throttle again and leaped off almost at right angles to my previous course. He shot past me, cutting his wheel hard. For a hairy second it looked as though he would go over, but he caught it, came on again.

This time he paralleled me, keeping twenty feet offside, I let him come alongside, inch a few yards ahead. When he swerved in on me, I was ready. I braked, swung to the right. My cat skidded, caught itself, then hit a freak bump that straightened her out just as I hit the pedal, I had a fast glimpse of the other car rushing in at me; then I hit, felt my car going up and over. I covered my head, rode out a shock that nearly snapped my neck, another, then went whirling off into an explosion of stars.

I was not out, just stunned. For a minute I could not understand why my head felt so heavy. Then I realized I was hanging upside down in my seat harness. I got a grip on what was left of the panel, unsnapped buckles, fell ungracefully to the crumpled surface that had been the car's roof. One door was sprung half open and bitter wind was whirling ice crystals in around me. I kicked at the door, got it open, crawled out into a glazed, porous surface of frozen snow. There were new ruts cut in it where the car had skidded; fifty feet away the other car sat, right side up but with the top crushed like a stepped-on top hat. Bright, pale flames were flickering somewhere inside. I ran to it, limping pretty badly—my weak right knee had gotten a nice twist—tried to get the door open, gave up and ran around to the other side. The door was open here; the driver was lying on his face half in, half out, not moving. From the angle of his left leg, it was badly broken. I grabbed his arm, hauled him clear, turned him over. He was one of the men who had been with Prune Face when he came for me with the gun—the one who had not fallen overboard.

The wind sawed at me; I could feel my frostbitten ears and nose beginning to burn again. I got a fireman's carry on the man, staggered across to my car, got inside and dragged him after me, wedged the door as nearly shut as I could. It was not warm here, but it was at least a shelter from the wind.

My playmate made a bubbly sound and opened his eyes. I waited until he had blinked a few times, gazed around and let his eyes rest on me.

"Why were you chasing me?" I asked him.

"To catch you," he said in a ghostly whisper.

"Here we go again. Look, pal, I've been brought a long way for something; I want to know what."

"It . . . so ordered . . ." His eyes were still open but while I watched the faint spark died from them. I grabbed him by both shoulders, shook him.

"Answer me, damn you! You can't die yet! I have to know . . ." His head lolled against his shoulder. I let him fall back, took a deep breath, shivered.

"OK, Irish, here you are, free as a bird," I said aloud. "Nobody within fifty miles. You can go where you want to go, do what you want to do . . ."

I was looking at his cold-suit; he was smaller than I, but I was prepared to make a few concessions.

It took me fifteen minutes to strip the suit from him, shove the pale body out onto the ice, wrestle out of my own makeshifts, and force myself into the tight, plastic-foam coverall. The boots were too small; I had to keep the flimsy ones I had. When I finished, I grabbed the emergency ration pack from its rack and crawled out of the wreck. I felt like a sausage packed into a undersized skin, but, except for my feet, I was warm enough.

The other car was still burning. As far as the eye could see across the twilight, it was the only break in the monotony of ice. The sun had set; the sky was an ominous, sulky violet—clearer than most of the world's atmosphere, but still nothing to get out the Brownie for. Back on the coast, the boys would be painstakingly following along my trail, noting every little break in the crust, every minute trace of a passing wheel. It might take them a few hours, but they would be along. I could creep back inside the car and make myself comfortable, and in due course they would arrive to take me back. They would not be too upset about my attempted escape. Nothing seemed to make them mad, any more than anything seemed to make them happy—or scare them, impress them, tire them. And then they would take me on to their Hidden Place just as they had planned all along.

That was the thing that bothered me most about these cold-eyed men. They were like a tide rising on a beach; you could fight and struggle and even mow them down with machine guns, but they simply kept coming. They were not very bright, not very strong, but in the end they had their way.

But not this time. They could follow the trail, and they would find the burning car, and the other one, and the dead man, but not me. A man on foot would leave no more trail on the ice than a fish did in water. If I kept up a good pace, I could be ten miles away in three hours. And if they found me after that, I would be frozen too hard for even Junior's big machines to dig any answers out of.

I picked a direction at random and started walking.

It was not easy going. The ice underfoot was as hard as Manhattan pavement, uneven as a rock pile, slippery as oil. I fell and got up and fell again. After what seemed like a long time I looked back, saw the two cars just a long rock toss away. The smoke from the fire streamed away to the left like a marker beacon; I should have taken the time to damp the fire out, but I was not going back now.

My feet hurt for a while, then went big and warm, as dead as fence posts. I stumped on, the wind more or less at my back, watching the sky ahead slowly fade into deeper shades of purple and burgundy and gold. I must still be several hundred miles from the Pole, I thought; farther south, the setting of the sun was a weeks-long process.

Maybe the theories were right; maybe Antartica was moving north, dragging the whole crust of the planet with it to the accompaniment of quakes and typhoons and rivers of lava, forcing new mountains up where the skin was compressed as areas moved poleward, opening vast new chasms where the lithosphere was stretched to span the increasing planetary circumference of equatorial regions. It was as good a theory as any.

It was the price the world had to pay, periodically, for its unique, life-giving structure. It wasn't like the Moon, or Mars, or Jupiter's satellites—a cold ball of solid rock. It was a living, pulsating complex of molten core, inner and outer mantles, thin crust with continents floating on seas of magma, oceans of free water, ice caps, an atmosphere ense enough to support hurricanes, ice caps that grew and waned—and all infected with that strange disease called life. Life thrived on change, variety—and periodically, life paid the toll. Nature always had her checks and balances, and now man knew another of her rules: a world where life thrives is by its nature a planet of catastrophe.

I was lying on the ice, resting. I did not know how I had gotten there; I did not remember lying down. It was very comfortable, except for the weights strapped to my feet. A faint glow twinkled far away across the dark ice. It was the burning car, still faithfully marking the spot. And here I was running for my life.

No, not my life. That was already forfeit. Running for my death—a private death, unassisted, with no cold, indifferent little men with bland, unremarkable faces grouped around to poke and probe and question, question.

I rolled over, got my dead feet under me. It was hard to balance, but I made it. I seemed to be standing on stilts. My legs ended at the calf. There was no pain, just the annoying sense of dead weight, dragging.

Something hit me in the face. It was not painful —more like a mattress falling from somewhere. I groped, felt ice under me, got up and went on. It was almost full dark now, the sky a blue-black wall where here and there stars winked between black cloud strata. If I kept on long enough, I would reach them, and then I could walk through rose-covered gates into a garden of sun-warmed grass, where I could lie down among flowers and sleep.

I awoke with a terrible sense of duty not completed, of a voice urging me on—to what, I could not remember. Pain crouched like a tiger on my chest, I tried to move, and my arms and legs stirred reluctantly, as though I were frozen into a block of ice.

Ice. I remembered walking, falling, walking on, while the sky turned black and stars gleamed just ahead. There was a star shining now, a steady yellow glow across the ice. It looked close—almost close enough to reach out to. All I had to do was go on—just a little farther—and I would reach it. It was so near, and I had come so far, it seemed a pity not to go on, just that little way. I got to hands and knees, tried to stand, went down hard on my face; pain knifed through the fog that had settled behind my eyes. I tried again, got to all fours, blinking at the light. It was a strange sort of mirage; I was awake now, aware of where I was, what I was doing. . . .

What was I doing?

Sure, I remembered now: I had been driving fast all day, and just at dark the curve had come on me unexpectedly, and the car had gone over and down among trees, and I had been thrown clear, and then the police had arrived, and there had been an ambulance, and lights, and a smell of neoform. . . .

No. That was wrong. The wreck had been a long time ago; before—

I remembered mountains shooting fire into the sky, and a storm, like a bombardment out of hell, and a city where the buildings lay shattered in broken streets, and a dead man who gave me a coin and the flies had buzzed, buzzed around me as I lifted him over the side. . . .

That was not right either. I could not remember what had happened, but that was not important now. What was important was the light, shining serenely through the darkness. . . .

I was walking. There was something wrong with my feet, but it was only necessary to move one leg, and then the other, being careful not to fall, and not to think, but just to walk . . . walk toward the dancing yellow light that seemed always to recede before me, beckoning me on. . . .

I dreamed I was crawling across a vast ice field.

I was all alone on the southern ice cap of a strange planet whirling silently through space and eternity. My enemies pursued me, but they were far away, and only some blind force made me crawl, moving my hands and knees like parts of some broken machine in which I was somehow trapped. It was an unpleasant, painful dream. I tried to open my eyes, but I was still crawling, watching the light that swelled and blurred ahead. I laughed at the idiocy of it—lying comfortably in bed, dreaming of ice and pain, and, aware that I was dreaming, not able to end the dream while the light beckoned me on. It was strange how the pain in the dream was as real as any other pain. Perhaps all pain, all life, was a dream, an endless creeping progress across an untamable phantom wilderness toward a goal that always glimmered out of reach.

But the light looked so close now, so real, a pale rectangle of yellow radiance casting a golden pathway on the snow. Just a little farther, a few more agonizing yards. . . .

My arms moved, without my willing them. My legs had quit now; I dragged them behind me like a broken-backed dog, clawed another yard ahead, and then another, and the glowing doorway was close now, close enough that I could feel the toasting warmth flow out in a wave from it as it opened for me.

For an instant, a part of my mind stirred awake, recognized the mirage. But what did it matter whether my golden door was real or not? I had attained it, and passed through, and a warmth more marvelous than the diversions of emperors washed over me like a benign wave and carried me with it out into an endless sea.

I had recently developed a habit of wincing when I opened my eyes, ready to tally up my latest aches, breaks and contusions, and review the events that had led up to them. This time was different. There was a mirage bending over me—a young face framed in glossy black hair; a face that smiled, and a soft hand that touched my cheek.

"Maliriss," Ricia said.

CHAPTER THIRTEEN

For a while after that I paid no attention to the passing of time. Ricia tended me like a little girl with a new doll while fever burned through me like a magnesium fire, faded away into a sort of soft haze in which I was half aware of being fed, bathed, soothed when the pain in my feet flared up and I ran from faceless men who pursued me with silent shouts through rivers of molten lead.

Then one day I was sitting up, eating soup with a spoon, and looking at two massive bundles of bandages that were my feet.

"I don't know where to start," I said to Ricia. "I don't know where the nightmares end and the delusions begin. I don't know where I am, or how I got here; I don't even know who you are. And you don't know what I'm saying."

"Yes, Mal, know," she said. She was nodding, looking pleased.

"You understand me?"

"Listen, Mal, learn Engliss word, many."

"Kid, you're a wonder." I caught her hand. "Look, maybe I've gone soft behind the eyes, but the way I remember it, I left you in a hotel room in Miami; a little more than two weeks later, I was hiking across the South Pole. The next thing I know—this!" I waved a hand to take in the bed, the room, the whole incomprehensible universe. "Did I imagine the whole thing? Am I in Miami now with the DT's and a case of trench foot from taking long walks in the rain?"

"Mo, Mal. Gonwondo, here."

"Gonwondo—that's what Junior called it! He said they were taking me to something called the Hidden Place—" I broke off. "But to hell with that. I'll chew through that later and sort out the facts from the fancies. What I really want to know is—how did you find me?"

She smiled, shook her head. "No, Mal. I find, no. You find me."

"I found you?"

"You come to me, Mal. Close now, we." Her eyes looked soft and dreamy. She took my hand, lifted it, touched the ring she had given me. "This call you to me, Mal."

I blinked a few times, feeling like a kid who's just flunked his IQ test. "Sure," I said, "it's a nice touch of sentiment, girl, but I'm talking about taking a stroll ten thousand miles from the nearest town and running into an old friend. How did you know—"

"Mal, no too many word. This call you, Mal. Believe." She looked at me with a worried expression, like a fond mother waiting for the baby to say "Bye-bye."

I patted her hand. "All right, Ricia. I'll believe."

In a few days—or perhaps "sleeps" would be a more precise term, since the windows stayed an opaque black—I was up and hobbling around the apartment. The frostbite had been the rough equivalent of second-degree burns, but Ricia had applied various balms with curious odors, and the healing was rapid.

There were four main rooms: the lounge, where I had found myself, just inside a heavy, vaultlike door; a dining room with a big, low table; the bedroom and an adjoining bath with a twelve-foot square sunken pool, and another spacious room that I dubbed the library, not that there were any books in sight. The floors were a hard, lustrous material with overall patterns in soft colors that varied from room to room. The walls seemed to be made of the same composition, with an eggshell finish that subtly and unpredictably changed colors.

The furniture was comfortable, but oddly proportioned, curiously put together from colored hardwoods with bright fabrics. There was music, too—haunting, not-quite-familiar tones built to a scale that seemed to have too many notes.

Ricia produced our meals from a well in the center of the big table in the dining room; there was no kitchen, no pantry, no heating plant, no doors. From somewhere, she got clothes for both of us—a loose sort of sarong for herself, a short robe with loose sleeves for me. They seemed to be new each morning. I asked questions and she showed me a closet that seemed to be empty when I looked inside. But the next morning, there were our new clothes again—not that Ricia was scrupulous about wearing them. She seemed to be as comfortable nude as otherwise.

It was an easy routine: I slept, woke, ate, lay on

my bed and studied the pictures on the walls, the hangings with their stylized representations of stick figures hunting dragons, the bowls in which the food popped up on the table, the food itself. The menu consisted of variations on a theme resembling sukiyaki, with large, shallow glasses of what seemed to be bland, faintly sweet wines.

"Where does it all come from?" I watched Ricia open the lid and lift out a hot meal. "How is it prepared? And what is it, anyway?" She laughed and told me to look for myself. I used the silver chopsticks to stab a bite-sized piece of meat from the bowl in front of me.

"It's good," I said."Well marbled, tender, nice flavor. It's a little like port and a little like beef, but it isn't either one."

She smiled, made motions like someone strewing confetti in the air, put two fists in front of her nose and swung them out in a grand gesture.

"Sorry—the sign language is worse than the other," I said. "I'll just eat it in ignorance."

On my first day up, I explored the apartment, ended in the room I called the library. It was a plain room furnished with seats along one side. The walls, I discovered, were lined with what looked like sealed storage cabinets. There were no latches, no handles to turn, no drawers to pull out. I tapped, got a hollow ring. Ricia was following me, looking a little thoughtful.

"What's all this for?" I wanted to know. "I can understand the rest of the place, but this stumps me."

She took my arm, tried to guide me back toward

the doorway. "No, Mal, not now look. Too much tired still."

"I'm not too tired to be curious."

"Not talk now. Mal—"

I took her by both arms, gently but firmly. "Listen to me, Ricia. You've been putting me off for a week now, and I've gone along because—maybe I didn't want to dive back into troubled waters myself. Let's stop kidding each other: There are things I have to know, and you can tell me."

"Mal—sick, you. Rest."

"First," I continued, "I want to know how you figure in all this. Who are you, Ricia, aside from being my ministering angel? Where did you come from? What do you know about . . . them?"

She stiffened, looking into my face.

"Better, Mal forget." She looked at me appealingly.

I shook my head. "Not as long as I'm alive."

She gave me a long, tortured look; then her shoulders drooped. She nodded slowly.

"I think, Mal, these are ones our legend tells of. The undermen, hide away deep in earth; but when bad time is come, then they appear. Sometime, take woman away to burrow deep in earth, do evil thing with her. Old man never see again."

"Fairy tales aren't—" I started.

"Live long there, in hidden places. And wait. Old men say, when bad time come, then again undermen come among us. Bad time here, now, Mal. And they are here."

"Legends," I said. "Folk tales. But these killers aren't pipedreams, Ricia! They're here, now! And they have a special interest in you. Why! There must be something you know that would shed a little light on this."

"Mal, under-men everywhere now. Take all place, make men slave. We stay here, quiet, live, forget."

"I wouldn't make a good slave, kid. I'm a little too used to independence. Don't hold out on me now. I have to know. What more can you tell me about them—and about yourself?"

"No, Mal, not think this thing. Rest, get strong."

"Sure, I'll rest—as soon as you've told me what I need to know."

Ricia looked sorrowfully at me. Then she sighed. "Yes, Mal. Better no, better stay here, happy and alone. But you are man; you must ask, and not rest." She led me to a chair. "Sit, look now. I show many thing."

I started to argue then went along, sat in one of the too-low, too-wide chairs. She went to the wall, twiddled things out of sight. The light in the room dimmed to deep gloom. A glow sprang up in the center of the room; I could not tell where it came from. It grew, resolved itself into misty shapes that grew solider, became a scene of sun-bright plains stretching away to wooded hills. Something moved at the center of the picture—a tiny, distant point that grew, became the bobbling form of a galloping animal. In the foreground, trees swept into view as the camera panned.

From the dappled shadows of the foliage, a man stepped out, trotted forward, away from the camera. He was a tall, dark-skinned, handsomely built fellow, dressed in close-fitting black. His black hair was cut short; he was carrying what looked like a weapon in his right hand. He was running fast now, angling out across the path of the approaching animal. I could not tell yet what the quarry was he had marked out, but it was big, even at half a mile. It was not a horse; the legs were too short in proportion to the body. I had about decided it was a big bull bison when it changed course, veered away to the right. I got a good look then; it was a black elephant, running like a trotter, right legs, then left legs, his trunk curled up between a pair of tusks that would have looked good over any mantle in town.

The lone hunter changed course to intercept the big bull. The camera followed, holding on him at about a hundred yards. He was racing along full tilt now, his head back, his legs pumping like pistons. The shape of the lumbering elephant was growing fast; his head swung around—an oddly shaped head, rising to a peak between the too-small ears. Then he was braking to a halt with all four legs, swinging around to face the man who was coming up fast now. The trunk went up—it looked shocking pink against the dark body—and the mouth opened. There was no sound, but I could almost hear the bellow of rage that went with the expression.

The man came on, while the shape of the animal grew—and grew—and grew some more. The hunter looked like a child against the tusker that towered up over him to a height of at least sixteen feet at the shoulder. And I was close enough now to see that I had made a mistake: the hide wasn't black; I was looking at a heavy coat of long, shaggy hair that hung down far enough to brush the grass tops.

The hunter had dropped back to a trot. Now he was walking, no more than fifty yards from the mountain of flesh that stood with its trunk still up, its yellow tusks curving out and away, two tiny reddish eyes watching every move. It swung its head restlessly from side to side, and again the mouth opened in a silent trumpet.

At fifty feet, the man stopped. He brought the thing in his hand around, lifted it, and I saw it was a horn with a flared mouth. At once the hairy elephant dropped his trunk, lifted it again to sample the air. The hunter moved forward, stopped when the trunk curled high. He blew another blast, and again the monster rocked back, swung his head from side to side, watching the man come on steadily until I thought he was going to climb a leg. He had the horn up again, and I sensed somehow that he was blowing softly on it now, crooning some kind of mammoth lullaby to the big fellow who stood over him like a mastiff over a mouse, rocking gently with one foot raised clear of the ground like a field dog on point.

A full minute passed. I could see the wind stirring the grass, the fluffy shapes changing form against the hills in the background. The man was swaying and the elephant followed the motion with his eyes—the camera was that close now.

Quite suddenly, the man lowered the horn, made a smooth gesture with his right hand. The immense animal took a step backward. The man walked in, holding his hand out. The restless trunk curled out, touched the hand. A moment later the man was stroking the massive organ that could rip a hundred-year oak nut out of the ground with one tug. Then he reached up, caught a tusk, pulled himself up and an instant later was sitting just behind the big fellow's head.

The mammoth did not like that much; he stepped sideways, shaking his head, and the man went flat, holding on the round, naked-looking ears. For half a minute the mammoth curvetted ponderously, while his trunk curled up and over to touch the man, as though not quite sure now how he felt about the proceedings. Then the man sat up, kicked his heels against the beasts's neck, and the ten-ton mount swung off at a brisk walk as though that was what he had intended all along.

The picture faded into a bright mist and I let out a long breath.

"What in the name of Phineas T. Barnum was *that!*" I called to Ricia.

"Look," she said. "More see."

The mist was taking shape again; this time it showed a view from fifteen feet above an avenue paved with glazed and colored bricks, laid in patterns that reminded me of the floors in the apartment. Dead ahead, the vast bulk of another shaggy elephant swayed, moving placidly down the center of the street. There was a gilded howdah strapped to his back, and under the fringed, peaked canopy a woman sat bolt upright, her arms folded. She had a beautiful, straight back, quite bare; the skin was a tawny olive color that gleamed in the sunlight. Her hair was blue-black, arranged high on her head in an ornate style woven through with strings of bright beads. Along the avenue, people with dark skin and barbaric costumes waved their hands and smiled as she rode past.

The buildings behind them were elaborate with bright colors against gleaming white, like something a fanciful baker might have made from colored sugar. Ahead, the avenue widened into a broad plaza faced on the far side by a building that went up into the clear sky like a lone skyscraper. The wide steps in front of the building were packed with people in fancy headdress.

When the elephant was a hundred feet from the steps, he stopped, went heavily down to his knees. The girl rose, slid down to the ground. She was wearing nothing but beads and loops of white silk fore and aft, but she had the figure for it. She raised her arms and turned around, and I said, "Hey. . . !"

She looked enough like Ricia to be her sister—or at least her cousin.

The scene faded, took shape again—this time showing a grassy slope above cliffs with white breakers churning at the bottom. A thing like a dragonfly rested at the top of the slope. It started moving slowly, coasted down the hill, lifted off just at the brink, soared out in a wide curve that swept it past the camera's vantage point, and I saw a man crouched in a frame of sticks and wire, his hair tossed by the wind, grinning from ear to ear. A second glider had launched itself now. It shot outward, climbing in a steady updraft, bucking and pitching. Abruptly one wing crumpled, folded back; the broken flyer dropped, spinning lazily, struck the sea far below with a lazy explosion of white water that made me wince.

Another picture was taking form; this time a gay-colored boat was mooring to a long jetty; it had a short mast, an open deck with a small deck house. Men stood on the deck, waving to those on shore. A plan was run out, and crewmen came across, leading what looked like a captive gorilla; then I caught a glimpse of the wide, pale face, the swift-darting eyes, a startling pale blue. It was a man, hairy as a sheep dog, with his hands manacled before him.

The show went on and on. I saw men with glittering short swords hack at each other in an arena decked with flowers; a giant tiger walking on a leash held by a girl who was the twin of the mammoth rider; a view from a balcony across a city that sparkled on a mountainside; an interior shot of a wide room with a polished floor where men bent over a long table with an array of glittering apparatus, a vaulted chamber that might have been a powerhouse.

When the misty sphere faded and the lights came up, I patted my nonexistent pockets for a cigaret I had not had for weeks.

"What"—I had to swallow—"what was it? *Where* was it?" I looked at Ricia. "*When* was it?" My voice came out in a dry whisper.

"My home," Ricia said. "My people." A look of desolate loss swept across her face, and she lifted her chin above it. "Gone, now. All dead, my people. Only me, now."

I hobbled into the dining room, lifted the cover of the food well, grabbed the wine glass as it popped up, drank it off. It did not change anything, but it was something to do to span the whirling seconds while my mind tried to find a floating straw to grab at. I had a second, then turned; Ricia stood there, looking concerned.

"Rest now, Mal," she put a hand on my arm. I took her hand.

"Sorry, girl, I've had my rest. We talk now." I led her into the lounge, sat her down in a chair, took the one beside it.

"These movies you just showed me: they were . . . real?"

"Oh, yes, real, Mal."

"They were made—here, on earth?"

She looked surprised. "Yes."

"Where? What country?"

"Gonwondo, here, this country." She pointed to the floor.

"Yes, but—"

"Not ice, that time, Mal. Beautiful land, my Gonwondo."

"Antarctica—before the ice." I was shaking my head. I did not hear a rattle.

"Mal, how long time?" She looked anxiously at me.

"God, I don't know, Ricia." I tried to remember what I had read on the subject. "The generally accepted figure is a few million years; some theorists say a few hundred thousand—and some say only ten to twenty thousand years. But from what I saw—mammoths and cave men—and if that cat wasn't a sabertooth, I'll turn in my junior woodsman's badge—that means anything up to a hundred thousand years, anyway."

"What is hunditausen?"

I took five minutes off to explain the numbering system to her. She looked at her fingers and large tears leaked from her eyes. She wiped them away impatiently and said, "Thousand, hundred thousand, same. All dead."

"These were your ancestors?"

She shook her head. "No. My people, my city, Ulmoc name. Me *I* am here, I ride Holgotha, I walk these streets, I see these sky."

"How?"

"Here, Mal." She pointed to the bedroom. "Long sleep. There is"—she made smoothing motions with her hands—"roof. Breathe"—she breathed deep—"sleep-air. Come, show—"

I followed her into the bedroom. She touched a spot that looked just like the rest of the wall to me, but a table like a morgue slab tilted out. A gray steel cover was hinged above it, with tubes leading to it.

"Lie here, Mal. Roof come down, sleep-air inside, cold, cold. Sleep long."

"But—what for?"

She looked stricken. "Bad time come, Mal. Sky turn from blue to black, sun red. Earth shake. Ice come from sky, many day, thousand day. My . . ." She shook her head. "Too many word, no, Mal. You wait, teach more—"

"Go ahead, you're doing fine. Your what?"

"Man, woman, old—me." She pointed at her chest. I shook my head. "I don't get that, but go ahead."

"My . . . old man. Take me here . . ."

I grinned in spite of the excitement pounding in my ears. "You're getting the hang of the vernacular now. Go on."

"Many people go in boat, thousand boat. But my old man, no. He is fear—for me, not he. I must sleep, wait, I must do, Mal. I say good-by, lie here. Darkness come.'

"I can't say that I blame him. Those boats didn't

look like anything I'd want to go to sea in."

"Have more boat, Mal. Big, big. But many bad thing, other land. Holgotha, Otucca, beast-man. He fear for me, Mal."

"Sure. So you told your family good-by and . . . died." I pictured her, lying alone in the dark and the cold, while the world circled the sun and cultures rose and died and the ice built up above her.

"Not die, Mal. Live on, and one day—wake."

"Then what?" I asked.

"I think soon old man come back. Very sick, Mal. Long time here, so sick. Long sleep no good. But house good, help, tell me what to do—"

"The house told you what to do?"

"Yes, house. Very wise, know all thing. Say to me, do that, I do, soon well. But old man—"

"I'm afraid you lost me."

"Come." This time she took me to the library, to the small niche at one side with a seat in front of it. She sat down, put her hands flat on the foldout tabletop.

"*Iklathu ottraha oppacu madhali att*," she said, as well as I could make out.

"*Optu; imruhalo soronith tatrac . . .*" a hollow voice rasped in a monotone. It went on, reeling off words. When it finished, Ricia said "*Accu*," and stood up.

"You see? House say ice falling above now; tomorrow, warmer; ice become water."

"It's some kind of automatic weather-report gimmick?"

"House know *all* things, Mal. Not house here—great house, there." She pointed.

"It's tied in to another machine? Some kind of

recorded information service?"

"Not know too many word, Mal. You see, not talk more now."

"What woke you up?" I cut her off.

"Ice go, make water, above." She pointed at the ceiling.

"The ice was melting, and the . . . machinery . . . was set to bring you out of it when the thaw started?"

"Maybe, Mal." She looked doubtful.

"Don't mind me, kid; I'm just talking to hear myself think. Anyway, you woke up; you were sick, but you recovered. Then what?"

"I must go, find old man. Take sea clothes, small food. Much ice above, but house make way through. Much water, soft ice, hard to go with sled . . ." She described what sounded like a self-propelled surfboard that she used to cross the slushy ice to the spot where the city had stood. There was nothing there but ice. She headed for the coast; she had decided to follow her father and the others. After a couple of days of cruising along the beach, she found a boat—a derelict, thawling out of the ice. She broke it loose, hoisted a sail and headed north.

Her story was halting, vague, interrupted by the frequent need to act out a missing word; but I got the picture of days of sailing, living on food concentrates and fish. Her sea suit—the green outfit she had been wearing when I found her—kept her warm enough. From her description, it was a lot more efficient and less bulky than my cold-suit.

She steered due north, missed the coast of South America by a few hundred miles. She had steady winds and fair weather—but no landfall. She had started to believe the whole world was flooded when she sighted islands—maybe the Azores. They had been evacuated, of course; she found no one there. She set off again, followed the wind. It brought her into the South Florida coast ten days later.

She saw the lights of Miami, landed the boat, went looking for people. She found them—but no one understood her language. Everything was strange: the people, the buildings, the animals—cats and dogs. She was hungry, but without money, nobody would feed her. Then one day a man came up to her and spoke to her in her own language.

She was overjoyed; she followed him. He led her into a dark alley and tried to kill her. She broke away, and ran. Three days later, in another dark alley she met me.

"It's a swell world," I told her. "You went under while the crust was going through contortions, and woke up in time to catch the next show. In between we had a few thousand years of nice weather, but you missed it. OK. Now, what about the men that tried to kill you. Any idea why?"

"No, Mal. I think first, nice friend. Then—choke me. I"—she acted out a punch to the jaw and a knee in the groin—"run away."

"Good for you, kid. But think: you must have some idea who they are, why they tried to kill you—and me, and the sailor. What about Sethys? The name mean anything?"

"No, nothing, Mal. Strange men."

"But they spoke your language."

"Spoke, yes." She nodded vigorously. "Speak strange, but understand."

"All right, there's one obvious tie-in—the sailor visited Antarctica; he swore the little men sabotaged the expedition and followed him. And you say they speak a language that was used here, sometime in the remote past. As for why they chased me. I walked into their conference in Miami and showed them the coin. A nice piece of strategy, that."

"Coin?"

"A gold piece, money. Like this." I rummaged in a drawer, found a stylus and pad, sketched the design on the coin as well as I could from memory.

"Gold," I amplified. "Yellow metal."

Ricia nodded suddenly. It was gesture she had gotten from me. "This is *grisp*, for . . ." She waved her hands, unable to express the function of money in pig latin.

"He said he picked it up here—in a building frozen in the ice. Sethys recognized it. He switched coins on me. I don't know why."

"Mal, swish?"

"Changed—he took my coin and gave me a different one."

"Yes, yes!" She looked excited. "Coin like ring, Mal. But bring him to *you!*"

"What does that mean?"

"Mal, wise men, my people, make ring, make little thing inside ring." She groped for words. "You, me, ring . . . together."

"What is it—magic?"

"Mal—ring made for woman, give to man. It call man to woman."

"You don't need a ring for that."

"Sethys have same thing, in coin. Give you, call him to you."

"In other words, as long as I carried the coin, he had a tag on me." I snorted. "And I thought we were hidden away at Bob's place like the bankroll in grandma's sock."

"You have *grisp* now?" Ricia caught at my arm.

"No. I guess I left it on the boat. Now, let's have your story. How did you get clear? You were a sick girl when I left you. I thought—"

"Yes, Mal, I sick. Lie, wait, long time, two days, night. Feel better, wait, dark, go off boat. Think one thing, go to home, away from strange men. I look Mal, find man—strange man talk my language."

"You went looking for those killers?"

"How else I get thing I want? Know him, now, not afraid. Get man alone. Fool man, learn many thing. Go to place of machine sail in air—"

"The jetport?"

"Yes. Find other man, take me in machine, sail in air long way."

"What happened to the first man?"

Ricia made motions graphically depicting a knee in the back and a broken neck. "Strong, me."

"My God, and I was worried about you."

"Come to place," she went on. "Johannesburg. Buy boat."

"Buy with what?"

"Dead man, plenty *grisp*."

"And then?"

"Sail south; come to Gonwondo, come here, to house."

"On foot?"

"Sled still there, Mal, same place."

"You must have some sense of direction, kid."

"Not need; have ring too." She smiled and held

up her hand, showing me the ring, the twin to the one she had given me. "Easy find sled; call to ring. Then come here, to house, wait. I know maybe Mal . . . dead." She put her hand on mine. She had a nice way of touching me, as though she could transmit her meaning through her fingertips.

"But if you alive, you come. I know maybe long time; think maybe go back on cold-bed; but wait, and soon you come."

"OK, I'll pass that for now. That leaves us with a few large questions still unanswered: who are they—Sethys and his gang? What do they want? Why did they try to kill you, then kidnap you? That place under the water—"

"Yes, Mal! Old place; long-ago house, like this—but water come, wise men fix, hold water back, I think."

"Yeah, it looked like a hurry-up job. But there was a lot of know-how there. These wise men of yours must have been first-rate engineers. But what was the idea of grabbing you in Miami and taking you there? If they wanted to kill you, why didn't they do it in the hotel?"

"Not want kill, Mal. Old man, evil and ugly, want . . . use me."

"Use you? For what?"

"For son." Her lip curled.

"You don't mean . . ."

"He talk, make much question. I talk, no. Then he tell, I make son for him, many son."

"That old devil couldn't even roll over in bed."

"Mal—very strange, old man. Son very important. Say many strange thing . . ." She shook her head impatiently. "No too many word, Mal!"

"All right, you're doing fine. Forget him; his

playhouse broke up; he's probably washing ashore on a mud flat about now. But we still don't know what it is these fellows want."

"Mal, you tell, sailor here, Gonwondo, find *grisp* . . . in house." Her eyes were bright with excitement. "What house, where?"

"He claimed they'd found a city under the ice."

Her fingers on my arm hurt. "Mal, city—*my* city! Ulmoc! Still there!"

It couldn't be; these glaciers move. They'd have scraped the rock to the bone. If there had been a city, it would be in small pieces now."

"But, Mal, sailor have *grisp*."

"There is that." I rubbed at my chin. "Hell, there's no point in trying to be logical. Maybe the snow fell and turned to ice and the mountains held it in place so it couldn't slide."

"Yes, Mal! Mountain! Every side! Ulmoc in . . ." She picked up a bowl from the table. "Like this, Mal."

"Maybe it's possible then. Maybe he really did find a buried city. And"—I snapped my fingers—"Junior told me something called the Hidden Place; maybe this was what he meant!"

Ricia looked at me anxiously, watching my lips as though she could read them. I got up, stumped painfully up and down the room. "They had to be headed somewhere. It could have been some kind of in-gathering; that ship was loaded with them. Maybe this is their big annual get-together. If so—" I smacked a fist into my palm. "Ricia, how far is this Ulmoc place from here?"

"Why, Mal?" She stood, looking worried.

"That's where the answers are."

"Mal, no! Stay here, safe, warm! Sick, Mal.

Rest!" She was close to me, her face turned up to me. Her eyes looked big and dark enough to dive into and get lost. This was one of the days she was wearing her chiton, but I was suddenly acutely aware of her feminine nearness.

"You act as though you really care." I tried to make my voice jovial but it came out cracked.

Her hands crept up my chest to my shoulders. "Yes, Mal, care." She kept her eyes wide open when I kissed her; her mouth was soft and startled under mine. Afterward she touched my lips with her fingers. "Care much, Mal. You stay, forget strange men."

"I'm not an invalid any more; at least I won't be in a few more days. I can't sit here, hiding like a hunted rabbit. For now, they've lost me—but they'll find us some day; they're that kind of boys. This is my chance—maybe my only chance—to slip up on their blind side. If this is the place my sailor friend was talking about—"

"Stay!" She threw her arms around me and squeezed hard enough to hurt. I patted her back, feeling like I had sneaked in under false pretenses.

"Listen to me, I think I may know a back way in—if the shaft the Navy dug is still intact. I can take your sled, go in at night, do a fast reconnoiter, and get out again before they know it."

"They kill you."

I took her arms and eased her back far enough to look at her. Her eyes brimmed like overfilled teacups. "Think about it for a minute. These baby-faced killers wiped out a couple of hundred men—Hayle's whole outfit. They hunted the lone survivor down and would have killed him, if he hadn't died first. Then they went after you. My guess is they recognized who or what you were—and that meant things to them. And last but not least, they killed Carmody, and Rassias—and made a nice try at me. It was nothing but dumb luck that I got clear. I'm a guy that will go the long way around to miss trouble every time, Ricia, but I can't duck this. If those lads are holed up just over the hill, I have to go see."

"Mal, take boat, go back, your city. Tell wise men all things, bring many good men."

"There's no one to tell. Hayle's expedition was the last gasp of organized government. There's nobody to get another. And if there were, I'd be laughed into the chuckle ward with my story. I have no proof—not even the coin. Nothing!"

"Say to friends, tell all things—"

"If our guesses are right—if they're there—I can get proof, I'll have something to show, then. Maybe there'd be a chance of getting away from here and organizing something. Maybe in Denver; I heard the Air Academy was still holding something together." Ricia was watching me, shaking her head.

"No, Mal," she whispered. "Safe, here."

"Could I operate your sled?"

"No!" She looked stubborn.

"Then I'll walk."

We argued the point for another hour, but in the end she went dull and rigid-faced and agreed to help me get ready.

CHAPTER FOURTEEN

Eight more days went by before Ricia led the way up the sloping, jointed tunnel to the surface and we stood together in purple twilight on the frozen slush surface twenty feet above the buried house. I was dressed in a blue-black shimmery suit like her green one; it was as light and comfortable as cotton, and kept out the bitter cold like a brick house. Ricia had supplied me with boots that seemed to be made of a sort of tough felt; inside them my feet were still a little tender, but warm enough. I had gloves and a cowl that fitted over my head like a hood of a parka. As a sample of Gonwodon science the outfit was impressive. I took Ricia's hands between mine.

"I won't get hurt, kid. Just a fast, sneaky look around, and then out; just long enough to pick up something more convincing than a few bruises to prove I ever met these boys."

"It will be dark soon. Time to start," she said woodenly.

"Yeah, just show me the sled and I'll be on my way."

She went past me, used a small pick on an ice-crusted mound. I helped her; in five minutes the sled was clear. It was flat, about the size of an air mattress, with a hooded panel at one end. It did not look like much. Ricia knelt by it, twiddled things; it made a sighing noise and lifted itself six inches from the ice. There did not seem to be any airstream coming from under it.

"How do you make it go?" I came to Ricia's side. She swung onto the sled.

"Get on," she said in a dull voice. I climbed on behind her. She leaned forward over the controls.

"I can't see a thing from here," I said. "Better let me get up there."

"It is not necessary," she called back to me. "I am going with you." She had learned a lot of English in the past week. Maybe I should start competing with Berlitz when the world calmed down again.

"Not a chance, girl. You're going back down in that nice snug burrow of yours and sit tight until I get back."

She swung around to face me. "I am not afraid for me—only for you."

"My God, Ricia, this isn't a chicken contest! I'm going in there because I have to!"

"I have to also."

"You're not going."

"Mal"—she leaned against me—"I will operate the sled, and help you dig; it will not be easy to uncover the shaft. And inside—how will you know the way, if I am not there? This is my city; I know its streets."

"Its streets are solid ice now; I don't need a guide. I'll play it by ear, and—"

"No." She was smiling at me, looking impish. I

wondered how I could ever have thought she was anything but beautiful. "We will play it by *my* ear."

"What's that supposed to mean? I'll have enough on my mind without looking out for you too."

She was pointing to a button set behind her ear like a hearing aid. "This is linked to the house library. It will speak wisdom in my ear."

I was in no mood to be impressed. The closer I got to bearding the quiet men in their Hidden Place, the less I liked the sensations it engendered under my ribs. I wanted to get it over with in a hurry now.

"Sure, your wise men were clever as hell. But we aren't trying to break the bank on a quiz show. Now just slide off of here like a good girl."

"You do not understand. This"—she touched the button—"is an instrument of the most fine . . ." Her English still slipped a little under pressure, and she still had an exotic way with her words sometimes.

". . . will detect sounds, sight, hidden things; all these it will relay to the library, and the library will advise us."

"Swell, the voice of conscience in your ear, ready with an oracular saying for every emergency."

"Even now it tells me things." She had a faraway look in her eyes, as though she were listening to a distant drummer beating out a rhythm I would never hear. "It says men are abroad even now; ten . . . *sarads* away, there—" She pointed out acros the dark ice.

"All right, let me have it then." I was humoring her. "Maybe it will direct me to the civic booze supply; I'll probably be needing a drink."

"No, only I can use it." She looked triumphant. "It speaks in my language, not your English."

"Go below, Ricia!" I took her arm, tried to ease her over the side. She resisted; she *was* strong. I got my leg under me to lift her and her eyes met mine.

"You would have me wait alone *again*, Malcome?" she asked softly.

I was holding her by both shoulders. I looked at her and thought about her waiting down there, if I did not come back, and the days going by and lengthening into years.

I let my breath out in a long sigh. "All right, kid. Let's get going. I want to finish this caper before the sun comes up."

Ricia held the sled six feet above the ice, raked it along at a speed that made bob-sledding seem sedentary. It was a good forty-mile run, I estimated; we made it in under an hour, the last few miles at a fast crawl.

We came up over a slight rise, down across an open stretch that showed up pale in the light of a few stars that had found a crack in the cloud layer. It took us half an hour, while Ricia pored over instrument faces, to find a pit scooped out in the ice like a crater dug by an air burst. Ricia maneuvered up to it, settled in and cut the switch.

"This looks like the spot," I told her. "It's just as the sailor described it."

"Grand Tower of the Sun is here, Mal." She

jumped off the sled, pointed to the ground at her feet. "The master steerer of the sled is centered here."

"Was that the tall building I saw in the picture?"

"Yes." She paused, listening. "Library tells me they are here," she said in a low, tense voice. "This is their Hidden Place—my city of Ulmoc!"

"Well, it's not hidden any longer. Let's see what we can do about clearing the shaft." My feet crunched loose ice in the hollow. I used the pick on it; it was a solid mass, thawed and frozen again. Ricia came up with a metal tube like a flashlight, aimed it at the ice. Water bubbled, boiled away from the cavity that appeared.

"You're full of surprises," I said. "And I was going to try it with hairpins and chewing gum."

"I do not know those tools. Are they better than my heat gun?"

"They're pretty versatile, but for a job like this you can't beat specialization. You're doing fine."

"Mal, you use too many words you have not taught me."

"I use too many words, period. I get gabby when I'm nervous." I watched while she cut a deep slot across the ice, then another beside it. I picked at it, broke a fifty-pound chunk loose, tossed it aside, and Ricia went to work widening the hole.

An hour later, six feet down in a slushy pit of porous ice, there was a sudden hollow crunch and a slab dropped from under us. I grabbed Ricia with one hand, the edge of the pit with the other. There was a hole in the floor of the excavation now; through it, the corner of a metal cage showed.

"This is it; that's the car the sailor was caught in." Ricia kicked more ice away, cleared the top of the car. There was an access door, frozen shut. I used a pick to lever it open. We dropped down inside the six-foot square cage. It was half full of ice forced in through the half-open door. I used Ricia's light, set now for a pencil-thin beam. It showed me an unbroken drop into a blue-black well that dwindled away to darkness far below. The cables suspended from the bottom of the car fell away in lazy loops.

"This is the end of the line for you, kid," I said. "There's only one way down, and that's via the cables. You wait up on top, by the sled."

"I will go down."

"Listen, girl, sliding down is easy—maybe. Coming back up is another thing. I can't climb a rope and carry you."

"I climb very well. Now we must go down, or go back together."

"You're not easy to discourage. Maybe I'm glad, at that." I squeezed through the door, dropped down until I was holding on to the door sill, swung my legs out and tangled them in the cables, lowered myself a few yards hand over hand. The ropes were a nine-gauge synthetic fiber, no bigger than my little finger and slippery with ice. They quivered as Ricia swung out above me.

"Stay close," I called up to her. "If you slip, I'll stop you."

"I will not slip," she said coolly. I grunted, got a loop of rope around my leg as a brake, and started down.

I tried to keep track of distance but gave it up after the first hundred feet. At any moment I expected to slam against a blockage in the tube or come to the end of the cable. My arms got tired and then numb, then ached again. I called to Ricia and she answered, sounding calm and a lot less winded than I was. Then my feet hit a sloping surface of loose ice. A moment later Ricia was standing beside me in what felt like a small cave hollowed out of the ice. She flashed the light around on glassy black walls—and stopped on a surface of gray stone with a tall, narrow niche fronting on a tiny balcony railed with twisted iron.

"Mal, it is"—her voice broke—"the Grand Tower . . ."

I put an arm around her shoulders, stared at the ancient wall. "Skyscrapers under the ice," I said. "I don't think I really believed it—until now."

She went to the niche, stepped over the railing, disappeared into darkness. I followed. The light showed us a tiny room with a narrow bed with carved head- and footboards, a squat table with an open drawer, rotted scraps of rug, a doorless opening in the opposite wall. There was an odor of suppressed corruption, like a cold-storage vault.

"This is where he found the coin. My voice was as hoarse as a sideshow barker's. Ricia was already at the doorway, flashing the light on a wall with blotchy painted murals.

"The ramp is this way." She led me along the hall, past doors closed on secrets preserved in deep freeze for an unknown number of millenia. A part of my mind told me that I was walking through a greater treasurehouse than archaeology had ever dreamed of, but the other part kept my hackles raised and my muscles tensed for a fast jump—in either direction.

We reached the ramp. It was wide, like a grand staircase, and wound down in a sweep around a central well. There was no guard rail. I took the lead, hugging the wall.

Five floors down, I saw the first sign of recent occupancy—a cast-off carton marked *U.S Navy—One Ration, Type Y-2 Caution. Not to be consumed after 1 Dec. 1990.* For a moment it gave me an almost comforting sense of human companionship. Then I saw the fellow who had been eating it.

He was lying on his face, ten yards along the corridor. I turned him over carefully; it was like handling a dummy in a store window. He was in good shape—a little dark and withdrawn-looking, his eyelids sunken, his cheeks drawn in—but the bitter cold was an excellent preservative. He was wearing a heavy parka and thick boots laced to the knee. The can of potted meat was still in one hand.

"He didn't die of starvation," I said. My voice seemed to echo like a shout.

Ricia pointed. There was a tiny black spot, almost hidden in the fold of the parka.

"Burn gun," she said. "*They* did it."

"What's a burn gun?"

She held the light out. "Like this, but more strong. It kills."

I unstrapped the forty-five from the dead sailor's waist, buckled it on. "So does this. Let's go."

Two levels lower we found two more men. One was a Navy rating lying curled on his side with his face frozen into an expression of agony like a tortured pharaoh and six burns that I could see without moving him. The other was a soft-looking fellow of perhaps fifty, with a round, oriental-looking face. He was dressed in a quilted suit and felt boots. There was a a large bullet hole in his chest. "Pay dirt," I said. "This is one of them. He's got the look." I went through his pockets, found nothing. There was no gun on the sailor's body.

"How many floors are there in this building?" I asked Ricia.

"Eight tens . . . and three," she calculated.

"Where would they be most likely to hole up?"

"They would take the rooms nearest the kitchens, would they not?"

"Unless they're living on concentrates. They didn't strike me as lads who cared a lot about creature comforts—except for the fat one they called the Primary."

"I think they could be anywhere. There are many apartments here. Only on the lowest floors are there rooms not suitable for sleeping—storage rooms and offices and spaces for the heat engines and other things."

"All right, we'll push on."

At the next floor, Ricia touched my arm. "There is warmth coming from there . . ." She pointed along a dark corridor.

"I don't feel it."

"The library tells me." Her voice was a tense whisper.

"Let's take a look." I unholstered the gun. Ricia

adjusted the light to cast a barely visible pink glow over the floor ahead. I eased off, breathing with my mouth open. Ricia walked beside me, silent as a shadow. We passed open doorways beyond which I caught fleeting glimpses of dark furnishings of strange proportions.

"Close, now," Ricia breathed at my ear.

"Better douse the light."

"Wait." The light dimmed to a sultry glow, went out. Something touched my hand.

"Fit this over your eyes," she whispered. It was a sort of visor, feeling like smooth plastic. I clamped it over my head without asking questions. Now I could see a bright puddle of radiance on the floor ahead from Ricia's light.

"Infrared," I told myself. "That's some bag of tricks you've got there, girl."

We moved on. Two doorways down, Ricia touched my hand. "In there."

I moved up beside the arched opening, listening hard, heard nothing but the blood beating in my ear.

"I think your library's got an overactive imagination," I whispered. "Why would—"

Ricia put a hand over my mouth—too late. Something stirred in the darkness—a sharp, sudden movement. I jumped back, pushed Ricia behind me. A heavy body slammed the wall where we had stood an instant before. The gun was ready in my hand, but I didn't want to use it. I stepped in, swung and connected with something as bristly as a bear. It grunted and clawed at me and I kicked it away, just as Ricia's light found it. I froze, staring at a tall, rangy man, bundled in grimy gray cloth and matted fur, his face pale and hollow-eyed in a snarl of beard. Blood was running down the side of his jaw, and he was showing his teeth in a snarl that could have been either pain or rage.

"Hold it—" I started. He did not wait to hear the rest. He swung wildly, missed, then kicked me hard enough to chip bone. I rushed him, slammed him back against the wall. "I said hold it, damn you!" I got out between my teeth. "We're on your side!"

He went rigid, blinking almost at my face. He was breathing hard between his teeth.

"Give us some light, Ricia," I snapped. The eerie glow of infrared brightened to an honest pink. The man I was holding squinted his eyes, stared into my face. Then he relaxed, let out a long, shuddering breath.

"Thank God," he croaked. "Addison got through . . ."

The room he had fixed up for himself smelled like a Hudson's Bay store just before the fur ship arrives. There was a rough pallet of rotted cloth and odds and ends of clothing in one corner, a pile of Navy ration cartons beside it. He was sitting against the wall, limp as a scarecrow now that the excitement was over.

"I've gotten careless lately," he nodded toward his meager effects. "I used to keep it all hidden, but they never come up here any more. They think I'm dead; I was content to keep it that way. A waiting game, that was all, until you got here." Even talking was an effort for him. I wondered how he had gotten the strength for his attack on me.

"How many men have you?" He glanced at Ricia, looked puzzled as he had each time he noticed her, then fixed his eyes on me. "I hope COMSPAC is patroling the entire perimeter of the continent. I didn't have time to say much to Addison, but I think he understood . . ." He faded off as I shook my head.

"Sorry, COMSPAC couldn't patrol Catalina Island today. There's no task force here. Just me—and . . ." I caught Ricia's eye. "This is Ricia. She led me here."

He straightened himself, made a move to get to his feet. Ricia knelt quickly beside him. His face looked worn and old; his beard was iron gray, shot with white.

"We will help you," she said softly. "We will take you with us to a place where you will be safe."

"Am I . . . am I dreaming this?" He touched Ricia's hand. "No, I see I'm not. You're as real as . . . life." He ducked his head in a caricature of a stately bow. "I am Rome Hayle, my dear."

"Admiral Hayle!" I looked at the gaunt face in vain for a likeness to the dapper officer I had met once in Guam. "Are you the only one . . . left?"

He nodded. "But"—he looked from me to Ricia—"who are you? How did you find me? How is it up above now?"

"Hold it, Admiral," I said. "I'll tell you the whole story—as much as I know of it."

". . . Ricia's bet paid off," I finished. "I woke up inside, damaged but alive. That was a couple of weeks ago."

"But in Heaven's name, why did you come *here?*

You knew this damnable place is infested with them."

"For information. We don't know anything—nothing we can prove."

"You'll never get out alive. You should have gone back with what you had. Now there are three of us in the trap."

"Why didn't they kill you?"

"They tried hard enough. But I found a hidey-hole—up there." He pointed to the ceiling. "There's a narrow crawl space above; I can enter it through the wardrobe ceilings—a trapdoor arrangement. Access space for heating ducts."

"What happened to your men?"

"Most of them were cut down at their posts before we knew we were under attack."

"They hit you from inside?"

"They came up from below, intercepted us at about the seventieth floor, down from the top of the tower. About a dozen of us survived their first attack. They came at us in absolute silence, firing. I shot one; managed to find cover. Got the remnant of my boys together and tried to pull back, but they pressed us from both sides. Four of us got clear, to the upper levels. They picked Hieneman and Drake and Ludcrow off over the next week. I fooled them. Rigged Ludcrow's body up, propped in a doorway. When they fired, he fell. They thought they'd gotten me. They went away, and I haven't seen them since—up here."

"Up here?" Ricia queried him.

"I've been down a few times. The first month I was quite active scouting them out, spying. Then I began to get a little weak. Lack of sunshine, and the damned cold, I suppose. Always shivering. Plenty of food, though . . ." His attention seemed to wander from his disjointed story, and he brought it back with an effort.

"They're not human, you know," he said, and I could hear the strain in his voice. I said nothing, waited.

"They call themselves . . . Womboids. They prey on us. They need men to live—I don't know how, but they need them. The way ticks need cattle."

"What else did you learn about them, Admiral?" I had the feeling he was close to some unseen edge, and that the wrong word would send him over.

"They don't care whether they live or die," Hayle said hoarsely. "As long as something they call their Primary is safe. All they want is food and a place to breed. That last is very important to them. The ones that haven't bred are in a sort of special, protected category, as well as I could gather. They're . . . tested . . . in some way. Those that don't pass are killed as casually as you'd swat a fly."

"How did you learn all this?"

"I listened. There's a big room where they gather to eat . . ." He described it. Ricia nodded. "The feasting hall; there is food stored there—enough for the whole city for a year or more. It was gathered there when the Long Winter began."

They bring captives here, I think. They spoke of the need for women. Not the way a man would speak of women—don't misunderstand me. The way a butcher would speak of a new supply of beef!"

"They don't *eat* human flesh?"

"It's not that either. I hate to think of it, but I believe they use them in some unnatural way to breed more of their own obscene kind."

"When you say they're not human, Admiral, you're speaking—"

"I'm speaking fact, man! They're no more human than a scorpion! Yes, they look human—they may even walk around in human flesh, but the spirit that moves them is as alien as a boa constrictor."

"He is right," Ricia said, and shuddered as with a chill. "I felt it, too."

"I agree they're a clammy lot, but to jump from that to Aliens Among Us is quite a leap. The fact is, we don't know enough about them." I looked at Ricia. "Is there a back way into this Feast Hall? Something they might not know about?"

"There are service routes leading to the kitchens. It is possible that they have not discovered them."

"You'll need a gun. I guess we can borrow one from the Admiral."

"Wait a minute," Hayle barked. "You're not going to try an attack on them? There must be hundreds of them!"

"Nothing so dramatic. I want information, proof that these Womboids exist—that they're a threat."

"Don't be a damned fool! You have to get clear, now, before they discover you! I'll write a letter for COMSPAC; they'll send a force in here big enough to take this place lock, stock, and barrel! We can't let one of them escape, now that we've found their nest."

"Sorry, I'm not leaving until I've got something

concrete. Tell COMSPAC they're a threat, you say. What kind of threat? Maybe they're a harmless secret society."

"Harmless! They killed my men!"

"Your men intruded on them, Admiral. I guess you could say the same of me. They don't seem to go out looking for trouble."

"Are you siding with these devils!" Hayle glared at me with red eyes.

"I'm trying to point out the futility of arousing any official interest in them without something more than a strange feeling to go on. *You* know this is something big; *I* know it. I can feel the threat in the air as thick as the smog over Naples. But we need proof."

"My letter—"

"They'll file it along with the UFO reports. I'm going down. Ricia, you stay here with the Admiral. If I'm not back in twenty-four hours—"

"Mal, do not speak foolishly. I am with you."

"You two are going down there, beard these vipers in their den? when you could get away clean, now?"

"You'll be all right here for another day, Admiral. Then we'll leave together."

Hayle stared at me. Then he got to his feet, painfully. "I've been without light, without the sound of a human voice for three months," he said heavily. "I'll not be without them again, as long as I can crawl."

I thought about it. "All right, Admiral," I said. "Buckle on a gun and let's get moving."

The route that Ricia showed us was a narrow, sharply spiraling ramp, almost lost at the far end of the corridor. We followed it down past arched openings at each floor, emerged into an echoing vault as big as the nave of a middlesized cathedral. Heavy equipment was ranged in dark rows along the center of the room. It looked like an abandoned factory.

"This is the upper kitchen," Ricia whispered. "Here the carcasses of Holgotha were prepared, and the hearts cut from the Riffa tree, and the great fishes . . ." She stared, caught in a dream of barbaric banquets served long ago.

"They're not here," Hayle was sniffing the air. "I could smell them if they were. We haven't descended far enough."

"There is another kitchen below," Ricia said. "But they have been here—and they are near. The library senses their warmth."

"What's this 'library'?" Haley asked sharply. I explained the miniature pickup and relay system. Hayle grunted. "Handy," he said. "Some day I'll want to know a great deal more about you, young lady, and about the people who built this fantastic pile."

Back on the ramp, we moved stealthily, pausing to listen every few yards. The walls were warmer here; I could sense it through my gloves. I sniffed, caught the taint of fresh decay. Beside me, Ricia put out a hand, touched my arm.

"Just ahead," she breathed.

"Give me the light."

She handed it to me. "Be careful." I nodded, waved her back. Hayle started forward.

"Stay here," I mouthed. He glared at me. I made a peremptory motion and turned away. He was a good officer; he took the order in silence.

Six feet farther, half around the next turn of the ramp, an arch opened on the right. The warmth and odor were stronger here. I poked my head out, looked into a long room much like the one above. If there was anyone in it, they were standing very still.

"I'm going in," I whispered. "If the coast is clear, you follow." I did not wait for the arguments; I started down the aisle between the giant cauldrons.

It was a hundred-yard walk to the small, square door in the opposite wall. I moved along, heel and toe, with my gun in my hand and my ears out on stalks. It was as silent as a deaf-mute's tomb.

At the door, I flattened myself against the wall and listened. There may have been a few faint sounds from beyond it—or maybe it was just imagination frisking in the dark. The door was a double one, hinged at both sides. I touched the nearest panel; it swung in, letting in light and a whiff of foul air like an opened coffin.

Tables were ranged in rows across a wide room with tall shuttered windows. Twenty or thirty men sat at the tables, dwarfed by the scale of the high, vaulted ceiling. At that moment, one of them looked my way.

I froze, holding the door as it was, half an inch open; the movement of closing it would catch his eye more surely than the displacement. He stared across for a long moment. Then he turned back; I thought he spoke to someone across the table, but I was not sure. He was at least fifty yards from me, and the light was a dim flicker from a crude flambeau on a stand in the space between tables. No one moved from his seat. I decided the man had not seen me.

Another man entered the room, went to a serving counter, scooped up food, took a seat alone at a table. Another man rose, went out the way the other had entered. Minutes ticked past, while nothing happened, I let the door close gently, turned to cross back to the ramp where Ricia and Hayle waited, and a yellow light bloomed, a heat-lightning flash; sound racketed and roared from the walls. I dropped, rolled behind a leg-mounted rectangle of cold iron with an odor of grease and mold as a second shot thundered, and a third. There were sounds of scuffling feet, of fists hitting flesh, the clatter of a dropped gun. Hayle snarled something that was cut off in the middle by a blow. Then silence.

CHAPTER FIFTEEN

I waited while five minutes crawled across the darkness. Feet scraped and voices muttered across the big room; lights swept the aisles, I pulled my feet in just in time. Someone came toward me; I held the gun ready, flattened myself half under a massive cooker. He passed me by two yards away, looking in the other direction. The voices and footsteps moved away to the far end of the room. Lights bobbed there. Some instinct said that for the moment the coast was clear. I crawled out, easy-footed it along, behind the big, dark ovens. Voices muttered in the distance; the door into the dining room opened, let in a wedge of dirty light, shut again. Feet came and went. They had not given up yet; maybe they had instincts, too, that told them they had not quite finished the job.

The archway beyond which I had left Ricia and Hayle was thirty feet away, and it meant crossing open ground. I got within ten feet of it before I realized a man was standing silently with is back to me, just inside the opening. I froze against the wall and waited, unable to go forward, unwilling to go back. Then he turned and disappeared. I followed, made the archway, saw him standing six feet away, looking past two bodies on the floor. In the first instant, I thought they were both dead; then I saw the glint of Hayle's eye, a tiny movement from Ricia. They were trussed in wire like giant, half-wound armatures. I slid around the edge of the wall, and Ricia saw me. The guard did not; his ears were tuned to some fancied sound from the ramp above. I could have taken him then, easily enough; then he stepped off, went up the ramp and out of sight.

I went to Ricia's side, knelt by her.

"He had a signaler. Do not let him see you! Go quickly!"

I was checking over the wires that bound her. There were hundreds of turns around her, cutting cruelly into her arms, her thighs, her ankles.

"No time for me, Mal! Listen! They spoke; they wait now for the instructions of their Primary. They do not know about you; they think that the old man and I are alone."

"I'll get these wires off."

"No! Find the one they call the Primary; he is their weakness! They spoke of the Chamber of the Dragon. I know the apartment they mean."

"The wires—"

"No time!" She cut me off. "There is a way out. Above the central bank of ovens there is a flue big enough for a man, I think. When you reach the kitchen above, go along the corridor to the far side, all the way to the end. There you will find a door decorated by carvings. He is there."

Someone was coming. I touched Ricia's face. "I'll be back," I said, then faded back against the wall, slipped through the archway and ran for cover.

It took me half an hour to work my way across to the big central unit. There was a wide hood above it. I climbed up, thrust my head and shoulders in; soot drifted down, and I resisted the impulse to sneeze. Metal handholds were set in the masonry. I used them, started up.

The kitchen above was laid out like the lower one, except that the units were bigger, designed to accommodate gargantuan haunches of meat. There were tables the size of badminton courts, pots big enough to render missionaries in platoons. I moved past them, through the door at the far end, along a dim-lit corridor at the end of which men came and went. The doorways gave me concealment. I advanced as a lone skirmisher, five yards at a time. The door Ricia had told me about was plain enough—a high double panel with a carved lizard with two heads spitting fire at a bare-legged man with a spear.

The traffic thinned. A single man emerged from the door, went away along the cross corridor. For the moment, the coast was clear. I did not pause to weigh odds; I dashed, made it to the door and through into dimness and stale-smelling warmth. A man jumped up as I came in, gaped at me for a moment—just long enough for me to swing on him, knock him back against the wall. I caught him, hit him again. He fought back, clawing at me with untrimmed fingernails, until I got my thumbs in behind the big tendons of his neck. I felt his larynx break, kept choking until he flopped a final flop and went limp. I lowered him, checked for a pulse, caught the last feeble flutter. Killing him bothered me no more than swatting a moth. He was one less live enemy at my back.

There was a heavy hanging across a doorway in the left wall. I flipped it aside, stepped through into an evil-smelling room hung with decayed splendor and almost filled by a vast bed on which a bloated caricature of a man sprawled, staring at me with bulging eyes.

I showed him the gun, moved across and put myself to the left of the entry. I had a weird sensation that I was reliving another confrontation. I could almost feel the pressure of the water beyond the walls. But this time it was ice, and the walls were old, old, reeking of time and forgotten things.

"Are you the same one?" My voice came out hoarse. He did not answer. I jammed the gun cruelly against one bloated foot and the giant leg twitched away. He wheezed, grunted. Thick fluid oozed from his slack mouth.

"You can talk." I aimed the gun at his head. "Who are you? What do you want from us?"

"I want . . . only peace, and silence." His voice was a high, thin sigh. "Why do you hurt me?"

"Don't pull that on me; I know about you, remember? Or maybe he was your brother. There's not much keeping alive, Fat Stuff, just my curiosity. Give me answers or it goes off now."

"I am the Primary," he squeaked. "Nothing must injure me."

I raked the gun sight down his gross thigh, as big around as a turbine shaft; it left a red weal across the doughy flesh. He gave a high squeal and quivered.

"Why did you kidnap me? What did you want with the girl?"

"Women are needed," he piped. "More women. Bring many women, I will pay you well."

I could feel sweat popping out on my face. A sense of unreality made the giant slug on the bed seem like some gross fantasy, a dream of greed and evil. I jabbed it again. "Talk, damn you!" I felt my voice rise, but it was not important; only the answers were important now. "Who are you? Why do you kill without warning? How did you get here? What are you?"

There was a quick sound behind me. I whirled, dropped as a wire-fine beam of vivid light crackled across above my head, and then my gun bucked and roared in my hand and a man leaned in the doorway, clutched at the hanging with one hand, crumpled slowly, the heat gun still lanced across. Behind me, the fat one screamed—an infinitely high, pure note of agony that ululated on and on, wailed down the scale to a choking rattle and died away like a moan of utter bereavement.

The man in the doorway fell, and his gun bounced clear. Smoke was rising from the bedding. A foul odor choked me. I staggered to my feet, saw the gaping, char-and-crimson wound that curved erratically down across the quivering bulk of the creature on the bed, laying open the vast paunch like a split melon.

As I watched, something stirred in the depths of the wound. A glistening black shape wriggled there, thrusting. A blind tendril like the head of a great soft worm poked clear, a sheen of blackish red. I jerked the gun up, fired again and again, saw the writhing shape spatter, twist away, jerking and whipping with an unclean vitality as foot after foot of its hideous length emerged from the ripped abdomen. I was not aware of slamming another clip into the gun, but later I noticed the empty magazine on the floor where I had thrown it.

I pumped every round into the slug shape, and still it coiled out, yearning across the filth-spattered floor toward me and I backed until the wall stopped me, then dragged a heavy chest from the wall, toppled it on the frightful thing. Pinned, it whipped and beat its slimy coils against the floor. And on the bed, the fat man, like a great burst balloon, sagged, an empty bag.

Time seemed to stand still. I was in the outer room, still hearing the restless slap of the slug against the floor. A man stood near the door. I raised the gun, clicked it emptily at him. He made no move. His mouth hung slack; his eyes looked past me vacantly. I ran past him, knocked him aside. Out in the corridor, more men stood. As I watched, one staggered, fell against the wall. The others ignored him. None of them seemed to notice me. I pushed through them, found myself face to face with the man with the shriveled skin, the one I thought I had drowned.

"Who are you?" I hissed. I caught his coat, a rumpled brown suit, and shook him. His gaze turned on me from some remote distance.

"He is dead," he said.

"Who was he? What does it mean? What was that—thing?"

"Now the long dream dies," he said. Then the intelligence went out of his eyes. His mouth opened slackly. I shoved him away, ran on. No one tried to stop me.

Ricia and the Admiral lay where I had left them. Their guard was gone—wandered away, they said. The wires had made ugly marks on Ricia's skin, but she was able to walk. Hayle staggered at first, but after the first hundred yards he found his feet again.

We passed Womboids, a few standing, or moving aimlessly along in the dark, but most of them lying like firing squad victims. I turned one or two over; they were dead, without a mark on them.

"It's as though they'd forgotten how to breathe," Hayle said.

"Maybe they did," I said. "I think that somehow they drew their strength from the . . . thing on the bed."

We tramped through the building, explored great halls and lavish apartments and vaulted corridors, and Ricia talked of the fetes and galas that she had known in the once-magnificent halls. We found the exit by accident; it was a sloping tunnel that led upward from wide double windows behind a terrace far up on the side of the tower. Half an hour later we stood on the ice crust under a dawn sky like spilled paint. Far away the sled was visible as a dark speck against the purple-and-red-dyed ice.

"We'll go to the house first for supplies," I said.

"Then to the coast. Ricia's boat will be there. In ten days we'll be home. After that—I don't know."

"Omaha," the Admiral said. "CINCNAVOP is there, and they'll be operating, you can depend on it. I don't know how much sea power the Navy can still command, but it will be enough."

"If they believe us," I said.

"They'll believe me," Hayle declared. "I'll see to that."

We made the crossing in fifteen days; the weather was good—barring the eternal black-clouded skies and occasional falls of volcanic ash. We rested, ate and talked, and Ricia spent hours studying a one-volume encyclopedia we found aboard.

"I can understand why they thought they had to kill my party," Hayle said. We were sitting on the tiny afterdeck, smoking and watching another violent sunset. "We'd stumbled onto their hide-out—their Hidden Place, as they called it. But why the persecution of Ricia? She was no threat to them."

"I have a theory," I said, "that they recognized her for what she was—a member of the ancient race. Naturally, they'd want to question her."

"But that implied they knew . . ."

"Certainly; the Primary spoke her language."

"I think," Ricia said hesitantly, "that he was . . . of my people. Beneath the swollen body I thought I saw the likeness."

"You mean he—as an individual—was God knows how many thousand of years old?" Hayle snorted. "That's preposterous!"

"No older than Ricia." I smiled at her youthful face.

"That's different. She was in a low-energy comatose state. The Navy's been experimenting with similar techniques for years."

"They're not human, remember, Admiral—your own statement, I believe. They *used* humans. The slug thing that I killed—I think *that* was the Primary—not the swollen thing that served as host."

"Why did the others . . . run down, when he died?" Hayle's voice was hoarse, as one speaking of the horribly dead.

"In some way, they were all linked to him. They existed to serve him."

"And what did *he* live for?"

"For the same reason we do—the instinct to survive. In our case, the race is made up of millions, billions of individuals. In his—I think he was the race: a single, immortal individual, supported like a queen bee by his Womboids."

"What for? They lived in secret; I think they must have inhabited that tower for ages—literally. They had no luxuries, not even comfort. They just lived, parasites on the human race. Perhaps we never would have discovered them, if the changes in the planet hadn't brought their Hidden Place to light. And if Ricia hadn't come on the scene, perhaps not even then."

"It seems they've been with us a long time," I mused. "I wonder where they came from, how they established their role in the first place."

"Perhaps they're invaders from some other world." Hayle half smiled. "Perhaps the flying saucers landed a million years ago. But, then, perhaps they've always been here, a product of the same slime that we came up from. Perhaps they learned to use us as hosts long before we were men."

"Strange—all that history to come to an end, because one creature died."

Hayle narrowed his eyes. With his beard trimmed and his cheeks beginning to fill out, he was looking like a tough old Navy officer again.

"They tried to keep him alive; they spent themselves like flies to protect him. Strange creatures—at once so deadly, and so inept. With all the technical wealth of the frozen city to draw on, one would think they'd have been more effective in surviving."

"I think they had no intelligence of their own," I said. "They used the brains of the human bodies they infested, just as they used their limbs. And remember, Admiral, they weren't human; their needs and drives weren't ours. They wanted nothing but a safe, dark nest for their Primary."

"Still, they ventured out; you saw them in Georgia, in Miami, in the Mediterranean. And the villa you found there—I suspect they had inhabited it for quite some time."

"Ricia's people knew them," I pointed out. "I suppose that house was built on shore, and somehow sealed before it sank."

"Those oldsters had an astounding technology." Hayle wagged his head. "Not like ours, but in some ways, surpassing ours—as witness the marvelous little communications devices Ricia has shown me. How could such knowledge have been lost so utterly?"

"That was a long time ago, Admiral. The ice came down, and ground everything to rubble before it. Weather and age and warfare and looting could account for the rest."

"And, do you not see," Ricia asked, "when human cities fell, the under-men alone, living long in their secret places, remembered the ancient wisdom. It would have made them kings among savage men. And they would have destroyed every reminder of man's former greatness."

"I wonder . . ." Hayle puffed on his pipe. "What we know of the habits of ancient rulers seems to fit the pattern: impassive, long-lived, ruthless, worshipped as gods—and always the immense harem—and their treatment of women as inferiors, useful only for breeding. Perhaps it's from them that we derived our concept of sex as something secret and evil, surrounded with ancient taboos.'

"A civilization that could build a city like Ricia's would have to leave *some* trace," I protested. "At least some legend, some tradition of knowledge."

Hayle was frowning. "There *are* anomalies," he said softly. "The ancient Arabs used storage batteries to plate their jewelry; the Greeks had an astronomical computer; even the bushmen and their boomerangs."

"There is another thing," Ricia said. "The minerals that your people have regarded as precious—the metals and stones. I think this is a racial memory of a lost technology. Silver is a conductor of electricity, better than copper. Diamond is a cutting tool; the ruby is necessary to the laser."

"And the fiber-reinforced metals," I suggested. "Sapphire 'whiskers' in a silver matrix, for example, and uranium."

"And gold, too," Hayle nodded. "Our satellites are plated with the stuff."

"Their value could not be explained by rarity alone," Ricia said.

"Hell, diamonds wouldn't be worth a dollar a pound if the supply weren't controlled by the producing governments," I pointed out. "And the same is true of most of the stones. Even gold is artifically supported. It was common enough among the South American Indians that they made ordinary drinking cups and ornaments from it."

"All this is theory," Hayle said. "When we've restored some degree of order to this catastrophe-wracked planet, then we'll investigate our cold-storage city. Perhaps then we'll learn the answers."

"Perhaps—and perhaps we'll never know. In a way, it's too bad the Primary is dead and his Womboids with him. There might have been a way to make him talk."

"We're well rid of the monster, and all his spawn," Hayle said harshly. "We will have our problems, God knows." He looked at the ruined sky. "But that's one curse we can live without."

Two days later we sighted the Louisiana coast. We made landfall west of a little town called Iowa, commandeered an abandoned car after digging it out of a mud bank. A few hours later we were on the outskirts of Omaha. Hayle took over, skirted the ruins of the city proper, took a winding route among black ash cones standing on the plain like chimneys, pulled up to a fence, much mended but still standing, surrounding a bare hundred-acre tract with a blockhouse and some sheds at its center. A squad of armed Marines watched us climb out of the car and come up to the gate. Hayle gave the password; the Marine sergeant used his talkie; then an officer came out of the blockhouse and looked us over. There was more corfab; then they opened the gate, formed up a box around us, marched us across to the building.

Hayle looked impatient, but kept calm. I was still wearing my .45, so it must have been just routine. In the blockhouse they frisked us, looked the gun over, let me keep it. There were happy smiles and salutes all around when a fat Commodore arrived via elevator from somewhere below, greeted Hayle warmly, ushered us all into the car. He was bubbling with questions, but Hayle gave him the old Academy smile and said he would save it for the official briefing.

We stepped out into a wide, immaculate, gray-walled room packed with electronic gear. The Commodore took us across to an office with rugs, pictures, a big desk, pushed a buzzer on the desk, offered drinks. There was a tap, and three men came into the room, all portly, gray-haired desk sailors with adequate braid on their cuffs.

"Gentlemen," the Commodore was saying.

Ricia touched my arm. "Malcome!" she whispered in my ear. "The library says—"

Someone was holding out a hand to be shaken. I took it, nodded replies to introductions.

"Mal!" Ricia said urgently. "That one—in the center—he is one of . . . them!"

I jerked as though a needle had hit me, remembering the dead Primary. Apparently the Womboids came in varieties. Perhaps through some kind of selective propagation, they developed some who could live independent of, though murmured something. The Commodore was talking:

". . . after so many months. I'm sure, gentlemen, that we shall all be most interested in what Admiral Hayle can tell us of what he encountered in Antarctica."

I was watching the officer in the center of the three, an Oriental-looking fellow with dead-black eyes. He had stepped back half a pace. His hand went to a side pocket; he palmed something, raised his arm unobtrusively.

I jerked the .45 from its holster, shot him in the chest, heard his gun bark, shot again as he slammed back, put a third slug into his head before they landed on me. I tried to yell; Hayle was staring, saying something. Then the door burst open and Marines spilled in. I caught a glimpse of knuckles, and my interest in the proceedings faded in a shower of lights.

The courtroom was a converted office, but no less ominous for that. Armed Marines lined the walls; grim-faced officers in tieless whites or dungarees sat behind the long table. Admiral Hayle sat at one side, two Marines with drawn guns behind his chair. I was still dizzy; my head buzzed like a burned relay. It had not taken them long to get a court together.

The Commodore was at the center of the judge's table, reading out the charges. It seemed that I had wantonly committed mayhem on the person of one General Yin, a military observer from a friendly nation. There seemed to be other, vaguer charges as well, having to do with breach of security, sabotage, false representations, kidnaping and treason. It did not interest me much. My head hurt too badly. I put a hand up to feel it, got a sharp crack across the arm from someone standing behind me.

I looked around. Ricia was not in sight.

"Where is she?" I came half out of my seat and was slammed down hard. The Commodore said something in a harsh voice; the other members of the board looked at me with impassive faces.

"Get up," a voice said behind me; a hard hand helped me, urgently. The Commodore glared. I looked across at Hayle. He was watching me, his face set in anger.

". . . brutal murder," the Commodore was saying. "Have you anything to say to this court before sentence is passed?"

Hayle was on his feet. "The man is in no condition to conduct his own defense. I'm warning you, Commodore, this kangaroo court—"

"You'll be seated or I'll have you removed from the courtroom!" The Commodore's face was blustery red. "I don't know your role in this murder plot, Admiral, but I can promise you we've no patience with traitors here."

"I've told you enough to make it plain that there's more to this than appears at first glance,"

Hayle stormed. "This man deserves a hearing!"

"He'll have his hearing! Be seated, sir!"

Hayle locked eyes with the Commodore, then sat.

"Where's Ricia, Admiral?" I called before a hand cuffed me.

"Shut up, you!" the man behind me barked.

"The woman is being cared for," the Commodore snapped.

"What happened to her?" I yelled.

"She was injured."

"Injured how? How badly?"

"Silence! If you have anything to say that bears on the issue here, speak up now!"

"I shot him because he wasn't human," I said. My voice sounded loud and hollow in my ears. Babble broke out. The Commodore gaveled it down.

"How did you learn that he was not human?" one of the board members asked. His eyes bored into me.

"I . . . can't tell you." Somehow, it seemed important to keep Ricia's library a secret.

"How did you know of the city under the ice?" another demanded.

"I was taken there—by them."

"By whom? Who do you mean by 'them'?"

"The Womboids. They—"

"How did you learn of the secret place under the water?" a third queried coldly.

I opened my mouth to answer, paused, trying to remember. I had not mentioned the sunken villa to anyone here, other than the Admiral. My eye went to him. He frowned, shot a look at me, shook his head. I looked back at the solemn faces of the board, and suddenly I knew.

The Commodore was human. The rest were Womboids.

The questioning went on for an hour; I gave half answers, vague answers. I was stalling, hoping for something, I didn't know what. My head ached; it was hot in the room. Hayle had objected again and been forcibly silenced.

The Womboids fired questions at me in a merciless cross fire. It was apparent that they were probing to discover how much I knew about them, and how I had learned it, rather than investigating the circumstances of the shooting. Even the Commodore was looking puzzled. He pounded the table, called for silence.

"This investigation is wandering far afield," he snapped. "This court has no interest in these fantasies. The man is either out of his head or seeking to create that impression. The question is simply: are there extenuating circumstances which might justify or mitigate the crime he committed. The answer is clear: No!" He looked across at me under beetled brows.

"The accused will stand."

I got up.

"This court finds you guilty as charged," he said flatly. "The sentence is death by firing squad—to be carried out immediately.

The door burst open. Three young officers—two Navy men and one Marine—strode into the room, each with a machine pistol across his chest. I swung around to face them, felt my teeth clamp, bracing for the shock. They brought their guns up, leveled them. The utter stillness was shattered by the racketing burst of fire that lanced from their muzzles. I staggered, saw the bright surface of the judge's table explode in splinters, saw the blank faces behind it open in unheard cries as they tumbled down and away in a rising dust cloud of broken plaster.

The silence rang with echoes. The Commodore was still sitting, his face as gray as the wall. Some of the Marines groped for holstered guns, raised their hands as the machine pistols swung to cover them.

"Everybody stand fast," the Marine captain said. "We've been the victims of a plot, but it wasn't the prisoner who was plotting. Admiral Hayle, will you assume command, sir?"

Hayle stood. "With pleasure, Captain."

Ricia was propped up in a clean white bed, looking a little pale, but bright-eyed and smiling.

"It is nothing, Malcome. The bullet from the little gun struck me in the side, but they have tended me well."

"It could have killed you. Damn me for not listening—I could have shot him before he got the gun up."

"It does not matter, Malcome. We are alive—and safe. The secret of the Womboids is known now; they have no more power to hurt us."

"There's no telling how many cells of them there are. We finished one off in Gonwondo; I think most of the Mediterranean group were killed. Now this bunch. They seem to be able to communicate in some way, so they'll be on the alert."

"We'll get them," Hayle said. "Don't worry about that angle, Irish."

"How did you do it, Ricia?" I took her hand; it was warm and firm. "Nothing I said got through; even the Admiral couldn't get a hearing."

Ricia smiled. "I convinced the good surgeon that he must make a special examination of the dead colonel." The smile faded. "He found—anomalies. The library told me that the judges were of the enemy. The rest you know."

"Astonishing thing, that." Colonel Barker, the army surgeon who had removed the bullet from Ricia's ribs, had come in time to hear her remark. "His heart seemed perfectly normal, until I probed for the bullet." His face twisted at the memory. "I found a bloody great worm in it—alive, mind you. Damned thing seemed to have roots, of a sort. Ran all through the body. Microscopic, of course. Never have noticed 'em, but for the young lady."

"You're full of surprises, Ricia," Hayle said. "How did you get him to listen to you—and you telling him his business at that? What kind of special powers of the ancients did you use on him?"

"No special power of the ancients, Admiral Hayle. Only the power that all women have." She looked at me and smiled a dazzling feminine smile. "A woman can always have her desire—if her desire is great."

I looked into her dark eyes and agreed.

THE END

Afterward #1:

THIS DYNAMIC PLANET

by

G. Harry Stine

Keith Laumer wrote *Catastrophe Planet* based on a scenario of a Planet Earth that occasionally suffered extreme convulsions. In view of what we have learned about our home planet *and other planets*, how valid is Laumer's scenario today?

Have geologists, meteorologists, seismologists, oceanologists, astronomers, planetologists and other "earth scientists" discovered anything new in that time?

Have they measured any new things, things that could not be measured or even detected fifteen years ago?

Have the Vanguards, Veneras, Rangers, Surveyors, Lunas, Lunar Orbiters, and Apollos given us any new data? While busily exploring space and other planets, have these far explorers increased our knowledge of our home world at all?

Indeed they have.

Everything we have done on Earth and in space during the past fifteen years has, in some way or another, contributed to what we know about our home world or has revealed to us what we do not yet know. The most rudimentary discoveries of other worlds, even close-up photographs of them, have given us an entirely new perspective on our unique planet.

The expansion of knowledge of our planet has not been exclusively the work of space exploration, but the maturing of a whole new group of sciences now called "earth sciences." They include not only the classical science of geology, but also oceanography, meteorology, seismology, and a long list of others.

In turn, the progress in the earth sciences has been due to the fact that we are doubling the amount of knowledge we possess every seven years. Thus, in the past fifteen years, we have quadrupled our knowledge of the Planet Earth *and everything else.* This simple fact is often ignored by many people because the consequences of this explosion of knowledge is difficult to grasp in the first place.

It's nothing really new. It just seems that way. The human race has been doubling its knowledge at an increasing rate for milennia. It's now beginning to show in a dramatic fashion that scares most people. There is an oft-quoted statement that 90% of the scientists who ever lived are now alive and working; *this has always been true.*

And with the march of technology has come entirely new measuring tools and detection apparatus. The now-ubiquitous laser, once upon a time in 1960 known as "an invention looking for a job," now forms the bulwark of some of the most precise instruments known—such as a measuring stick thousands of kilometers long accurate to a quarter wavelength of light.

How do these advances impact Keith Laumer's planetary catastrophe scenario?

Have they produced new information to indicate it's a possibility or merely a figment of a writer's very fertile imagination?

First of all, there is nothing wrong with Laumer's catastrophe scenario either from the literary or the scientific point of view. When it comes to either one, one must apply the pragmatic approach.

From the literary point of view, *Catastrophe Planet* is a good adventure yarn based on a scenario generated by the very best scientific data and evidence available when it was written. The Womboids are, of course, strictly amusing speculation; though there is yet no evidence that points to such a possibility. Laumer has achieved what many writers—especially "main stream" writers who attempt science-fiction—never manage to attain: the elusive "suspension of disbelief" on the part of the reader.

Scientifically, the planetary catastrophe scenario is now only one of a number of valid scenarios that have been created as a result of new information. We've learned a few things about our planet in the last fifteen years.

We know that Earth is a dynamic planet and always has been a dynamic world.

The only difference between Earth-change scenarios today is the wide variety of ways in which the planet can be dynamic and the time scales in which these various forms of dynamic change could take place.

We always knew our home world was dynamic —even before our ancestors began to recognize it as a planet.

Vulcanism, seismic activity, violent meteorological activity, climatic changes, and even the regularity of the diural and seasonal cycles were events that had enormous impact upon humanity and still do.

Life may have started on Earth just because it is a dynamic planet, as Laumer points out.

There has certainly been a dramatic change in the Earth because of the existence of life on the planet. Earth is now believed to have had a "reducing atmosphere" until approximately two billion years ago, an atmosphere much like the atmospheres we find today on Venus and Mars. These atmospheres, probably much like the early Earth's, are mainly carbon dioxide with very little oxygen present. However, Earth is the only planet in the Solar System—with the possible exception of Mars during some portions of its precessional cycle—where liquid water can exist; the water probably came from vulcanism. So did copious amounts of carbon dioxide. At some point, plants grew and multiplied to the point where they took the water and carbon dioxide of the primordial Earth and, through photosynthesis, literally created the present oxidizing atmosphere that still surrounds us today. *That* was probably the most catastrophic and dynamic change ever to have occurred on Earth, but it probably took eons. It took a long time because there was limited energy available to create the change.

And we'll speak more about the role of energy in

creating change and in the rate at which change can take place.

We need to pause momentarily to review the meaning of a "catastrophe." The world comes from the Greek language where its root means to turn down or overturn. It means a great and sudden calamity or disaster. To whom? One entity's catastrophe may be another's windfall. What happened to all those life forms that had evolved in the primordial Earth's reducing carbon dioxide atmosphere; have they done as well in the past two billion years in an oxidizing atmosphere? And the term "sudden" is also relative. To a race of ants whose individuals live but a day, sundown is a catastrophe. A "galactic catastrophe" may take place over many human lifetimes. We shall have to settle the question in human terms: a catastrophe is a disaster insofar as humans are concerned and its sudden calamity takes place in a very short percentage of one's expected life span—say, from a few seconds to a few weeks.

By and large, the human race has managed to cope with all of the catastrophic changes of Planet Earth. Otherwise, you and I wouldn't be here to talk about it.

Humanity evolved on this dynamic planet of change. Our ancestors built civiliations surrounded by the tremendously energetic forces of the planet, and perhaps *because* of them.

The change of seasons with the apparent motion of the sun in the sky and the march of the stars across the heavens at night were things that ancient people looked upon with awe because these pheneomena were regular and inexplicable.

The regular cycles of the planet permitted the development of the calendar which was vital to successful agriculture. Agriculture in turn was vital to the development of civilization where people began to record past events and current knowledge for the purpose of passing these important tools along to their offspring to enhance the chances of survival of the next and future generations. Without civilization, mankind was foredoomed to continue as bands of nomadic tribes, passing along folk knowledge only by word of mouth. Without permanent repositories for written knowledge and records, human beings were forced to re-invent the wheel every few generations as word-of-mouth stories grew twisted in re-telling. But this is an old story and one that has been written about at length.

What hasn't been thoroughly studied yet is the effects on civilization of the sort of catastrophic events that form the basis for *Catastrophe Planet.* Although the human race has finally reached the point where its members can create planetwide catastrophes with massive exchanges of thermonuclear weapons—it's as yet unclear whether or not humanity can make catastrophic changes on other than a temporary, localized basis except with thermonuclear weapons—we are still very much at the mercy of a large number of natural catastrophic possibilities ranging in both their effects upon our lives and upon our scientific and technical abilities to do something about them either by prediction or prevention.

Volcanos and volcanic activities are part of our human heritage. We know a great deal about volcanos, and yet we are continually reminded of how little we know about them and how little we can do about their effects on our lives. Each generation is reminded of their power and catastrophic capability to change the local environment. Every generation has its Mount St. Helens. In the past, it's been Vesuvius, Krakatua, Mount Lassen, Popocatapetl and others. Even in an age of fifty megaton thermonuclear bombs, the power of vulcanism astounds us. Mount St. Helens blew off its north face with an explosion estimated to equal more than a hundred megaton thermonuclear explosion. The shock wave of that eruption was recorded thousands of kilometers away and was plainly visible on weather satellites 36,100 kilometers away in space. The cloud of ash and debris was tracked for more than three thousand kilometers, leaving in its wake a blanket of ash that literally demolished mankind's finest machinery. Air filters were clogged. Paint was abraded off the wings of airplanes flying through the diffuse cloud. Turbine aircraft engines of high precision were ruined by brief exposures of several minutes to the ash. When wetted, the ash set up into both a fine adhesive and mortar.

Even our mightiest technology stands dwarfed by a mere mountain. . . .

In the past of memory, Mont Pelee destroyed the city of St. Pierre, Martinique at 7:50 A.M. on May 8, 1902 in less time than it takes to read this. Thirty thousand peole ceased to exist in an instant, leaving only one survivor, Ludger Sylbaris, who had been jailed in solitary confinement in a cell that effectively sheltered him.

Is there anyone who hasn't heard of the legendary explosion of the volcanic islet of Krakatua in the Sunda Strait between Java and Sumatra? At 10:00 A.M. on August 27, 1883, the island literally exploded, sending *twenty-one cubic kilometers* of rock eighty kilometers into the ionosphere and producing air pressure waves that were recorded around the world. The *tsunamis* or great sea waves produced by the explosion killed 36,000 people in Java and Sumatra. The explosion itself was *heard* 5,000 kilometers away. The island, what's left of it and what's been rebuilt by volcanic action since, is still in eruption.

The equally legendary Vesuvius thirteen kilometers southeast of Naples, Italy, has produced a major eruption at least six times in this century alone. On August 24, 63 A.D., Vesuvius buried the cities of Pompeii, Stabie, and Herculaneum. In spite of a history of nearly continuous paroxymal eruptions of Vesusius, people still live on its slopes and tend their vineyards there.

We know about earthquakes that tremble and heave the solid ground we have become so accustomed to thinking of as firm and steady forevermore. Again, the sheer power inherent in these seismic convulsions awes us because a single small tremor signals the release of more energy than we have bottled up in all the thermonuclear warheads in the world. A major quake running from five to seven on the Richter Scale involves unimaginable amounts of energy. The catastrophe of earthquakes have changed the face of civilization countless times in history.

Hardly a year goes by without at least one major earthquake occurring somewhere in the world and creating untold damage and the deaths of hundreds or thousands of people. In 1980 alone, both Algeria and northern California experienced major earthquakes. At noon on September 1, 1923, a major earthquake hit Tokyo, Japan, levelling 54% of the brick buildings in the city and causing the destruction of 700,000 houses by fire; 74,000 people were killed, more than were killed in the atomic attack on Hiroshima 22 years later. At 5:12 A.M. on April 18, 1906, 435 kilometers of the San Andreas Fault in California underwent slippage that caused earthquakes felt from Los Angeles to Coos Bay, Oregon, killed more than 700 people in San Francisco, and caused more than $400-million in damage.

With all our advanced technology, we still cannot accurately predict the onset of vulcanism or seismic activity. These terrestrial catastrophes are still as capricious as ever. Our attempts to reduce them to the predictability we have worked out for the diurnal and seasonal cycles has come to naught. Vulcanology and seismology are still emergent sciences that haven't yet attained the precision of astronomy; they are not yet developed to the point where they can pass the Swartzberg Test developed by Harry Swartzberg at RCA over a decade ago: "The validity of a science is its ability to predict."

But the vulcanologists and seismologists are working hard at it.

Both volcanos and earthquakes come about as natural consequences of the structure and dynamics of the planet. We know a great deal more about these in 1981 than we did when Laumer wrote the novel. In fact, even our philosophical concepts of natural planetary change such as exhibited by volcanos and earthquakes has changed.

As recently as a hundred years ago—in spite of volcanos and earthquakes which were certainly an indication of dynamism on the part of Earth—the general concept of Earth was as a static, immutable, unchanging place. Save for a few islands like Thira (Santorini) that blew up, cities such as Pompeii that were destroyed by volcanoes, or towns such as Port Royal, Jamaica, that slid into the sea because of an earthquake, the world was considered to be much as it always had been.

But the evidence to the contrary was there and had been seen by people for centuries. There were those curious objects known as "fossils" that appeared to be living organisms turned to stone; these could be dug up in many places. Greek scholars began to recognize the essential nature of these fossilized life forms, but the superstition of the Christian era gave fossils a supernatural interpretation. The idea that fossils might represent the remains of former life forms that had been mineralized began to take form about two hundred years ago with people such as Lamark, Linnaeus, Culver, and William Smith. The importance of fossils took on a new light with the publications and acceptance of Wallace and Darwin.

Fossils and the rock strata in which they were found posed serious problems to the unchanging Earth concept. Fossils of fishlike animals and other organisms of obvious aquatic origin were discovered thousands of kilometers from any ocean and thousands of meters above sea level. How did they get there? What were the processes that formed the layers of rock in which they were found?

The geological processes that twisted, bent, sheared, and thrust these layers of rock were obviously the result of enormous forces. Because people think in short time spans—after all, *nothing* really existed before you were born, regardless of what the books say—these visible exhibits of tremendous energy release had to be incredibly violent if they occurred in short periods of time.

Such short and violent geological processes were known: vulcanism and seismic activity.

And the concept of brief, violent, and catastrophic geological activities was born.

Nobody stopped to consider the amount of energy required to create such short-term violent changes or where such energy might come from. Or whether or not there was sufficient energy available from these sources.

This has led to the "rapid catastrophic school" of geology, and a great deal of science fiction—such as *Catastrophe Planet*—is based on it. There is nothing wrong with the catastrophic school of geology, it's valid, and there is a definite probability that such catastrophic and violent changes could take place. The reason for saying this is our relative ignorance of macro-processes on a planetary scale. Our ignorance is further reinforced every time a spacecraft, manned or unmanned, lands on or flies by another planet or satellite, adding new data and posing new questions. Our Solar System has turned out to be far from understood, and our knowledge of planetary processes is yet rudimentary.

However, we're dealing with the release of enormous amounts of energy when we speak of planetary processes. A major earthquake can involve hundreds of thousands of cubic kilometers of solid rock. When one has to blast three cubic meters of rock from the earth to build a backyard swimming pool, one begins to gain some appreciation and perspective for the energy requirements of a simple, major earthquake.

The Planet Earth, after all, is a very large object even though it is one of the smaller planets of the Solar System. It is a roughly spherical body with an average diameter of approximately 12,756 kilometers. It has a mass of some 5.9765×10^{22} kilograms. The amount of energy required to change its orbit about the Sun or its rotational rate, or to precess it so that its rotational axis is changed is enormous. All of the water in Earth's oceans—some 1.315×10^{21} kilograms—is only 0.022% of the Earth's mass. Moving this water would hardly make any change in the Earth's angular momentum of 5.209×10^{27} kilogram-meter-seconds.

But moving the Earth's crust around might.

One of the consequences of the catastrophic school of geology was the dynamic Earth concept. Obviously, a lot of rock had been moved around in the ancient history of the planet. How?

In 1912, Alfred Wegener put forth the idea that all the continents of Earth were once one large land mass he called "Pangaea." It's an immediately obvious hypothesis because anybody with a map or globe of the world can see at once that the east coast of South America seems to make a perfect fit into the west coast of Africa. However, it's not so easy to get such an obvious fit anywhere else.

Today, Wegener is recognized as the pioneer of the new "plate tectonic theory" of the movement of the crust of the Earth. It took a lot of scientific progress, new instruments, and much exploration to verify the "continental drift" theory of plate tectonics.

Plate tectonic theory hypothesizes that the surface of Earth is made up of crustal plates floating on the semi-liquid magma rock below. These crustal plates range from 8 kilometers thick beneath the oceans to more than 50 kilometers thick at the core of a continent under a major mountain range. There are 8 major continental plates and numerous minor ones. They appear to wander over the surface of the Earth propelled very slowly by convection currents in the liquid magma beneath them.

Where two tectonic plates are spreading apart, a rift valley appears with a string of volcanos. This is happening right now along the middle of the Atlantic Ocean. Measurements made with satellites indicate that North America and Europe are getting further apart by a matter of centimeters every year. Where two crustal plates collide, they may buckle upward to form mountain ranges such as the Himalayas about 10 kilometers high, or they may slip over and under each other to form an ocean trench 10 kilometers deep. This is still a very small dislocation in terms of the thickness of plates and of the diameter of the planet. (If one were to make a true scale model of the Earth the size of a billiard ball with all vertical dimensions in perfect scale, the surface of the model would be mirror smooth and the Earth's crust in scale would be thinner than an egg shell.)

Insofar as we know, these plate tectonic changes take place over very long periods of time. Where the Arabian Plate is colliding with the Asian Plate along a line running through the Persian Gulf, maps have shown us over the period of 200 years that the Persian Gulf is slowly closing up. The Tigris and Euphrates Rivers each used to empty individually into the Persian Gulf; today, they join one another and must flow almost an additional hundred kilometers to reach the receding Gulf. In a few million years, a new mountain range rivalling the Himalayas will grow across the nothern margin of Asia Minor. We now know that the "California Island" consisting of Los Angeles and that part of the Golden State west of the San Andreas Fault is moving slowly northward with respect to the rest of North America. At the present rate, Los Angeles will slip beneath the ocean in the Aleutian Trench 50 million years from now.

It's quite unlikely that these events will occur sooner than this, but one must remember that the slippage and movement rates are based only on recent measurements made in the past quarter of a century, a mere blink of the cosmic eye. There is nothing that says it couldn't happen more quickly. But it would take a prodigious amount of energy to move teratons of rock quickly. Although nothing in our historic experience tells us that catastrophes of such magnitude can occur in such short intervals of time, there is also very little that tells us that they *can't*.

We're still learning.

With new data, new theories, and new methods and new equipment to make measurements, earth scientists are well along toward an understanding of the phenomenology of volcanos and earthquakes, natural catastrophes in which opportunism and just plain good luck rule when it comes to getting data. It won't always be the case, and some day in the next fifty years, vulcanology and seismology will at least reach the 1981 level of predictability of the weather.

Thanks in large part to the space program and our ability to rise above the Earth and view it from the high ground of orbit, we are beginning to move the science of meteorology into the "true science" category of those that pass the Swartzberg Test. Our increased ability to predict the weather has been due to the information we've obtained from an ability to view the weather patterns of the entire planet.

Before the days of weather satellites, meteorologists were limited to surface observations of temperature, humidity, barometric pressure, dew point, cloud cover and cloud type made at isolated locations on land. They were sharply restricted in their ability to make accurate weather predictions. They could guess at the future weather, but the term "guess" is extremely unscientific so the word "forecast" is used instead although it means just about the same thing.

With weather observations limited to a few hundred locations on a continent and with difficult communication of the data to a central location, meteorologists were necessarily completely ignorant of the weather over 72% of the earth's surface: the oceans. And the great oceans of Earth, unique in the Solar System, are the genesis of the weather patterns over most of the Earth.

Meteorologists also had no data from the polar regions where much of the Earth's water is locked up in seasonally-changing polar ice caps whose freezing and melting have much to do with the energy imbalance required to drive the weather machine of the world.

And save for a few locations where balloons could be launched regularly to detect the winds of the troposphere and lower stratosphere, meteorologists had no means for obtaining vertical profiles of the atmosphere.

Thus handicapped, it was no wonder that meteorologists couldn't predict the great storms, hurricanes, typhoons, and other meterological catastrophes that plagued civilization in the past and, on many occasions, actually changed the course of history, too.

Meteorological catastrophes are no longer the great killers they once were, at least not in the United States or other parts of the world where modern meteorology and communications can locate disasterous weather before it strikes populated areas and get the word out to activate precautions ranging from evacuation to sheltering. Even in the face of modern techniques, hurricanes continue to devastate the Carribbean and typhoons tear up the Pacific Ocean regions. Blizzards still sweep the Great Plains of America and "blue northers" blast their frigid paths across the Texas Panhandle, freezing cattle and people.

And often dangerous weather systems can be quite small and treacherous, highly localized in their effects and often unseen by meteorologists and their instruments until it's too late. Tornadoes still destroy and kill in the mid-continent "Tornado Belt" of the United States. Violent thunderstorms only a few miles in extent can cause flash flooding in the American West.

A severe thunderstorm or thundersquall can be frightening enough in its intensity on the ground. In an airplane in the air, regardless of the size of the airplane, such phenomena can be stupifying in their intensity and power. Hail stones can demolish the wings of the strongest airplanes. Updrafts can carry an airplane to altitudes far beyond the point where occupants require supplemental oxygen to remain conscious. Lightning strikes can completely disable electrical systems and radio equipment. And severe turbulance can rip the wings off in an instant. The violence of a thunderstorm is something that one encounters in an airplane once; either one may not be lucky enough to encounter anything else. Survivors give thunderstorms a wide berth thereafter.

But volcanos, earthquakes, and severe weather are all phenomena that are natural to our highly dynamic planet. We have learned that there can be other catastrophic natural happenings that are totally unpredictable.

"I can more easily believe that two Yankee professors lie than accept the notion that stones can fall from heaven," said President Thomas Jefferson in 1808 when told that a meteorite fall had been located by two Harvard professors.

But stones *do* fall from heaven . . . unannounced and unpredictably. We've seen enough of them fall and have recovered enough of them to know beyond a shadow of a doubt that meteorites have their origin in outer space.

Fortunately, all of the meteorites that have hit the Earth during recorded history—with the possible exception of the Tunga fall of June 30, 1908 which was a meteorite approximately a hundred meters in diameter and produced an explosion equivalent to a ten megaton thermonuclear bomb—have been small objects such as those of the Sikhote-Alin shower of February 12, 1947 which produced more than a hundred small craters, the largest being 90 meters across and approximately 12 meters deep.

Meteorites have hit people who have survived to tell about it.

By and large, all these have been small catastrophes.

What are the chances for a really *big* meteorite hitting the Earth?

It's happened before.

The Barringer Meteor Crater in Arizona is about 1.2 kilometers in diameter and 200 meters deep. A meteorite a mere 25 meters in diameter hit the Arizona plateau near the Little Colorado River more than 10,000 years ago. The energy released in the impact was equivalent to a 2.5-megaton bomb. It must have killed every living thing within a hundred kilometers.

There are other places where meteorites have

struck the Earth and left evidence of their craters Osel, Estonia; Box Hole, Australia; Haviland, Kansas; Odessa, Texas; and Wolf Creek, Australia, to name but a few.

Yet we see through telescopes our Moon literally pock-marked by uncountable meteorite impacts. Mariner and Voyager spacecraft have returned pictures showing Mercury, Mars, Callisto, Rhea, and other planets and satellites of the Solar System covered with impact craters. Why not the Earth, too?

Because Earth is a dynamic planet.

Most of the meteorite craters except the very large ones and the most recent ones have been obliterated by the dynamic planetary process we call weather. The persistent forces of erosion eradicates them.

Yet there is ample evidence that the Earth has been struck by *huge* meteorites in the past. Canada is dotted by at least ten remnants of circular crater formations whose geology leaves no doubt that they were formed by meteor impacts; these remnant craters still exist because they are part of the ancient Canadian Shield of rocks, some of the most primordial geological structures still exposed on the surface of the Earth.

But a real catastrophic meteorite impact occurred unknown millions of years ago to leave the "fossil" crater at Vredevoort, South Africa. It is a ring of geological formations fifty kilometers in diameter, the layers of Earth turned up at the edge of this ring measure almost fifteen kilometers in extent. Other geological studies of the rocks in the region confirm that the Earth was struck at Vredevoort by a planetoid approximately two kilometers in diameter. The resulting release of energy at impact was enormous—equivalent to about a 250,000 megaton thermonuclear bomb.

The phenomena accompanying the impact of such a very large meteorite involves more than the release of energy when it hits the Earth. As such a large body encounters the atmosphere, it will create a huge atmospheric entry plasma around it like an Apollo capsule returning from the Moon. Only this is bigger, brighter, and lots more energetic. For hundreds of kilometers around, this plasma sheath will create electromagnetic effects including not only St. Elmo's fire but a lethal dose of X-rays as well. On impact, it would create the biggest earthquake yet known accompanied by an incredible atmospheric shock wave. The show isn't over yet, for soon it will rain rocks—secondary meteorites composed of pieces of the planetoid and pieces of Earth ejected from the impact site by the explosion. Within a matter of days, there wouldn't be a living thing within a thousand kilometers of the impact site.

And four out of five times, such a large meteorite will fall in the Earth's oceans. Contrary to the thought that such an impact would be more benign than a land strike, it's worse. In addition to the quakes triggered by this shock, there will be tsunami sea waves rebounding around the Earth. The impact will not only vaporize several thousand cubic kilometers of ocean water, but smash through the crust on the ocean floor to the hot liquid magma of the Earth's interior beneath. A blazing wound in the ocean floor results. A waterfall of ocean two kilometers high rushes in, is promptly changed to steam which rises into the stratosphere and stays there. Before the rush of waters cools the white-hot hole in the Earth, some 16,000 cubic kilometers of ocean water have been evaporated. This eventually falls as rain, enough to provide an average rainfall of more than 3 centimeters everywhere on Earth.

But it won't rain immediately. All of the heat trapped in the evaporation of that water keeps the cloud up there for a very long period of time . . . over the entire planet. Weather forecast for the indefinite future: 100% cloud cover, strong chance of rain, temperatures decreasing, strong chance of unseasonal snow and ice storms.

During the Earth's long 4.5-billion year history, the probability of the planet having been struck by very large meteorites indicates that there have been a least a thousand strikes of this magnitude.

Could such a catastrophe happen again?

Yes.

Most everyone who knows a little bit about our Solar System from private studies, a school course, or contact with astronomers also knows that there is a planetoid belt between the orbits of the planets Mars and Jupiter where there may be more than 40,000 pieces of rock ranging in size from several hundred kilometers in diameter down to pea gravel or smaller.

What many people do not know is that there are planetoids whose orbits go closer to the Sun than the orbit of Mercury and thus cross the Earth's orbit. Thirteen of these "close approach" planetoids have been discovered to date, five of them have been lost and not seen after being discovered, but they're out there somewhere. Others such as Icarus, Geographos, Betulia, and Hermes have been spotted again and again, and their orbits are now well known. All of them can pass within ten million miles of the Earth. Calculations made of Hermes' orbit indicate that this planetoid about a kilometer in diameter could come to within 360,000 kilometers of Earth—a distance closer than our Moon!

Dr. Fred S. Singer, an astronomer and early space pioneer, once calculated that there was a better than 50% probability that we would be able to witness the impact of at least four planetoids more than a kilometer in diameter on one of the planets of the Solar System in the foreseeable future.

In fact, seismic instruments of the ALSEP equipment left on the lunar surface by Apollo astronauts in the 1969-1972 time period have recorded several meteorite impacts on the Moon.

The Earth can be hit again and probably will be. However, the probability of Earth being hit by a meteorite more than ten meters in diameter is slim. But the possibility exists.

And the consequences to life on Earth could be staggering, depending upon where the meteorite hit.

There have been several "discontinuities" in the archaeological record of fossils found in terrestrial rocks. Whole species have simply disappeared. The demise of the dinosaurs was apparently sudden or at least took place over a short period of geological time. Could these discontinuities have resulted from major meteorite strikes on Earth? We'll probably never know for sure, but it could have happened that way.

It is doubtful that the impact of even the Vredevoort meteorite could have caused something as drastic as a major shift in the Earth's rotational axis or rotational period because of the energies involved. But the consequences of a major meteorite impact in terms of radiation from the atmospheric entry plasma sheath, the heat and pressure of the impact atmospheric shock wave, and the possible changes in the Earth's climate or weather patterns because of the added heat energy all could have had major roles in changing the course of evolution by wiping out life over a whole continent or even over the whole planet to some degree.

As long as the human race is bottled up on Planet Earth with no outposts or colonies elsewhere in the Solar System or even around other stars, we will be at the mercy of unanticipated, unpredictable astronomical catastrophies such as meteorite strikes.

But there are other catastrophes that can be developed into plausible scenarios.

The Sun appears to be a steady, constant object in Earth's skies, coming and going with a regularity that is now well documented and shining its benign rays upon the planet in a constant manner. The Sun is an operating fusion reactor that converts hydrogen into helium through the process of fusion at a rate of 657,000 tons of hydrogen per second. This produces more than 80,000 horsepower per square meter of solar surface continuously. At the Earth's distance from the Sun of 150-million kilometers, this energy amounts to 1.94 calories per square centimeter per minute, a number known as the *solar constant*. But it isn't constant. It never has been. It's an average value. The Sun changes from minute to minute, day to day, year to year. Solar flares erupt and sunspots march across its luminous surface, often in regular eleven-year cycles. Solar astronomers have been observing and measuring the Sun for about a century, and it has been only in the past quarter of a century that they have had the measuring instruments and the satelite platforms to permit more careful measurements of a larger variety of solar phenomena. As a result, we really know very little about the Sun, which is a risky situation because of the overarching effect this small star has on all life on Earth.

Our planetary atmosphere and magnetic field protect us from the radiation outbursts that accompany solar flares. The protons and electrons of these outbursts are trapped by the Van Allen Belts and eventually result in the spectacular auroral displays seen near the Earth's poles where the magnetic field lines dip strongly and steeply into the ionosphere. But could there be a really *big* solar flare of such intensity and power that its radiation could penetrate the Van Allen Belts and affect living beings on the Earth's surface?

Probably.

We don't know that much about solar dynamics yet, which makes such a scenario probable. But we can't predict it, nor can we yet assign numbers to it. Solar dynamics hasn't yet advanced to the point where it can pass the Swartzberg Test.

But could the solar constant undergo a *really* radical change from the current 1.94 $cal/cm^2/min$?

Probably.

From what little we know of stellar mechanics, the Sun is an average, middle-aged star known as Class G0. It probably has a lifetime of another ten billion years before it uses up its hydrogen, blows off its photosphere, expands into a red giant, and finally settles down to being a white dwarf star.

Ten billion years? We'll worry about that later!

Or will we?

We don't yet know enough about stellar mechanics to say for sure that a major change could *not* occur in the solar output, either increasing or decreasing the solar constant. There is no way to predict the possibility of this sort of solar catastrophe, nor any way to know which way it would go. It could happen tomorrow. It could be happening right now and we wouldn't know about it for another nine minutes, that being the length of time required for light to traverse the 150-million kilometers between the Sun and the Earth.

Thus, any major change in the solar constant could have—and may already have had—long-range implications for the terrestrial climate, making it warmer or bringing on an ice age. We don't know enough about it yet. We do know that a small change in the amount of solar energy reaching the Earth's surface or the upper atmosphere can have a definite effect upon weather. The volcanic explosion of Krakatua in 1883 threw so much volcanic matter into the upper atmosphere that the solar constant (the "pyroheliometric value") at the Earth's surface decreased 10% and the average worldwild temperature decreased almost a half-degree Celsius, resulting in 1884 being the "Year Without A Summer." (The effects of the eruption of Mount St. Helens may be felt in 1981, but again they may be measurable only on highly sensitive instruments; we'll have to wait and see.) But these changes caused by vulcanism interacting with the solar constant are not "catastrophic" in the sense that they result in a major change overnight or even within a few weeks.

We can, of course, create an "ultimate scenario," and several science-fiction writers have done so. It's not necessary to postulate a man-made catastrophe resulting from a massive strike-counter-strike exchange of multi-megaton thermonuclear weapons. Old Sol can out-do us any time, and may. There is a *slight* chance that the Sun may become a nova.

There is a critical point in the life of any normal star such as the Sun when it has used up about 40% of the hydrogen in its core and converted it to helium in the fusion process. At that point, the core collapses and its temperature rises to about 200-million degrees C. where the helium "ash" of the former fusion process becomes a very lively fuel. This is known as the "helium flash" or "popping the core." The star can then either blow up as a nova or collapse into a blue-white dwarf. Stellar astronomers still don't know enough about the helium flash to be able to predict what will happen. But either way it goes is bad news for Earth.

The Sun itself can go on being a reasonably stable and normal star for ten billion years. Yet the Earth can still suffer an astronomical catastrophe: another nearby star can blow up, becoming a nova or a supernova. There are many novas that take place in our galaxy every year, but they are as a firecracker to the violence of a supernova which can produce in a brief period of time as much light energy as an entire galaxy of billions of stars. Astronomers can see many galaxies beyond the Milky Way and have observed many supernovas. On the average, a supernova occurs in a galaxy every few centuries. Supernovas have been observed in our galaxy in 1054, 1572, and 1604. We're due for another one any time now.

The occurrence of a supernova within a hundred light years of the Solar System could produce enough hard radiation to bathe the Earth in X-rays, gamma rays, and cosmic rays to the extent that life could be imperiled if not destroyed. Certainly, the supernova radiation bath would cause genetic mutations.

Could such nearby supernova explosions have caused the archaeological "discontinuities" of the past? Perhaps. We may be here in our present forms today because of a nearby supernova. Although the time may be coming when humans will control the destinies of stars, this may have been an occurrence when the stars actually controlled the destiny of *homo sapiens*, a far cry from what is claimed by astrology.

Could such an interstellar catastrophe happen?

Yes.

And we have no idea of the probability. The supernova that spells drastic change for us may already have occurred years ago in our galactic neighborhood; we won't know about it until the radiation reaches us at the speed of light . . . perhaps tomorrow.

Oh, yes: Our Milky Way Galaxy could be

exploding, too. Astronomers are already observing other galaxies that seem to be exploding. If something started to happen in the galactic core today, we've got 15,000 years before the message reaches us. Or it may already be on the way. . . .

Since the only survival remedy in the face of such overwhelming astronomical catastrophes is exactly the same as the remedy now open to us that will provide salvation from terrestrial calamities, we've got to get our eggs out of one planetary basket, get into space, and then keep going on and on in space to spread life and intelligence as far and wide as we can lest some cosmic catastrophe blow out the candle of life and the flame of self-aware intelligence.

The only road to immortality of intelligence, species, and life itself that we now know about is to forge into the universe and go as far as we can as rapidly as we can, knowing that there are untold and unpredictable dangers forever lurking *everywhere* in the universe, waiting to swallow up perhaps forever this spark of self-awareness we believe ourselves to be. For until and unless we find other intelligent life elsewhere, we must behave as though we are the *only* self-awareness in the universe.

Rather than cower before catastrophes as our primitive ancestors would have done, we can rise and confront these catastrophes.

We may not be able to overcome them and insure our collective survival, but we can try.

And maybe that's what this is all about after all. . . .

—G. Harry Stine

Afterward #2

SHAKING UP SPACE

by Frederik Pohl

The other day in Seattle I had the pleasure of paneling with two distinguished theoretical physicists. Roger Freedman teaches the subject at the University of Washington; George Harper writes about it, for publications like the *Brit. Astron. Journ.* and *Analog.* Mt. St. Helen's was shaking and belching off to the south, along the Oregon border, the first volcanic activity in the lower 48 states in my lifetime; and while George Harper was explaining how everything came to be born out of the universal ylem and Roger Freedman was telling us how it would die, in the decay of protons thirty decillion years from now ("Oh, thank God! At first I thought you said thirty billion!"), I was trying to look intelligent enough for the company I kept. Actually, it was an extraordinarily stimulating occasion. Apart from the volcano and the cosmologies there was a Richter 5.0 earthquake going on just off the coast, and besides we were at a science-fiction convention. (Norwescon III, and I was Fan Guest of Honor— but that's a whole other story.) And while Harper was drawing pictures of doughnut-shaped cosmoses and Freedman was explaining what quarks do to nuclear particles, I was thinking about the relationship between earth shakes and astrophysics. You don't believe there is one? Well, actually there are several, but let's start with the one I was thinking about.

The way you locate the epicenter of an earthquake is with seismographs. A seismograph is essentially a sturdy and solidly mounted little piece of machinery which contains a weight that is free to wobble when something shakes the instrument; the weight moves a lever arm, and the lever scribbles a pen (or some other recording device) over a moving sheet of paper (or sometimes film) when it feels the tremor. If you clock the moment when each of a group of widely separated seismographs reacts, you can then plot a circle around each instrument. The source of the vibration lies somewhere on each of those circles. The point where the circles intersect is where the earthquake took place. Scientists have been doing that for a good long time with earthquakes. Last year they did the same thing with a vastly different class of objects on a vastly different scale.

On the 5th of March of 1979 a very brief, very intense burst of gamma radiation passed through the solar system, and was registered on a number of instruments. Nine of them happened to be aboard satellites scattered around the system. (None of them were put in those orbits for the specific purpose of monitoring that burst, because no one knew it was going to take place—chalk it up as another fringe benefit of the general space program.)

What that burst of gammas came from is a fascinating question, to which, unfortunately, there are at the moment no good answers; it may be that we have discovered still another class of intensely radiating objects, unlike anything ever detected before. But almost as fascinating is what happened with those nine space observations. The time of each was quite accurately measured. And by plotting the time when the burst was received at each point in space in the say way that earth tremors are plotted in seismology, the point of origin of all those gammas was identified. It turned out to be an object called N49. It is an old supernova remnant, and it is not located in our galaxy at all. It's in the Large Magellanic Cloud, a quarter of a million light-years away.

Think a minute about what that feat of location implies. It is as though someone had popped a flashbulb near Marble Arch in London, and we, in Seattle, had pinpointed it there, and not at Tower Bridge or on Hampstead Heath, by timing the light received at nine photoelectric cells—tiny ones—small enough so that all nine would fit in a circle about the size of the point of a pin.*

To be sure, the technology involved in this space observation is remarkable. But for that technology to work requires something even more remarkable: the thing Einstein told us about three-quarters of a century ago, the invariant stability of the speed of light.

*For the purposes of this discussion I am neglecting the fact that the curvature of the earth puts an awful lot of rock in between London and Seattle, and I would appreciate it if you would do the same.

There has never been a more law-abiding traveler than the photon of light. It speeds not, neither does it slow down, and it keeps its place in line. That gamma burst leaped from the surface of the burned-out supernova almost a quarter of a million years ago, and for all those years each individual particle marched in step, in a column less than two hundred miles long, so that the whole thing arrived in order at the neighborhood of our Sun 1,4000,000,000,000,000,000 miles away. If some of those photons were faster or slower than the others by as little as one part in one quintillion the location experiment would have failed. Now, that's what I call a sure-enough *constant.*

Such invariant constants are what the mathematical models of science are built on.

Since the human race has been around for what is no more than the wink of a gnat's eye in cosmic time; a lot of things that look pretty constant to us aren't, really. (Not even the atom is stable over the long periods Roger Freedman was talking about.) The quantity H_0, Hubble's figure expressing the rate of expansion of the universe, is only more or less constant—it will not possess the same value a billion years from now that it has now. (That's what the little subscript "o" is for, so it can be written as H_1 or $H_{1,000,000,000}$ as the universe ages.) According to some heavy thinkers like Paul Dirac even *g*, the force of gravity, isn't constant either, although that's still arguable. The real constants are the ones that *never* change—*pi* and *e* and *h* and all the rest—and they not only make science possible, they do the same thing for life. For if the values that describe, for instance, the charge, mass and other parameters of nuclear particles were anything other than what they are, the atom would be a quite different thing. Chemistry would happen in a different way, and perhaps it wouldn't happen at all. And if chemistry didn't happen, neither would life.

And yet—some of them really do seem rather capricious. Can you think of any reason *why* light should always travel at the same speed? Or granting that it does, why that speed should be 186 thousand miles a second and not, say 185? A few constants seem to make intuitive sense. For instance, it is hard to imagine any circumstances in which the ratio of the circumference of a circle to its diameter should be anything other than 3.14159 et cetera. Others do not. If there is a logically necessary reason why *c, e, h,* the mass ratio of the proton to the electron, the fine-structure constant and others should have their present values, I personally do not happen to see it.

Indeed, some thinkers, like Tong Tang at Cambridge, suspect that at least some of these values are pure accidents. Tang thinks it is possible that they may have been caused by random fluctuations in particle density in the first few microseconds after the Big Bang, and if the exploding universe had expanded in slightly different random directions we would have a whole other set of "invariant" constants.* This is

*As some may recall, I have been playing with this notion in a novel called *Beyond the Blue Event Horizon,* which is why I don't intend to do so at much length here.

an intriguing thought, because some of those perhaps-accidental constants are a real nuisance. If *c* were a thousand times its present value, for instance, those old science-fiction stories about hopping over to Alpha Centauri on a weekend might be almost possible. If we could change them, at least temporarily or locally, we might be able to do ourselves a lot of good, one way or another.

We might even be able to get to that fusion-powered Beulah Land the nuclear-power people have been promising us. Long years ago, around 1954, when the first British reactor was built at Calder Hall and the outlook for fusion power seemed more immediately hopeful than it does now, one of the English physicists was asked what he would do if it turned out that the fundamental physical laws prevented small-scale nuclear fusion reactions. "Why," he said, "we'll just have to change the fundamental physical laws."

If Tong Tang's conjecture is correct, those "fundamental physical laws" were defined at a point so early in the history of the universe that most particles had not yet come to exist and even the four fundamental forces—gravity, electromagnetic, weak and strong/nuclear—were essentially interchangeable.

Is it possible to create that sort of environment again? Even very briefly, in a very small space? Not bloody likely, one would say; but plasma physics has a long way to go before its limits are understood. I would personally bet against the attainment of cheap nuclear fusion power, by this means or any other, within the next half century or so . . . but you never know. I would have bet against the programmable hand-held pocket calculator, too, and now I own a couple.

I said there was more than one connection between shakings of the Earth and astrophysical events. Another such lies in a book called *The Jupiter Effect*, by John R. Gribbin and Stephen X. H. Plagemann, which I have been reading with more than usual attention lately.

The reason I have been reading it is that it relates to a story I am writing, but it's worth a read on its own merits. I start by saying that I don't believe things are going to happen exactly the way Gribbin and Plagemann predict; but I have no way of being *sure*.

What Gribbin and Plagemann say is that in the early part of 1982 most of the planets will be on the same side of the Sun, an event which only happens once every 179 years or so. This, they say, will impose strains on the core of the Sun, where the nuclear reactions take place which cause it to emit heat, light and other radiation. These strains, they suggest, may cause it to change its radiation levels in such a way as to slightly heat up the atmosphere of the Earth. The increased heat will cause the atmosphere to swell. The swelling will increase the moment arm of the Earth's effective radius (like a skater sticking her arms out to slow her spin down). Not much. But enough, perhaps, by means of coupling through friction with mountains, trees and wavetops, to make a slight "glitch" in the Earth's diurnal spin. (These glitches do happen, although it is not clear just why and not many other people think they are related to solar radiation.)

All that is interesting and, if not always consensual scientific wisdom, at least reasonable speculation. It is the next step that is the killer.

There exists, Gribbin and Plagemann say truly, places on the Earth's surface where immense stores of seismic energy are stored up, waiting for a trigger to release them. The stored energy comes from the slow crawl of the Earth's tectonic plates, moving but stuck at the edges by friction; the trigger need by only quite tiny, just enough to break the sticky part loose. A glitch might be big enough. And then all that stored energy will shake the Earth with great violence—will, be, in fact, an earthquake, and a big one, and the place that Gribbin and Plagemann think most likely to suffer is California, where the San Andreas fault has been waiting for decades for an excuse to break loose.

As they put it in the book:

> A remarkable chain of evidence, much of it known for decades but never before linked together, points to 1982 as the year in which the Los Angeles region of the San Andreas fault will be subjected to the most massive earthquake known in the populated regions of the Earth in this century . . . in 1982 'when the Moon is in the Seventh House, and Jupiter aligns with Mars' and with the other seven planets of the Solar System, Los Angeles will be destroyed.

Ray Bradbury, A. E. Van Vogt, Forrest J. Ackerman, H. L. Gold, Harlan Ellison and all you other dear friends in Los Angeles—are you listening?

Well, I already said I didn't believe it would happen exactly that way. I'm quite doubtful about some of the links in the chain of reasoning—notably the change in nuclear reactions because of the position of the planets, on which the exact timing of the event so firmly depends. Even if the pull of the planets did in fact play hell with the fusing core of the Sun, I do not really think it would at once knock out Los Angeles. There is the matter of the missing solar neutrinos.

On thinking it over, I am not sure just how much reassurance the missing solar neutrinos will give anyone, but let me run over the situation anyway. As you all know, for some years scientists have been trying to detect the flow of neutrinos that really ought to be coming out of the Sun if it is indeed fusing hydrogen into helium in its core the way it is supposed to be. The task of detecting a neutrino is not easy, since it is so tiny and chargeless that it slips right through most matter without a trace. The "telescope" for observing the Sun's neutrino flux is a great big tank of cleaning fluid at the bottom of a mine shaft. The way you observe it is to wait for the odd neutrino to interact with the odd atomic nucleus, and watch the spray of particles that comes out. This has been going on for a number of years now. Although watching for these infrequent events rates high among the most boring jobs in the world, it is not quite as boring as the job that is about to begin of standing by ten thousand gallons of protons (in the form of ordinary water), waiting for one of them to decay every six weeks or so. A fair number of neutrinos have in fact been caught and counted.

But not nearly enough.

So something is wrong—either with the "telescope" or the theory . . . or maybe with the Sun. Because one reasonable hypothesis is that the telescope is doing its job and the theory is right on, but the Sun has stopped fusing.

It is easy to see that this has unpleasant implications. If the Sun has stopped fusing hydrogen into helium, then it has either switched over to some other nuclear process or it has stopped generating energy entirely. In the first case, we don't know what to expect, which is worrisome. In the second case we know exactly what to expect, and that is even more worrisome, because it implies that the Sun will go out.

Probably you are now breathing a sigh of relief; after all, you looked out the window this morning, and there it was, still shining. Well, that's not really any guarantee. Energy generated at the core of the Sun does not spring to its surface, and thence to your window, at 186,000 miles a second all the way. Before it gets to the surface of the Sun it needs to fight its way through some very dense material, and the process takes just about a million years. So it is at least theoretically possible that the Sun's engines could be turned off now, but that it will be a million years before we know it.

(You may be breathing another sigh of relief, because you're not going to worry about something that won't show up until the year

1,001,980 A.D., are you? Well, don't feel *totally* secure. The neutrino telescope has been going for less than ten years. There is nothing to say that the Sun's fire didn't go out 999,990 years ago and we'll start to shiver tomorrow. I don't *really* think this is the case, either—it's easier to believe that the theory is somehow wrong. But there it is, just one more damn thing to worry about.)

Anyway, that's the reason why I don't expect the Gribbin-Plagemann Jupiter Effect to smite Los Angeles as soon as the planets wheel themselves into position, in the spring of 1982. Events at the core of the Sun are not really likely to affect its radiation that quickly. Even if the events actually do occur.

But I wouldn't feel too relieved about that, either. Not if I lived in Los Angeles. Everything Gribbin and Plagemann say about the San Andreas fault is gospel. It's sitting there, waiting. It has been storing up energy for around a century—a little more, in the southern portion around Los Angeles, a little less near San Francisco—and it is well overdue to go off. As to that, the only place where my opinions differ from Gribbin and Plagemann is in the nature of the trigger, and the time when it is pulled. I don't think the time of maximum danger is the spring of 1982. I think it is every minute of every day, including this one.

—Frederik Pohl